WONDERFUL YOU

Alex George worked as a lawyer for eight years before becoming a full-time writer. He lives in the USA with his wife and son. *Wonderful You* is his fourth novel.

For automatic updates on your favourite authors visit Harpercollins.co.uk and register for Author Tracker.

T0317959

Also by Alex George

Working it Out
Before Your Very Eyes
Love you Madly

ALEX GEORGE

Wonderful You

HarperCollinsPublishers

HarperCollins*Publishers*
77–85 Fulham Palace Road,
Hammersmith, London W6 8JB

www.harpercollins.co.uk

A paperback original 2005
1 3 5 7 9 10 8 6 4 2

Copyright © Alex George 2005

Alex George asserts the moral right to
be identified as the author of this work

THEY CAN'T TAKE THAT AWAY FROM ME
Lyrics by George Gershwin & Ira Gershwin
© 1936, 1937 (Renewed 1963, 1964) Chappell & Co, USA
Warner Chappell Music Ltd, London W6 8BS
Reproduced by permission of International Music Ltd.
All Rights Reserved

IT HAD TO BE YOU
Words by Gus Kahn and Music by Isham Jones
© 1924, Reproduced by permission of EMI Music Publishing Ltd/Remick Music Corp,
London WC2H 0QY

This novel is entirely a work of fiction. The names, characters
and incidents portrayed in it are the work of the author's
imagination. Any resemblance to actual persons, living or
dead, events or localities is entirely coincidental.

A catalogue record for this book
is available from the British Library

ISBN: 978-0-00711-796-3

All rights reserved. No part of this publication may be
reproduced, stored in a retrieval system, or transmitted,
in any form or by any means, electronic, mechanical,
photocopying, recording or otherwise, without the prior
permission of the publishers.

This book is sold subject to the condition that it shall not,
by way of trade or otherwise, be lent, re-sold, hired out or
otherwise circulated without the publisher's prior consent
in any form of binding other than that in which it is
published and without a similar condition including this
condition being imposed on the subsequent purchaser.

Thanks to Christina George, Cathy Hoey, Catherine Davidson, Sharon Bassin, Nancy Woodruff, Celeste Cole, Lee Sargent, Bennett Adams, Katie Espiner, Jennifer Parr, Bruce Hunter, Nigella Lawson, Deborah Silver, Richard Lewis, and Louis Barfe.

To my family

To my family

ONE

Exactly two months after her wedding day, Catherine Shaw spent her lunch hour queuing for tickets to see *La Bohème* at the Coliseum. It was to be a surprise for her new husband, an impromptu anniversary present. She bought the last available seats for that evening's performance, high up in the Gods.

Andrew Shaw was cautiously delighted. He had never been to the opera before.

That night they climbed the stairs and crammed themselves into their seats at the top of the huge theatre. Andrew did his best to follow the action on the distant stage, but all he really wanted to do was to turn and look at his wife. No drama could compete with the spectacle of her radiant face as the music swelled up towards them through the darkness.

At the interval they struggled down to the bar.

'Isn't it wonderful?' breathed Catherine, her eyes shining.

Andrew nodded. 'Tell you what, though. Next time, we'll buy seats downstairs.'

'Downstairs?' said Catherine.

'In the stalls, or somewhere. I'm almost getting a nose-bleed where we are, it's so high up.' He grinned.

1

'This isn't about the *seats*, Andrew,' said Catherine. 'It's about the music. The *art*.'

'Yes, I know,' he replied, 'I'm just saying –'

'I realise what you're *saying*. You're more interested in sitting in the right place than in listening to the music.'

'Not at all. I'd just like a better view.'

'It's an *opera*, Andrew. It's not about the *view*.'

'Jesus, Cathy, all right. Sorry I mentioned it.'

She looked up at him, her beautiful face clouded by bewilderment. 'Why can't you just *enjoy* it?' she asked.

Eventually Andrew had persuaded her to return to their seats. She had cried softly for much of the second half, moved beyond words by the tragic beauty of it all. By the time Mimì died in the final act, Catherine's face was streaked with tears. On the way home on the Tube she wept loudly on Andrew's shoulder. He put his arm awkwardly around her, unable to meet his fellow passengers' eyes. He was sure that people thought she was drunk.

That was Catherine, back then. That was her all over.

She was everything that Andrew was not: impulsive, romantic, boiling over with passion. She tore through life, scattering propriety and reserve. She laughed and cried with equal amounts of defiant abandon, oblivious to the more cautious sensibilities of those around her. Often she would do both simultaneously, screeching hysterically while tears rolled down her cheeks.

Her question that night fluttered at the edges of Andrew's consciousness for weeks afterwards: why couldn't he just enjoy the opera? In fact, he *had* enjoyed it – but just not with the dazzling, flamboyant intensity of his new wife. Beside Catherine he felt colourless, sluggishly inadequate. Andrew wished that he could join in the procession of emotions which paraded ceaselessly across her beautiful face. He would

2

watch her tears fall in quiet wonderment, hating his own dry-eyed dispassion. Happy endings, tragedies, it didn't matter. Catherine was riotously moved by everything.

Catherine often played the piano in the evenings. It was, she said, the best antidote to a day full of egocentric authors and dull-witted publishing executives. A stream of music flew from her elegant fingers, wrapping their sitting room in sound. She played waltzes and sonatas, études and fugues, barcarolles and mazurkas. Every tune had its own tale to tell, and Catherine coaxed these stories from the thickets of black notes on the page in front of her.

She always finished by playing the same, mournfully elegant piece. As the delicate patterns of notes filled the room, Andrew could sense Catherine retreat into herself. Only when the final notes had faded away into silence would she look up from the keys.

Catherine's playing enchanted and perturbed Andrew in equal measures. At the piano she inhabited another world, one that he would never know. He watched as she caressed the keys to life, and wondered whether he would ever be able to keep her.

Then, one day, Catherine stopped playing, and the light which had burned so brightly inside her went out.

Even now, all these years later, Andrew still languished in an agony of ignorance, unsure what had happened. Catherine's spirit had been extinguished along with the music, smothered by the silence. All that remained was a weary indifference. She became unrecognisable from the woman who had burst into tears at the Coliseum. Andrew watched, helpless, as his marriage descended into silence. When he looked at Catherine he no longer saw an irrepressible life-force, but the tired mother of his children, the reluctant co-owner of a shared history. Without the lifebelt of her passion to rescue

3

them, they had sunk into the treacherous waters of quiet predictability, their lives dulled by pernicious routine.

Andrew knew that the old Catherine was still there somewhere, locked away inside the unhappy woman he shared his life with now. That was enough for him. He carried on, doggedly affectionate. When she looked through him as if he weren't there, Andrew stood up all the straighter, and sustained himself with his memories of how it had once been. He wasn't going to give up on his grand romance, the love of his life. What had they told each other all those years ago? For better, for worse – all that stuff. And so he had loyally persisted, perhaps obstinately, perhaps a little heroically, refusing to admit defeat.

Which was why this business with Clara was so disappointing.

TWO

Andrew Shaw watched the Armani-sheathed procession with gloomy resignation.

One by one they filed into the room and moved silently to their places around the table. As they sat down they immersed themselves in useless industry, working hard to ignore their neighbours, like strangers in a slow-moving lift. Pads were repositioned; thick, expensive pens anxiously toyed with. Blinking eyes scrutinised the bespoke cherrywood table top.

Andrew's titanium PowerBook purred quietly in front of him. Florence grinned her gap-toothed, pixilated grin, unaware that the left side of her face was peppered with a rash of gnomic icons. Toby stood next to her, the weight of the world on his seven-year-old shoulders. Andrew looked at his children in silent stupefaction. They were all Catherine – honey-haired, emerald-eyed, implausibly perfect. Every trace of him had been eradicated, as if they were trying to cover their ancestral tracks. Andrew felt his heart creak, overloaded with pride and regret.

When Toby was five months old, Andrew had watched him claw at the cartoon giraffes which were printed on his play mat. Toby had screamed with rage as he tried to pick them up. He had not yet learned to distinguish between two-dimensional images and three-dimensional objects, and couldn't understand why the smiling giraffes always escaped his tiny fists.

Andrew now knew how his son had felt. He was struggling with his own giraffes.

He idly scratched the silver mouse pad and watched the cursor dance. The black arrow mirrored his wandering fingertip exactly. Andrew was gratified to see every twitch of his digit manifested simultaneously on the screen. He derived quiet solace from this localised display of absolute power. The arrow floated across Toby's face, a sluggish ghost. Andrew had read somewhere that this computer was so powerful it could operate rocket launchers and programme nuclear warheads. He wiggled his forefinger; the cursor shimmied beneath his son's chin.

Toby hated to be tickled. He would struggle away from his father's clumsy hands with a sharp yelp of complaint. But with his laptop, Andrew could perform the remote, electronic version without risk of filial censure. An e-tickle. Rocket launchers could wait.

Joel Flaherty was the last man to sit down. He gave Andrew's shoulders a brief caress before sliding into the adjacent seat with a complicit wink. Andrew smiled at Joel, wishing that he would stop pawing him in public. Joel spent a significant proportion of his day benignly molesting the entire workforce, administering a wide repertoire of hugs, rubs, massages, and general laying-on of hands. He only got away with his incessant fondling because he exuded an aura of profound sexlessness. There was a drably pristine flaccidity about him.

As usual, Joel was dressed in black jeans, which might have been marginally too tight, and a black polo shirt, buttoned up to the neck and wrists. What little hair he had left was scraped optimistically across his pinkly translucent pate. Joel's vanity had never quite come to terms with the catastrophe of his hair-loss. He had tried to compensate for his premature baldness by cultivating punctiliously topiar-ised sideburns which tapered to a sharp point in the middle of each cheek. The twin arrows pointed portentously towards his mouth, obliquely (but incorrectly) suggesting a Delphic quality to the pronouncements which issued forth from it. It was all rather embarrassing. Andrew wished that Joel would try to look more like a proper chief executive and less like Ming the Merciless.

Joel cast his eyes up and down the table. 'OK, people, let's begin. The good news is that for the eleventh consecu-tive month, viewing figures are up. The median figure on the twenty-day period to the end of May is up 1.2% on the equivalent figures for the preceding month, having factored in the relevant QRRs.'

A murmur went around the table. Everyone already knew that the figures were up, because everyone had read the confidential e-mail which Joel's hapless personal assistant had mistakenly forwarded to the whole company two days earlier. But everyone was also pretending that they had deleted the e-mail without reading it.

'Overall market share over the same period has increased by 0.3% to 28.2%,' continued Joel, as if murmuring a sanc-tified litany. '*Tilly!* remains the most-watched programme on daytime terrestrial television, and it's still growing. The only question is by how much, and of course we won't get a really clear picture of that until we number-crunch the SAFs.'

Andrew frowned. The man on his left, an associate producer called Damian, scribbled something on his yellow pad and nudged it towards him. Andrew peered at the pad out of the corner of his eye. On it were the words SEASON-ALLY ADJUSTED FIGURES! Andrew pulled his mouth into a half-yawn and blinked in a bored way to show that he knew very well what SAFs were. But that exclamation mark, thought Andrew darkly.

Joel was still analysing the latest statistics. 'The new demographics aren't showing as much of a move as we would like away from our core audience.' Like every television programme which started at 10 o'clock in the morning, *Tilly!*'s audience was divided into two principal groups: students who wouldn't get off the sofa, and pensioners who couldn't. 'Until we can demonstrate a significant shift towards the ABC1s, then the network is stuck in a rut with the advertisers. During Q1 we did make some inroads, but that seems to have fallen off again during Q2. As you might imagine, our Swedish friends are keen to see an improvement.'

Q1, Q2. SAFs. QRRs. Andrew hated all the snappy corporate acronyms, those flashy agglomerations of randomly clustered letters. They were just empty spells, incanted to obscure dreary actuality with illusory punch and pizzazz.

JKMN. Just Kill Me Now.

Andrew's mind drifted away, tuning out Joel's voice. A typhoon of bored antipathy churned inside him as he surveyed the sharp-suited herd in front of him. Look at these self-satisfied idiots, he thought. My friends and colleagues. Good Christ. Suddenly Andrew remembered that he and Catherine were going to a concert at the Union Chapel this evening. Fauré's *Requiem*. Annabel Sulzman, God help them all, was singing a *solo*. Afterwards he would be expected to spend hours agreeing politely how fantastic it had all been. And of course Richard would be there too. Andrew's spirits took another dive.

Joel was still talking. 'Now. On to other matters. Esme?'

The girl sitting next to Damian cleared her throat. 'As

8

you know,' she said, 'we're looking to roll out webcasts of the show over the internet, and that process continues next month with the next round of beta testing.' Esme had a gap between her front teeth, something which Andrew had always found very sexy – although she wasn't in the same league as Clara. But then very few were.

At the thought of Clara, a fresh wave of bewildered disquiet crashed through him.

'We anticipate that by Christmas the webcasts will be downloadable by anyone in the world, from anywhere in the world,' continued Esme. 'It will give us an immediate, pan-global presence.'

Joel nodded in approval. 'This web thing is exactly what we need,' he said. 'It sends out all the right messages. It says we're up-to-date, we're contemporary. It says we're *now*. Because we don't just cater for students and the blue-rinse brigade, right?' Half of the people in the room nodded in agreement; the remaining half shook their heads, also in agreement. After a moment, the nodders stopped nodding and began to shake their heads; at the same time, the shakers stopped shaking and began to nod. Quiet confusion reigned.

Joel looked down the table at the show's star. 'How will that feel, Tilly? Knowing you're being watched in Guadalajara?'

The queen of daytime television smiled back at Joel, but not so hard as to pose any serious threat to her make-up.

Tilly Tyler had been stranded on the tundra of late middle age for years. On screen she still exuded a certain desiccated glamour, but Andrew knew the effort required to preserve her from the cruel talons of time. Every day her skin was slathered in layer upon layer of unguents, dripping with toxins and foul-smelling chemicals. Her wrinkles were then grouted with several applications of beige powder, and on top of that, a garish kaleidoscope of make-up was thickly applied. By the end of the process, she was more efficiently preserved than a sheep's brain pickled in formaldehyde.

'Joel,' said Tilly glacially, 'I go to bed every night *dreaming* of Guadalajara.'

Joel's face fell, causing his sideburns to point slightly downwards.

Catherine Shaw stood in front of the cooker, stirring butter and chocolate together in a saucepan, missing her children.

She watched the glistening squares of yellow and brown as they collapsed warmly into each other. It was at this point in the afternoon when she began to feel an ache in her heart, an unbridled physical longing to see Toby and Florence again. The last hour before their return dragged by impossibly slowly. She wanted to touch their small hands and smell their hair, witness afresh the tiny miracles she had wrought. Their simple embrace was a haven. Catherine wanted to cling to them and never let go.

In a bowl Catherine beat together four eggs, some vanilla extract, and caster sugar. Brownies for tea: she was hoping to delay Toby's inevitable flight to his bedroom when he returned from school, which meant competing with his electronic games and magic tricks. Toby treated Catherine with cagey politeness, as if she were a distant aunt who might be charmed into dispensing a present or two. She added walnuts and flour to the other ingredients and carefully poured the mixture into a baking tray. As she slid the tray into the oven, the telephone began to ring. Catherine quickly crossed the kitchen. An afternoon call was a sinister herald of unscheduled news, an ominous portent of something gone wrong.

'Hello?'

'Cathy, it's me.'

'Annabel, how lovely.' Catherine closed her eyes. The dreaded telephone call, the one she would remember for ever, wasn't upon her, not yet. 'How are you? Ready for tonight?'

There was a heavy sigh. 'I've been sitting here all afternoon wondering what on earth I've got myself into.'

Catherine sat down at the kitchen table and began to read the front page of the newspaper. 'Why don't you get your mat out?'

'This is no time for yoga. What I need is a stiff drink. Several, actually. But I daren't.'

'You'll be fine. You know you will.'

'I don't know. I mean, I must be mad. My solo is supposed to be sung by a prepubescent boy, not some woman in her mid-thirties.'

Catherine pulled a face. Annabel was thirty-nine. 'Is Richard looking forward to tonight?' she asked.

'Richard? I suppose so. He's exhausted, actually. Just got back from the States. Yet another book tour. Sixteen cities in fourteen days.'

'Yikes. That sounds horrendous,' said Catherine, glancing at the kitchen clock. 'Anyway, look, you'll both come for a drink afterwards, won't you? To celebrate.'

'Try and stop me,' said Annabel.

Catherine kept her tone light. 'And the great traveller?'

'Don't worry. He'll come, jet-lagged or not. As if he could ever stay away from you!'

The two friends laughed.

Catherine put down the telephone. On the granite worktop was a knife. She picked it up and peered at her reflection in the steel blade. Her large green eyes gazed uncertainly back. She turned and looked through the French windows at the strip of unmown grass between the flowerbeds. It had been a lawn once, before the children were born, an elegant venue for evening drinks and *al fresco* dining. Now it was a rumpled quilt of mysterious hillocks and dark-bellied

11

divots of turf, occupied by an army of abandoned toys. In the middle of the grass stood a yellow and blue climbing frame. Its asymmetrical angles reminded Catherine of a giant Cyrillic letter. A red slide emerged from one side like a lasciviously unfurled tongue. Andrew had wrestled with the component parts of the climbing frame for an entire weekend, grimly refusing all offers of help. The assembly instructions had been in German. Catherine still couldn't bear to watch Toby clamber through the matrix of poles as he took command of his imaginary castles and tanks. All she could see were the metal joints creaking beneath his weight. Andrew had never been one for practical things.

Beyond the climbing frame lay Catherine's greenhouse. The afternoon sun dazzled hotly in the panes. She considered tidying up the rainbow of plastic scattered across the garden, but decided not to waste her energy. All efforts at containment were ultimately futile.

Instead, Catherine went upstairs to the bedroom. She climbed on to a chair and removed a shoe box from its hiding place on top of the wardrobe. She sat down on the bed and took off the lid.

The box was filled with things which Catherine Shaw had stolen.

She silently surveyed her booty. After a moment she pulled out a slim bracelet of white gold and slipped it on to her wrist. Catherine had taken it from Annabel's jewellery box about six months ago, while she was waiting for Richard to finish in the shower.

Catherine wasn't a proper thief. She didn't shoplift luxury goods, or burglarise strangers' homes, or siphon off bank funds with elegant computer fraud. Her criminal career was strictly small-time. She had no interest in big-value items. Still, she did like to look through her loot. Fingering the evidence of her crimes gave Catherine the proof she needed that she was not the person that other people believed her to be. The box, brimming with bald culpability, quietly re-assured her that she was still alive. Its sweetly stinging shame drew her into sharper focus, but it was the wild purple rush of danger which pushed her on to each new theft. The risk of being caught – of gambling so much for a meaningless private thrill – was necessary ballast, a critical counterweight which prevented her from capsizing into the ocean of dis-affected boredom which surrounded her. With each new transgression came fresh exposure to the incalculable risks of the mundane; it was not fingerprints or brilliant detec-tive work which would undo her, but a poorly-timed trip to the lavatory, an unscheduled return for a forgotten book. Each time she survived, Catherine felt a little more in control. The nearer towards the precipice of disgrace she edged, the easier it became to step back again on to the solid ground of bland respectability.

Sometimes she dreamed of being caught. She imagined her cool confession, detailing every sin, enumerating her crimes for the shocked consideration of all. She wondered whether Andrew would ever be able to forgive her.

Perhaps there was altogether too much to be sorry for.

Catherine took Annabel's bracelet off her wrist and held it up to the afternoon sunlight which fell through the bedroom window. She decided to wear it to the concert that evening.

The oven's timer buzzed. Catherine put the shoe box back on top of the wardrobe and hurried downstairs to the kitchen. When she opened the oven door, a small black cloud of smoke escaped. She extracted the tray and examined its charred contents. She prodded sadly at the unyielding surface of the brownies.

There was the brittle click of a key in the front door. Moments later the house filled with Florence's excited cries, and Catherine's yearning to see her children evaporated at once. Instead she was swamped by wordless anxiety. Toby and Florence represented indefinable, and therefore illimitable, risk. Their small, unpredictable existences were always poised for chaos, constantly threatening to destabilise everything they touched. Now that they were here, back within Catherine's orbit, she craved the worry-free calm which their arrival had shattered, seemingly for ever.

Toby was the first to appear at the kitchen door. 'What's that smell?' he asked.

She looked at him and smiled. 'I've baked some brownies for you.'

'Oh, yum,' said Toby politely, not moving from the doorway.

'How was school?'

Toby looked at his shoes. 'I got into a fight with Henry Rosenthal at lunch.'

'Oh dear. What happened?'

'He called me a quiff.'

Catherine frowned. 'A quiff? Are you sure?'

Toby nodded. 'He said, "Shut up, *quiff*".'

'What had you done to make him say that?'

'Well, I called him a yid,' explained Toby.

Catherine's hand went up to her mouth. 'Oh, Toby. That's awful. *Why*?'

'James Macintyre told me to.'

'Toby, do you know what a yid *is*?'

After a moment Toby shook his head.

'Did it not occur to you to find out before calling – who was it?'

'Henry Rosenthal.'

Catherine closed her eyes. '– before calling Henry Rosenthal one?'

'But James Macintyre *told* me to,' said Toby again.

'So you just did what he said,' said Catherine flatly.

14

Toby looked away. 'He's the leader.'

'Oh, he is, is he? And why's that?'

'Because he's got a *gun*.'

Oh damn, thought Catherine.

'A toy gun,' she said.

'Well, yes, obviously a *toy* gun,' sighed Toby.

'Lucky old James Macintyre, then.'

'If I had a gun,' said Toby, blinking, 'then maybe *I* could be the leader.'

'No, Toby. The answer is no. No guns.'

'But I haven't even –'

'And promise me you won't *ever* say things to people unless you understand what you're saying. Otherwise you'll get into all sorts of trouble.'

Toby sighed the heavy sigh of the perpetually misunderstood.

'Now, stop hovering by the door,' said Catherine. 'Come in and have a brownie. Then it's time for your piano practice.'

'Oh, Mummy. Do I *have* to?'

'Most certainly you do.' It was the usual battleground for their afternoon skirmish: guns and pianos, pianos and guns.

'James Macintyre doesn't have to practise the piano,' mumbled Toby.

Catherine said nothing.

'His dad says that playing the piano is for *girls*.' The word hung in the air, a single horrified syllable, dripping with wounded accusation.

Before Catherine could reply, Florence raced past her brother and wrapped herself tightly around her mother's legs. 'Mummy!' she sighed.

A few moments later Sinead peered around the kitchen door. 'Everything all right, Sinead?' asked Catherine.

'Yes, thanks, Mrs S,' answered Sinead.

Catherine loathed the Mrs S business.

15

Sinead had joined the Shaws under the apparent misapprehension that life as a north London au pair in the twenty-first century was similar to that of a scullery maid in Edwardian England. Her craven subservience – the *us* and *them* of it all – sat ill with Catherine's liberal credentials. She felt put-upon by this poor Irish girl. She had done everything she could to persuade Sinead to call her Catherine, without success. Mrs S was the reluctantly agreed compromise. Not very PC, this Mrs S.

When she was not looking after the children or performing her other domestic chores, Sinead usually stayed in her bedroom at the top of the house, although sometimes she would float through the rooms, a furtive presence, silently observing the Shaw family as they loudly pursued their lives. Catherine resented this sporadic surveillance, sure that Sinead was totting up their transgressions and calculating their collective atonement. Catholics had always given Catherine a crippling moral inferiority complex. Still, she did her best to be friendly. *Noblesse oblige*, and all that. She had tried everything to get Sinead to talk, from polite enquiries about life back in Ireland to soap opera gossip. She had even abandoned Radio 3 and instead pretended to jig around the kitchen to Capital FM. Sinead had responded insipidly to all these overtures, refusing to reciprocate with the nuggets of intimacy which would make them friends. Their relationship had remained obdurately business-like. Catherine still knew nothing about Sinead except that she went out with a boy in Kilburn twice a week. Catherine always lay awake, waiting for her return, listening for a second pair of footsteps on the staircase.

Catherine bent down to kiss the top of her daughter's head. '*Dog!*' shouted Florence. The Shaws did not have a dog. She escaped Catherine's clutches and ran into the garden, gurgling with unexplained laughter.

'I don't see why *I* can't have a gun if everyone else has one,' complained Toby, finally approaching the kitchen table.

'Oh Toby, I've explained it all before. Guns are bad, you know that.'

'But I don't want a *real* one,' said Toby.

Catherine tried to pierce the top of the brownies with a knife. 'What do you want a gun for, anyway?' she asked. 'Why do you want to kill each other all the time?' Finally she broke through the brownies' tough exoskeleton and began to hack away at the disintegrating biscuit beneath.

Toby shrugged. 'It's what boys do, isn't it?'

And therein lay Catherine's problem. Toby was right. It was what boys did. She knew that she was trying to stem the irrepressible tide of nature. There was something hard-wired into boys' psyches which made them go around pretending to shoot each other, just as girls liked to play with dolls. Catherine knew that Toby wouldn't turn into a sociopath just because he played with plastic guns. If anything, he was more likely to be irreparably damaged if he *didn't* play with them: he would be ostracised by his peers and become a loner. He would start wearing black. Then he would start dismembering small animals in his bedroom.

Catherine could no longer remember why she had imposed the embargo on weaponry, but it didn't matter any more: right or wrong, she wasn't going to back down now. She refused to compromise her principles, whatever they were.

'It might be what other boys do,' she replied, aware of Sinead's silent scrutiny from the kitchen door, 'but not you.'

Toby folded his arms across his chest. 'Anyway,' he said, 'James Macintyre's dad says that guns don't kill people. *People* kill people.'

Catherine stared at her son. 'What utter rot,' she declared. 'James Macintyre's dad sounds like a prize idiot.' She put a plate down on the table in front of him.

Toby looked at the two unevenly hewn slabs of burnt biscuit which were stacked one on top of the other. 'I'm not really hungry,' he said after a moment.

'Of course you are,' said Catherine briskly. 'And the next time James Macintyre tells you to do something, you stand your ground. Even if he has got a gun.' She walked around the table and put her hands on his shoulders.

Toby reached up and squeezed her fingers. He twisted around and looked at her with worried eyes. 'Mum?'

'Yes, sweetheart?'

'What *is* a quiff?' he whispered.

Finally, it was Andrew's turn to address the meeting. He stood up and looked along the table. Nobody met his eye. He cleared his throat.

'The highest rated show of the last quarter was *My Lesbian Mother Stole my Girlfriend*. Not *Secrets of a Successful Soufflé*. Not *My Third Nipple Hell*. But *My Lesbian Mother Stole my Girlfriend*.' There was an indifferent silence. 'Let me remind you all what happened in that particular show,' said Andrew. 'Adrian was a milkman from Bromley. Nice boy, still living with his parents. He was going out with a hairdresser's apprentice called Kelly-Anne. They'd been together for about three months, happily enough by all accounts, until one evening, Adrian came back from the pub to discover Kelly-Anne in bed with his mother, Dawn. Dawn and Kelly-Anne declared that they had fallen in love and Dawn said that her marriage of twenty-seven years had been a sham. She promptly kicked Adrian and his father, Dan, out of the house, and Kelly-Anne moved in. Now, Kelly-Anne's mother, Cindy, was furious. She didn't much like Adrian, but Adrian's mother was *far* worse. Anyway, we got them all together to talk about it.' Andrew paused. 'It was after this show, you may remember, that we began insisting

18

that our guests sign legal disclaimers before going on set. As it is, we eventually managed to settle everything out of court.'

The room was silent. Damian had started scribbling notes on his pad and passing them to Esme.

'Now, who knows?' said Andrew. 'Maybe their sordid little problem could have been peacefully resolved if they had been left to sort things out in private. But because *we* got involved, that's a matter of pure speculation.' He looked around the room. 'After his mother humiliated him on the show, Adrian, our milkman, vowed never to talk to Dawn again. Dawn and Dan are getting a divorce, which I understand is proving acrimonious. Kelly-Anne was so angry with Dawn for calling Cindy a slag on national television that she promptly fell out of love again, announced that she was, in fact, heterosexual after all, and moved out. Adrian, not unreasonably, wouldn't speak to Kelly-Anne, and her mother refused to let her move back in. As a result, Kelly-Anne shacked up with *Dan*, and so now Adrian isn't talking to his father either. The last I heard, he's given up his milk round and has gone to a religious retreat on the Isle of Sheppey.' Andrew stuck his hands into his pockets, struggling against the tsunami of apathy which was threatening to overwhelm him. 'I'm appalled to tell you that Freddie is absolutely delighted. I spoke to him this morning, and he is one *happy* Scandinavian.' Freddie Larssen was the Overseas Corporate Development Officer of the Swedish multinational media conglomerate which had purchased the share capital of Andrew and Joel's small television production company three years previously. The deal had simultaneously made them both millionaires and indentured slaves. Whilst they still in theory exercised executive control over the company's operations, Andrew and Joel now spent most of their time glancing anxiously over their shoulders to check that Freddie Larssen was happy.

'Freddie loved *My Lesbian Mother*,' continued Andrew. 'He said that it was a fabulous example of what we do best. He said it showed why *Tilly!* is the most popular show on daytime television.' He paused. 'No matter that we ruined half a dozen lives to do it, because that's *what we do*, isn't it? People watch *Tilly!* because they like to be reminded that there are people out there who are more miserable than them. It doesn't matter how depressed you are, you're bound to feel better if someone admits on national television that, I don't know, *My Wife Sleeps with Men for Money Because I'm Poor and my Cock is the Size of a Peanut*.'

More silence.

'Anyway,' sighed Andrew, 'the word from Stockholm is that they want more of the same. No more inspirational stories of survival against the odds. No more warm-hearted celebrity interviews. No more slimming tips, no more novelty talent contests. What we are looking for is more insults, more threats of bodily violence, that kind of thing. Here's a new principle to guide you all: from now on, the sweetest sound on our show will be the swear beep.' At one point during the *Lesbian Mother* show Kelly-Anne's mother had delivered a diatribe of such mesmerising and unremitting vulgarity that viewers were treated to an uninterrupted whine of electronic disapproval which lasted eighteen seconds. 'With immediate effect, that machine has to go into overdrive. Freddie wants *half the show* to be drowned out by the bloody swear beep.'

'Beep,' said Joel.

Andrew ignored him. He pointed at the floor. 'There is only one direction for this show, and it's *down*. They want us in the gutter, as deep as we can go. They want us to plumb new depths of exploitation, tastelessness, and tackiness. Ideas on my desk by Wednesday morning. The more degrading the better.' Andrew sat down.

20

'Actually,' said Tilly Tyler, 'I have *one* idea.'

'Tilly,' sighed Andrew. 'Please. Do tell.'

Tilly waited until all eyes were upon her. 'I thought that we could combine two old features,' she said. She held up one jewel-encrusted hand. 'We have the regular *Precious Pet* slot.' She held up her other hand. 'And we have the regular *Marvellous Makeover* slot.' Tilly brought her hands together with a dry slap. 'Why not put them together?'

Andrew closed his eyes and pinched the bridge of his nose. He could feel the twitching tail of a migraine at the back of his neck, the first stirrings of the monstrous beast. 'Together?' he said.

'*Marvellous Makeovers of Precious Pets*.'

Andrew knew at once that *Marvellous Makeovers of Precious Pets* was a good idea. (The concept of a good idea in the context of *Tilly!* was a highly refined and rarefied thing. All good ideas were – this was how highly refined and rarefied the concept was – terrible.) *Marvellous Makeovers of Precious Pets* was as brilliantly terrible as anything they had done. It couldn't have been more nauseatingly bland, more gut-wrenchingly naff. It would, Andrew knew, be a dreadful success. But still. Orders were orders. 'Sorry, Tilly,' he said. 'It's not really what Freddie has in mind.'

Tilly Tyler's mouth puckered into a petulant *moue*. 'Why ever not?'

Andrew threw his hands into the air. 'Where's the pain?' he demanded. 'Where's the degradation?'

Beside him, Joel shifted carefully in his seat. 'Andrew –'

'Giving a red setter a French pedicure is not going to set our viewers' black hearts racing, is it?' said Andrew.

There was a moment's silence.

Andrew sighed. 'Look. You all know the rules. What Freddie wants, Freddie gets. And he does *not* want legions of contented pet owners.'

'What if animal activists stormed the stage half-way through?' suggested Damian.

'Activists?' said Andrew.

'Let's say you're giving a golden retriever a bikini wax. That would constitute cruel and unusual treatment, surely.'

Esme leaned forward. 'They could kidnap the dog. In the name of, you know, animal liberation. We could have a hostage situation, live on air.'

'For God's sake,' said Andrew. 'We produce a mid-morning chat-show, not *Animal Hospital* meets *Die Hard*.'

The others ignored him.

'Think of the coverage we'd get,' said Damian. 'Every other media outlet would be forced to run the story. And we could do a deal with the activists so we can deliver a happy ending just in time for the next morning's papers.'

'Perhaps,' said Tilly modestly, 'I could negotiate the dog's release.'

'Brilliant,' said Esme. 'Save a dog – instant sainthood.'

'I know someone who's an animal rights campaigner,' said Damian.

Andrew looked at him. 'You *do*?'

'Well,' said Damian, 'she's a vegan.'

'Good enough,' said Tilly briskly.

'Perhaps we should just hire actors,' said Esme. 'It might be simpler if we didn't have to bother with *real* activists. You know. They might object.'

Esme had a point, thought Andrew. Apart from anything else, if real activists had any idea how many defenceless animals had been sacrificed in laboratories on the altar of Tilly Tyler's cosmetic vanity, they would be more likely to kidnap her than the damn dog. He took a deep breath. 'This is all very interesting, but it's really not what Freddie wants.'

Tilly turned towards him, her eyes granite. '*Bugger* Freddie,' she said loudly.

Andrew coughed. 'Alluring though your suggestion is, Tilly, I'm not in a position, either literally or metaphorically, to –'

'Can't you at least *ask* him?'

Andrew's eyes met Tilly's across the table. They gazed at each other for several seconds.

'No,' said Andrew eventually. 'I can't.'

Tilly leaned back in her seat. The corners of her mouth twitched fractionally upwards. 'Oh, that's right,' she said. 'I forgot. I'm talking to Andrew Shaw, the man who's never faced up to a single challenge in his life.'

There was a collective intake of breath from around the table.

Andrew blinked. 'Excuse me?'

'If you're really too spineless to talk to Freddie,' said Tilly, 'then I'll call him myself.' Her gaze danced with mockery and threat. Andrew knew the game was up.

He held up his hands. 'All right, all right. I give in. I'll talk to him and make him understand. *Marvellous Makeovers of Precious Pets* it is. But can we *please* forget the pet hostage scenario?'

Damian and Esme exchanged disappointed looks.

'Right then,' said Joel, standing up. 'I think we're done. See you all next week.' At this everyone began to make their way to the door. Andrew did not move. He stared fiercely at his laptop, his cheeks nuclear. Florence grinned back at him, her guileless smile compounding his gloom.

When he was the only one left in the room, he put his head in his hands.

It was never supposed to be like this.

THREE

Andrew's mother towered over his childhood like a gentle colossus, eclipsing everyone else from view.

Rosa Shaw – fragrant, flagrant Rosa! The proudest addict you ever saw. She swept across Andrew's memory, a half-smoked cigarette between her fingers, a trail of smoke languishing in her wake. Even now, the faintest caress of distant tobacco fumes could bring her crashing back to life – reincarnated by the very things which killed her.

Her father, a dour Scot, had been a civil servant in the Foreign Office. The early years of his marriage to Rosa's mother were spent in various sweltering outposts of the crumbling Empire, he efficiently administrating, she subsisting in bored luxury. Rosa, their only child, was born in Dhaka, in 1929. She had a troop of dark-skinned servants to tend her and a mongoose as a pet, but no friends to play with. Her mother, elegant and remote, read long Victorian novels and ordered hampers of *foie gras* from Harrods. When Rosa was seven, the family returned home to the chill granite crucible of Aberdeen, where her parents' cheerless *froideur* was an easy match for the winds which gusted off the North Sea. Without a phalanx of attendants to quarantine their spirited daughter, they soon sent Rosa away to a boarding school on the south coast of England. Not once during the ten years which followed did they make the six-hundred-mile journey to see her, preferring to pursue their existences unimpeded by childish caprice. Three times a year Rosa made the long, lonely train journey from Sussex to Scotland, and back again. As she watched the English countryside roll past the train window – all those miles which her parents had so carefully put between them! – she vowed that her life would be different.

And so began a rebellion which would last until the day she died. She began a distancing more meaningful than mere geography. She rejected everything that her parents held dear – their dutiful, grim-faced Presbyterianism, their puritanical abstinence, their pride in their small, wet country. But most of all she rejected their cold dispassion. When, years later, Andrew was born, she adored him with a matchless love. Every caress and kiss eclipsed her own lonely childhood a little more.

Like other mothers of a willowy Bohemian temperament, Rosa convinced herself that her son was an exceptionally gifted child, despite all the evidence to the contrary. Andrew was actually impregnably normal. In fact, he was mean. Every exam score, every class position, was pitched exactly on the average. Andrew toiled away anonymously in the middle of the pack, never failing, never excelling. He was an anthropological incarnation of a mathematical concept. But being Mister Average was of no use to him. Rosa's manifest devotion was something of a burden; he desperately did not want to disappoint her. And so he tried to hide his relentless mediocrity from Rosa by throwing a cloak of misdirection up around him, embarking on a campaign of wilful precocity. He borrowed Walt Whitman and Robert Frost anthologies from the library and left them lying about his bedroom for Rosa to find. He listened, grudgingly, to Joni Mitchell rather than Status Quo. His hair curled subversively beyond the prevailing acceptable length. For a while he even sported a moustache, its near-invisible hairs as downy as a young fawn's. He amassed an impressive collection of crushed velvet loon pants.

But it was all rather a struggle. Andrew was painfully aware how ridiculous he looked, even at the rayonned fag end of the 1970s. He longed to dress in regulation flares and tank tops. He dreamed of clandestine trips to the barbers for a neat trim. The books of poetry went unread, of course; instead Andrew secretly gorged himself on fat airport thrillers. Still, he kept loyally plugging away, trying to be the son Rosa wanted him to be.

As a result, Andrew's undistinguished university career was shrouded in a fog of marijuana smoke. Most of his waking hours were spent lying on the floor of other people's rooms, reverentially passing a succession of tightly-rolled joints and listening to Jethro Tull albums. His friends all smoked pot by way of rebellion; Andrew did it out of a sense of filial duty. It gave him tremendous headaches.

When his friends began to talk about CVs, job interviews, salaries and private pension schemes, Andrew listened with quiet envy. There was nothing he would have liked more than a lucrative office-bound career, but he knew that it would break his mother's heart. Instead he hurtled towards graduation with fatalistic abandon, his future uncluttered by job applications. That autumn, his old university friends cut their hair and began to swagger around the Square Mile with phones the size of bricks glued to their ears. This was at the beginning of the eighties, when the whiff of impending fortune lingered on every street corner. In the absence of any better ideas, Andrew moved into a cramped studio in Bayswater and began to write a novel. He tried not to think about the monstrous salary he was foregoing as he sat slumped in front of his typewriter, wallowing in self-righteous penury.

A year and a half later, there was a book, of sorts. Casting himself as the Faulkner of the West Country, Andrew had created a ponderous family saga set in Weston-super-Mare. The family in question were haberdashers by trade, locked in improbable battle with a rival retailer of superior sewing accessories. There was much commercial derring-do, industrial sabotage, and some carefully researched stuff about ribbon manufacturing. There was also an affecting sub-plot that centred around a small dog with a degenerative muscle condition. (Andrew had never actually *read* any Faulkner.)

He expended so much emotional energy on his *magnum opus* (every hesitant tap on the keys an effort, every word a torture!) that by the time it was finished he had convinced himself that this was indeed what he had been destined for.

Andrew would be a *novelist*.

Rosa was the first person to read the completed manuscript. She loved it, of course. Together mother and son sent copies to the ten most prestigious literary agencies in London. Andrew retired to his tiny Bayswater studio and waited for the telephone to ring, preparing himself for greatness.

The disappointment of the months which followed had remained with him ever since. He retreated to his parents' house and watched as Rosa harassed the literary agencies on his behalf. Nobody was interested in Andrew's book. With each successive call, Andrew could not help blaming her, just a little bit. In the past, the sheer force of her will had been sufficient to bring about everything she had wished for, but this time not even she could conjure up a miracle of the magnitude required. Because the truth was that

27

Andrew's novel really wasn't terribly good. It wasn't spectacularly awful, either. It was just cripplingly average.

Finally, Andrew had slipped the last remaining copy of his manuscript into an unmarked brown envelope and pushed it out of sight beneath his bed. In the years which followed, the envelope followed him across London, a silent reminder of his abandoned dreams.

He drifted listlessly, trying to decide what to do next. When Joel Flaherty, one of his old dope-smoking friends from university, called him up and asked him out for lunch, Andrew had nearly refused. Joel had somehow stumbled into a job as a market analyst at a large Japanese investment bank, and Andrew had no wish to listen to endless tales of ridiculous remuneration packages and corporate largesse. But he couldn't afford to eat out in restaurants, either, and Joel had promised to foot the bill.

Joel looked gaunt and grey, exhausted by the corporate feeding frenzy which gripped the City. But he was also bored. He was twenty-five years old, he told Andrew, and had already made enough money to retire on. He was looking for a new challenge, something *fun*, and here was his idea: this new daytime television thing. It was a fresh market, waiting to be tapped. Whoever got there first would clean up. Joel had some ideas, but he needed a partner, someone to provide the artistic input while he took care of the business side of things. Andrew was the creative type. Was he interested? At the time Andrew was working in a large department store, selling children's shoes. After a mean-spirited display of apparent indecision, he had grudgingly accepted.

It soon became apparent that Andrew had finally found his calling. In the arena of mass-market television, it was his very ordinariness, for so long such a torment, which was now his most valuable asset. Possessed with a genuinely plebeian sensibility, he discovered a flair for predicting trends in popular entertainment. His unerring instinct for the lucratively naff catapulted their company, Trident Television, to success, and it soon became one of the foremost independent television production companies of the decade. And, of course, his mother was delighted. Television wasn't the *Arts*, exactly, but it was the Media, which was the next best thing.

All of Andrew's subsequent success had stemmed from that lunch, and Joel Flaherty's generous offer. Joel had flung his old friend a lifebelt, and Andrew had never really been able to forgive him for it.

FOUR

Inside the greenhouse, Catherine was breathing.

She sat with her eyes closed, perched at one end of a thin blue rubber mat. Her legs were crossed, each foot resting on the opposite thigh, soles facing skywards. Her arms fell loosely by her sides, palms open towards the sun. She felt poised, a composition in three dimensions, elegantly symmetrical, gracefully still.

The blue mat was unrolled along the narrow concrete corridor which ran down the middle of the greenhouse. On either side of this central aisle, Catherine's orchids were arranged on trestle tables, a colourful infantry standing guard over her privacy. The flowers possessed a shockingly feral quality, sinuous beasts of exotic ferocity. Their jaws dripped with colour. Catherine filled her lungs with their sweetly-scented air.

The warm light of London's early evening flooded through the glass. The distant cries of children playing in neighbouring gardens caressed the fringes of Catherine's consciousness. She focused on the four stages of each breath she took. *Puraka, abhyantara kumbhaka, rechaka, bahya kumbhaka.* With every *kumbhaka* – the deliberate suspension of the

30

cycle between inhalation and exhalation – Catherine half-heartedly tried to channel her latent inner powers, as Rahsaan had taught. Even in the privacy of her own greenhouse, Catherine couldn't help feeling self-conscious about this part of the routine. She was never exactly sure which latent inner powers she was supposed to be channelling.

Still, Catherine's breathing exercises soon delivered a warm, golden calm from deep within her, radiating outwards in serene waves. She focused wholly on the air which she pulled into her lungs, visualising the rich deposits of cosmic energy, *prana*, willing it to infuse every cell of her body with its vital life-force. As she silently urged the *prana* onwards, her tranquillity grew. She dived down into a deeper inner consciousness. One by one, her troubles slipped away until there was nothing but the reassuring rhythm of her breath. The world outside was a dream's flight away now; she started to float blissfully free of her quotidian moorings. Her mind became a dazzling blank. As her breaths grew deeper and less frequent, a quiet ecstasy began to spread from the centre of her chest, liberating her, liberating her, liberating –

'Mrs S?'

Catherine opened her eyes. Sinead was standing at the door of the greenhouse. Catherine blinked, struggling to adjust to this brutal intrusion from the world she had been trying so hard to forget. The interruption made her want to burst into tears of frustration, but it was the blistering constancy of her need to *escape* which filled her with real sorrow.

'Sinead? What is it?' With a wince Catherine unhooked her feet from her thighs.

'It's Florence,' said Sinead. 'She wants a story.'

Catherine sighed. 'Well, Sinead, *read* her one. That's what we pay you for, isn't it?'

31

Sinead shook her head sombrely. 'I've tried, Mrs S. She wants *you* to read it.'

'For God's sake, Sinead, she's two years old. You can't let her bully you like this.'

'No, Mrs S,' agreed Sinead, hanging her head in contrition.

There was a brief silence.

'Oh, for heaven's sake,' said Catherine. She stood up and began to stride towards the house, Sinead trotting obediently behind her. As Catherine stepped into the kitchen she could hear Florence's hysterical screeching as it ricocheted down two flights of stairs. Catherine climbed the stairs to her daughter's bedroom, quietly delighted. How fine it was to be wanted so much!

Trident Television's offices occupied five cramped floors of a Georgian town house in a quiet mews in Soho. The building was in an advanced state of decrepitude. Paint flaked off the walls in extravagant curlicues of disrepair. The corners of the foot-weary carpets had begun to curl up in defeat. Corridors and stairways were the correct width for the proper reception of Georgian society, but woefully inadequate for a modern-day office.

Alone in his tiny top-floor office, Andrew Shaw dreamed of huge, sleekly modern foyers, decked out in proto-minimalist chic. He fantasised about soaring atria of excessive greenness, frond-heavy jungles of non-deciduous plant life. He yearned for an exotically verdant, ostentatiously redundant office space, filled with the indigenous flora of the rainforests. Mango plants. Some of Catherine's orchids. Perhaps a colourful family of parakeets to flit gracefully twixt palm tree and coconut leaf. Andrew knew how people calibrated success in the television industry; his Amazonian paradise would earn him more credibility than a shelf-load of Baftas.

For the moment, though, Andrew was confined to the congested reality of his fern-free working environment. His office was fashionably austere, but only because there was no room for any of the shiny accoutrements of the high-flying media executive. On the wall hung a framed copy of Tilly Tyler on the cover of the *Radio Times*. She was clasping a microphone in a mildly suggestive pose and winking slyly at the camera, exposing a wrinkled, cerulean eyelid. Andrew had positioned the picture behind his desk so that he didn't have to look at it all day.

Andrew lowered his head over his desk. His face hovered about an inch over the speckled foam of his full-fat cappuccino, his consolation for his earlier humiliation at Tilly Tyler's liver-spotted hands. He lowered his lips until he was kissing the top of the wobbling froth. He remained motionless for a moment or two, and then inhaled the shimmering knoll of foamy milk in one mammoth slurp. He gurgled with pleasure as it slipped down his throat. Tilly really was a poisonous old trout, he thought. As her fame had grown she had become increasingly obnoxious. The show's success depended on her, and everyone knew it. Most of all, Tilly knew it. Consummate professional that she was, she did everything to cultivate rumour and paranoia that she was contemplating another gig with a rival network. The prospect was unthinkable, and so occasionally Andrew and Joel were forced to endure these small humiliations to keep Tilly sweet.

Andrew's laptop beeped, and Toby and Florence disintegrated, replaced by his e-mail inbox. A new e-mail had just arrived.

It was from Clara.

How ru 2day?

Andrew hit the Reply button and began to type.

OK, I suppose.
Much teeth gnashing at my colleagues.

After a moment's thought, Andrew leaned forward and changed

colleagues

to

employees

He stared at the screen for several minutes, and then he typed, slowly, deliberately,

xA

and immediately clicked Send, before he could change his mind. A grey box appeared on the screen and Andrew watched the computer's running commentary on the progress of his missive as it was translated into a million electronic impulses and squeezed through his telephone line and out into the world.

Andrew sat at his desk and waited.

Two weeks earlier he had shown his face in a local wine bar at the leaving drinks for an assistant floor manager on *Tilly!* and had delivered his standard farewell speech, fulsome with praise and regret. (It always made Andrew feel like a priest, this clueless delivery of another stranger's eulogy.) While he was speaking, he noticed a tall, pretty brunette watching him. A few minutes later she tapped him on the shoulder and asked if he wanted to buy her supper. Hypnotised by this display of self-confidence, it seemed to Andrew that to refuse would have been quite impossible, entirely against all laws of nature. Blinking back his fear, he had called Catherine from the echoing sanctuary of the gents ('Where are you?' she had asked, 'in a *cave*?') and then guided Clara to a small trattoria on Frith Street. Clara, it transpired, had gone to school with the departing assistant floor manager. They failed to eat much of their food but managed to drink two bottles of Barolo. At the end of the evening they had exchanged cards and two lingering kisses, one on each cheek.

It was all innocent enough, until Andrew failed to mention anything of it to Catherine when he returned home that night. His last-minute decision to say nothing suddenly threw the evening into sinister shadow. By the following morning Andrew had realised his mistake, but by then, of course, it was too late. He had missed the window for such disclosures. Catherine's first reaction to any subsequent admission, no matter how casual or off-hand, would be to ask why he had failed to mention it straight away. And to that he had no answer – at least, none that he could contemplate giving to his wife.

Ten years of worshipful devotion and unwavering fidelity – and suddenly this.

Two days after their dinner, Clara had sent Andrew an e-mail, loaded with erotic obliquity. Andrew read it again and again in quiet stupefaction. After an unequal struggle with his conscience, he wrote back.

Andrew and Clara had then embarked upon a torrid electronic correspondence. E-mails flew down the wires, pithy and coy. They jousted, they parried, they teased. Of course, he told himself, it was just a bit of harmless fun. There was nothing to feel guilty about. It wasn't as if anything had *happened*. Still, that didn't stop Andrew from being crucified by shame with every treacherous peck at the keyboard. But nor was he able to stop himself. He was drawn irresistibly back, intoxicated by the furtiveness of the exchange.

Clara filled him with dizzying hope and ineluctable fear. Finally, her reply appeared on the screen.

Oh dear! r they not playing ball with your plans 4 world domination?
syla

A twist of regret played on Andrew's lips. Yesterday he had written Clara a long e-mail, mocking the programme which had made him rich. He had ridiculed *Tilly!*, the people who made it, and the people who watched it. He had told her how he wanted to take on new, more challenging projects – historical dramas, political documentaries, that sort of thing. It was all rubbish, of course, but Andrew wished that he had been rather more circumspect. The e-mail now sat, out of reach, on the computer of a girl he hardly knew. That's what you got for trying to show off, he told himself ruefully. It would take no more than a few seconds to send his message proliferating across London, an endlessly self-replicating paean to his idiocy. Ridicule and derision were two clicks of a mouse away.

Rather than think too much about this quietly ticking cyber time-bomb, Andrew typed,

syla?

and pressed Send.

Even if Andrew really *had* wanted to take on more interesting projects, the Swedes would never have allowed it. He was hemmed in by every treacherous clause of the employment contract which the Scandinavians had insisted he sign when they had bought the company. The tightly-worded paragraphs prescribed and proscribed in relentless detail, trussing him up in a thicket of unyielding legal verbiage. His job description, *Creative Director*, was a hideous joke. There was no longer an ounce of creativity in what Andrew did. His job was quality control: he was contractually obliged to ensure that there was no raising of standards. Andrew was trapped, lashed to the monstrous beast he had created.

Andrew tapped his fingers restlessly on the top of his desk, waiting for Clara's answer. Eventually, the computer announced the arrival of her reply. Andrew reached for his mouse.

See ya later, alligator

read the message. Andrew sighed. Clara only used the argot of cyberspace because she knew how much it irritated him. He wrote,

God. Must you?

This time the response was almost immediate.

Oh, absolutely. lol.
:-)
xC

Andrew let out a low whistle. The stupid sideways smiley face and the

xC

constituted definite progress. He stared into space, lost in thought. Suddenly the day's accumulated frustrations and humiliations began to press down, suffocating him. Tilly's withering comment echoed in his ears. *The man who's never faced up to a single challenge in his life.* Was that really how people thought of him? Well, he'd show the smug bitch. He'd show the whole lot of them.

He began to type.

Fancy grabbing a bite to eat next Monday evening?

He pressed Send.
Nothing happened.
Shit, shit, shit.

Andrew sat in front of his computer, suddenly helpless, an unwilling hostage to the elephantine labyrinth of nefarious gates, interfaces, POP servers and electronic impulses which stood between him and Clara. He could picture her sitting in front of her computer, trying to decipher those nine words, wondering how many layers of hidden meaning lurked behind them. Andrew hit the top of his desk with his fist. A telephone call could so easily have conveyed the lightness of the offer, the take-it-or-leave-it casualness of it all. But as he stared at his message, desperation seemed to shriek out of every pixel. He waited anxiously.

lovely offer thanx but am bc

bc?

Andrew groaned. *Busy.* The bastardised, crabbily compressed lingua franca of e-mail made Clara's response sound clinically dismissive. Well, if you can't beat 'em, he told himself. Breathlessly, he typed

hot d8?

A minute later:

hardly. my sister + I have got tix 2 c jules and the plum
yawn. :-o

Andrew stared at the screen in bewilderment.

oh, right

he typed cautiously, unsure whether *Jules and the Plum* was
a film, a band, a dance collective, a modern opera, or something even more terrifyingly hip. Then, a few moments later,
disaster struck:

r u jealous?!?

Andrew swore loudly. The only thing for it was to flirt
like mad and hope she'd forget his flash of naked paranoia.

madly. can u blame me?

An age.

when you put it like that . . . no. lol.
wot about 2nite?

Andrew felt his palms spontaneously dampen. Tonight!
Suddenly he remembered the concert in the Union Chapel.
Anguish and relief barrelled through him simultaneously.

ah, sorry, plans already hatched

sounded suitably rakish, he thought. Best not to go into too
much detail about the bloody Fauré. He paused for a moment,
fingers poised over the keyboard.

but I can offer you lunch on Tuesday, if that suits

'Andrew?'

Petrushka, his personal assistant, was peeping nervously around the door.

Andrew's head snapped up. 'Yes?'

'Can we go through your diary for next week?'

'My diary?' mumbled Andrew. His eyes drifted back to the PowerBook's screen, which remained inscrutably empty.

'Andrew?' pleaded Petrushka.

tues lunch sounds divine. e me avec details.

xxx

C

Three xs! Sweet Jesus.

'*Andrew*?'

'Oh, Christ, Petrushka. All right, all right.' Andrew closed his laptop and smiled at Petrushka, who was still half hidden behind the door. 'Sorry. Just having a bit of a moment. You were saying?'

Petrushka stared at him as if he had two heads. 'Your diary –'

'My diary. Of course. Of course. Sorry. Come on in.'

Andrew Shaw smiled his broadest smile, which was haunted by a shadow of dread.

Lunch next Tuesday!

Florence, already in her pyjamas, was standing on her bed, clutching a blue dog with large ears. When she saw her mother her screams grew louder, and Catherine's honeyed meditation on the glories of motherhood was obliterated. 'Florence?' she said. 'It's *me*.' Florence continued to wail. Sinead arrived at the bedroom door. Catherine turned on

40

her. 'I thought you said she wanted me,' she complained.

'She *did*,' replied Sinead, gazing impassively at the screaming child.

With a sigh, Catherine stepped forward and picked Florence up. Still yelling, Florence began to hit her mother over the head with the blue dog. When her daughter's fit showed no sign of abating, Catherine put her back down on the bed and retreated. Florence lowered her head into her pillow and emitted a low moan of unmitigated pathos.

Toby appeared, looking interested. 'What's wrong with Florence?' he asked.

'Nothing,' said Catherine. 'She just wants me to read her a bedtime story.' At this Florence gasped a mournful *Noooo*, and began to shake her head.

'Are you sure?' asked Toby.

By now Catherine's yoga-enhanced equanimity had completely disappeared. Bitterness and disappointment swelled within her. 'Go to your room, Toby,' she said irritably.

'But I just –'

'*Now.*'

With a pointed sigh, Toby retreated. Florence continued to snivel. Catherine felt her nerves begin to fray. All she wanted was for the crying to stop, as if her daughter's tears were the catalyst for some greater ill, the precursor to the inevitable unravelling of her world. She leaned her head against the wall and breathed deeply. *Puraka, abhyantara kumbhaka, rechaka, bahya kumbhaka*. Florence's cries grew louder. Catherine clenched her fists. Her fingernails cut into her palm.

Sinead stepped forward. 'Shall I try again, Mrs S?'

'Yes please,' said Catherine. She looked at her watch. 'I'd better go and get ready for this evening.'

In the shower Catherine turned up the temperature to

near-scalding. As the boiling needles of water pummelled her skin, she chastised herself for taking the capricious whims of her children to heart. She wondered bleakly whether this was actually no more than she deserved.

Forty-five minutes later, Catherine had completed her make-up and had donned a black trouser suit. She slipped on the stolen bracelet, confident that Annabel would be too preoccupied with her performance to notice. Catherine raised her chin, examining herself critically in the mirror. She un-buttoned her jacket and scrutinised the soft contours of her breasts beneath the ivory silk of her scoop-necked top. Even after the cataclysm of two pregnancies, she had nothing to be ashamed about. Beneath the outfit her saucily-engineered Gossard sculpted and enhanced in unrepentant deceit. She looked quietly sensational.

Catherine was looking forward to seeing Richard this evening. It had been a long two weeks while he was in America.

With a final glance at herself in the mirror, Catherine closed the bedroom door. At the top of the stairs, Sinead was standing outside Florence's bedroom, her ear pressed to the door. Catherine raised a quizzical eyebrow.

'She's asleep,' whispered Sinead.

'I didn't say good-night,' sighed Catherine.

'I said it for you.'

Unable to look Sinead in the eye, Catherine turned and tiptoed towards Toby's bedroom. She tapped on the door. 'Toby? Darling?' There was a long, accusatory silence, followed by a pointed thud as Toby dropped something on the floor to let Catherine know that he'd heard her. '*Toby?*' Catherine was always astonished at her son's obdurate ability to hold a grudge. 'I'm going out. I'm meeting Daddy and we won't be back until late.' Defiant, unrepentant. Catherine counted slowly to ten, and then, more slowly, to twenty.

Finally she turned to go. The silence chased her down the stairs.

In the hallway Catherine checked her face again in the mirror. Sinead hovered nearby, waiting for her to leave. Nobody wants me, thought Catherine sadly. 'Andrew will have his mobile with him,' she said. 'I'll make sure he turns it on after the concert.' Catherine turned and flashed a tight, desperate smile. 'How do I look?'

Sinead gazed at her for a few moments, then shrugged. 'Nice.'

'Oh, thanks,' cried Catherine, falling gratefully on the single, non-committed syllable. 'Well, Sinead, I'll see you when we get home.' She lingered by the front door, unsure what she was waiting for. Another kind word, perhaps, something for her to enjoy on the journey.

'OK,' said Sinead, yawning. 'See you.'

Catherine flung open the front door and escaped.

FIVE

Outside the Union Chapel, people were milling cheerfully about. Catherine scanned the faces of the crowd. There he was, leaning against the railings: six foot six, broad shoulders, a huge slab of a head, Easter Island proportions. His large, craggily patrician features broke into a smile as she approached.

'Hey, stranger,' he said. 'Wow, look at you.' Catherine stepped forwards to wrap her arms around him, but he held her at a polite distance and delivered a prim, dry kiss on her cheek. She gazed in confusion at his blandly affable expression. 'So how've you been?' he asked.

Catherine took a slow step backwards. 'You know. Busy. Bored. How was America?'

Richard Sulzman shrugged. 'You know. Busy. Lucrative, I guess. My publicist is an asshole, though. All very rigorous and efficient, of course, but then so were the Nazis.'

'And Annabel?'

'Annabel? She's a bag of nerves.' Richard spoke in his low New Jersey drawl, his vowels burnished and softened by two decades in London. 'But she'll pull it off.'

'Of course she will.'

'Here.' Richard handed her a folded sheet of paper. 'I got you a programme.'

Catherine opened the programme. She scanned the words, failing to read a single one. 'So,' she murmured, 'we're playing the gallant husband this evening, are we?'

Richard looked away. 'Come on, Cathy. It's her big night.'

After her children's behaviour, Catherine scarcely felt able to withstand another rebuff. 'Her big night,' she said.

'You understand,' coaxed Richard, coolly unfazed.

He was wrong. Just then, Catherine didn't understand. 'I haven't seen you for *weeks*,' she said.

'I know, I know. Me too.' Richard looked about him as he spoke.

'My God,' she breathed. 'You're absolutely terrified.'

'Please let's not be awful to each other.' Richard's languid ease had vanished. His body was rigid now, straining away from her. Catherine continued to stare blindly at the programme.

'Look,' said Richard after a moment, 'we should really go in. We don't have reserved seats and I –'

Suddenly Andrew was standing in front of them, running a hand through his hair. 'Catherine, sweetheart. Richard, hello. Am I late?'

'Actually, you're right on time,' said Richard.

Catherine's stomach twisted.

They filed into the church and squeezed into a pew near the front. Catherine sat between Richard and Andrew. An expectant hush descended. A door opened and the choir and musicians filed silently in, all wearing black turtleneck sweaters. The singers scanned the crowd. There were some covert grins, a few cheerful winks. In the tenors Catherine recognised a man she had once stood behind in the queue at the delicatessen on Canonbury Lane. After a moment, the door opened again and the soloists and the conductor entered.

They were dressed in white turtlenecks. As Annabel walked to her chair, Richard began to clap loudly, his heavy hands conjuring a rolling percussive boom out of the air. Each blow felt like a spiteful punch to Catherine's head. She wished she could reach over and touch him, signal her contrition, but the narrow space between them yawned impossibly wide.

The conductor turned towards the audience and acknowledged the applause with a small bow. Catherine glanced at her watch and thought of her sleeping daughter. Florence would wake up in the morning and remember nothing of this evening's tantrum, her memory banks erased by sleep. Catherine wasn't so lucky. She could not shrug off her daughter's fury with such ease. Her reservoir of painful memories was expanding by gradual accretion. Every missed connection was meticulously catalogued, every carelessly inflicted hurt unblinkingly filed.

Catherine glanced towards Andrew. He was looking around him, only half-listening to the music. Richard stared straight ahead, his jaw set in a rictus of furious concentration. In this packed church, Catherine Shaw was drowning in her loneliness.

'Really?'

'Really.'

'*Really*?'

'Annabel, it was wonderful. You were great.'

Annabel Sulzman beamed. 'Really?'

Catherine's smile slipped a little. '*Tell* her, Andrew,' she said.

Andrew realised that both Annabel and Catherine were looking at him. 'Have either of you heard of *Jules and the Plum*?' he asked.

'What?' said Annabel.

'*Jules and the Plum*. Have you heard of it?'

46

'Andrew.' Catherine's voice was strained. 'We were talking about Annabel's solo.'

'Oh yes,' said Andrew.

'So what *did* you think, Andrew?' asked Annabel, shifting forwards in her seat. She had changed out of her pretentious white turtleneck sweater, and was now wearing a dark blue blouse which Andrew thought might be partly sheer, if you caught it in the right light.

'I thought your solo was – astonishing,' he said.

Annabel flicked a few stray strands of hair out of her eyes with a well-practised manoeuvre. 'Really?'

Catherine rolled her eyes.

'Really. I thought you sang wonderfully well,' said Andrew.

Annabel ran a coy finger up and down the stem of her wineglass. 'You didn't think the phrasing was a bit rushed on the second verse?'

Andrew shook his head. 'Not at all.' In fact he hadn't heard a note of Annabel's solo. He had lost all interest in the concert by the end of the first song.

What was he doing, actually, arranging lunch with this girl?

There seemed to be a certain inevitability about Andrew's invitation to Clara. It was the act of majestic stupidity which he had been hurtling towards all day. The e-mail had been an instinctive gesture, two rebellious fingers flipped at good sense and responsibility. It had also been a doomed attempt to salvage some self-respect after his humiliation in this afternoon's meeting, a hopeless, belated gesture to prove Tilly wrong. But now, after a few hours' sober reflection, Andrew had begun to suspect that he had made a terrible mistake.

His serenity was being besieged on two separate fronts. Sniper units had been peppering his confidence with volleys of self-doubt. Clara was young and beautiful. Clara was

47

alluring. Andrew remembered that she also smelled terrific. All this merely fuelled his sense of foreboding. Andrew knew that Clara was *way* too much of a good thing. To flirt with her was to flirt with ridicule.

While he was struggling to prevent these isolated ambushes from coalescing into mass insurrection, Andrew also had to fight a beleaguered rearguard action against the waves of guilt which had begun to bear down on him, dropping devastating daisy-cutters of shame. He could no longer plead the defence of harmless chitchat. The long shadow of culpability cast by next Tuesday's lunch date was inescapable now. He looked across the table at his wife. Tonight Cathy seemed half hidden behind a veil of sadness. Andrew felt a sharp stab of self-loathing in his gut. She deserved better than this.

Richard arrived back at the table with the remaining drinks. He had been in a terrible mood all evening. 'Jesus, Annabel,' he growled, 'you're not *still* talking about the damn concert, are you?' He sat down next to Andrew and took a swig of his heavily-iced bourbon. 'We've all told you how wonderful you were. Twice.'

'I'm just trying,' said Annabel, 'to see where I can improve for next time.'

Richard put down his glass and looked at his wife. 'Next time?' he said.

Annabel nodded. '*Your* work might be the subject of dissertations and scholarly analyses, Richard, but we're not all so lucky. For *my* little forays into the artistic firmament, I have to rely on my friends for feedback.' She gestured at Catherine and then, after a pause, at Andrew.

Richard sighed. 'Annabel –'

'I just want to become a better singer,' said Annabel. '*Mea culpa, mea culpa.*'

Andrew felt a twinge of irritation. *Mea culpa* meant *it's my fault*, which was not the same thing as saying *sorry*. He

48

turned to Richard. 'Have you heard of *Jules and the Plum*?' he asked.

'Andy,' replied Richard heavily, 'do us all a favour, and take your head out of your ass for once, OK?'

'What?' said Andrew.

'Listen,' said Richard, leaning towards him. 'I haven't heard of *Jules and the Plum*. OK? So yes, well done. Another one in the eye for the philistine megalomaniac imperialists. We Americans are still as uncivilised as ever. So, bravo. Your point is made and understood.'

'Jesus, Richard,' said Andrew.

There was a pause. Annabel and Catherine stared at Richard. Richard stared at Andrew. Andrew stared at the table. Around them the bar was buzzing with animated Friday-night chatter. The quartet sat silently at their table, an island of sour chill in a sea of effusive *bonhomie*.

'Well, aren't you going to enlighten me?' said Richard after a moment. 'Tell me about Jules and his damn plum.'

Andrew glanced across the table at Catherine. 'How's your wine –?'

Richard placed an enormous hand half-way up Andrew's thigh and squeezed it. '*Please*,' he whispered. 'I want to *know*.'

'Richard,' said Catherine softly.

'For God's sake,' said Annabel crossly. 'This is supposed to be my celebratory drink. The least you could do is to rein in your cultural inferiority complex for the evening.'

'Listen, look, the thing is, I don't know anything about it either,' said Andrew. 'I – I just heard someone mention it earlier today. Thought you might know what it was. That's all.'

After a moment Richard withdrew his giant paw and picked up his drink, not looking at Andrew.

Christ, thought Andrew, what was all *that* about?

*   *   *

Richard Sulzman was, according to the blurb on the jacket of his latest bestseller, probably (Andrew loved that *probably*!) the most important novelist currently working in English. He had published eighteen novels, three obscenely fat compendiums of essays and journalism, and four collections of poetry. He had won the Pulitzer Prize when he was thirty-one. His work had been translated into fifty-one different languages. A few weeks ago Andrew had idly googled *Richard Sulzman* and to his dismay had registered 158,000 hits. Richard's books were no longer merely published; instead they were exploded on to the collective consciousness by stunning campaigns of pan-global cultural carpet bombing. Millions were spent to ensure that housewives in Melbourne and cattle ranchers in Montana would all be discussing everything he wrote. He was critically acclaimed, a multimillion bestseller, a literary deity, a walking media event. Andrew knew that, sitting next to him now, he should have been basking in the reflected glamour of Richard's celebrity, but instead he was lacerated by every curious half-glance from across the room. Millions of people watched *Tilly!* every day, but nobody would ever recognise *him* in a wine bar.

Richard's talent, celebrity and wealth tormented Andrew with the corrosive bite of envy – his own, abandoned novel still gathering dust in its envelope – but it was Catherine's participation in his success which had sharpened his antipathy towards the American to the point of bilious neurosis. Before she had gone on maternity leave to have Toby, she had edited Richard Sulzman's last five novels, including the famous *Hamster* trilogy – widely regarded, apparently, to be his most enduringly brilliant work. Catherine and Richard were a formidable team, a celebrated literary double act. She had even become well-known in her own right: framed on the wall of the Shaws' downstairs toilet was an interview with

Catherine and Richard from an old weekend colour supplement. They were discussing *How We Met*, or *Our First Meal*, or something equally trite. Having to suffer Richard Sulzman's pompous manner in the flesh was enervating enough, but Andrew simply could not tolerate all that smug self-importance in the sanctuary of his own loo. He chose to go elsewhere.

Living in the same postal district, the Shaws and the Sulzmans had become frequent guests around each others' dinner tables. Andrew's heart used to beat blackly as the conversation soared over his head into a stratosphere of unpardonable literary pretension. (Nobody ever wanted to talk about *television*.)

Worse, every day Catherine would come home from work dazzled afresh by Richard's genius. She was fiercely loyal to him, and responded coolly to Andrew's worried barrage of jocular put-downs. Richard, of course, flashily expressed his gratitude and admiration for her in his books. One panegyric in particular had unsettled Andrew. The words had squirrelled away inside him, and there was no budging them now. It was at the beginning of the second novel in the trilogy, *Hamster at Home*:

> To Catherine Shaw, flawless editor, magician, alchemist, and saviour – my Egeria. She brings me sympathy, wit, relief, and the inexpressibly treasured gift of enduring friendship.

And this hyperbolic rot about *his* wife had been translated into fifty-one different languages, and then replicated, by the million, across the globe! The idea still made Andrew feel nauseous. Who or what was an Egeria, anyway? He could never bring himself to look it up.

* * *

51

The whisky seemed to calm Richard down. After a moment he looked up. 'My God. Andy. Shit.'

Nobody else called Andrew 'Andy'. Andrew assumed that Richard's over-familiarity was simply an inevitable consequence of being an American, although occasionally he wondered whether Richard did it because he knew how much it irritated him. 'Are you all right, Richard?' he asked stiffly. Richy. Rich.

Richard nodded heavily. 'I'm fine. Well. A little tired, maybe.' The huge hand which had recently been cutting off the blood supply to Andrew's lower leg now landed squarely in the middle of his back with a conspiratorial thump. Richard winked. 'Blame the jet lag.'

'Jet lag,' said Andrew. 'Right.'

'Buddies?'

'Buddies,' agreed Andrew.

Richard extended his hand. Andrew shook it, mortified with embarrassment at this schoolboy ritual.

'You're worse than a child,' Annabel told Richard.

'Don't worry,' Catherine said, putting her hand on Annabel's arm in sisterly collusion. 'I think they'll play together nicely for a while.'

Annabel was staring at Catherine's wrist. 'Annabel?' said Andrew. 'Is everything all right?'

Annabel's head snapped up, a look of confusion on her face. 'What? Oh, yes. Fine.' She frowned as she looked away.

Richard finished his whisky. 'So, Andy, how's business?' he asked.

Andrew knew what was coming next. 'Business is doing fine, thanks.'

'Still going strong with –?'

'*Tilly!* Yes. Still going strong, thank you.'

'That's great.' Richard paused. 'I imagine you'll be looking

52

for new projects soon, won't you? Stretching your wings, new challenges, that sort of thing.'

'No, not really,' said Andrew.

Richard leaned forward. 'Have you ever considered films? You know, full-length features?'

'Look, Richard,' said Andrew, 'Trident is a small, independent production company. We simply don't have the resources to –'

'Ah, yes.' Richard nodded encouragingly. 'Resources.'

'Or the experience. To do feature-length films.'

'But Andy, you realise what I'm doing here? I'm offering you *Cock*.'

'Yes, and obviously I'm flattered, but I really don't think we're right for the project. We really couldn't do *Cock* justice.'

Unlike most of his other novels, *Cock*, Richard Sulzman's post-apocalyptic masterpiece, had never been adapted for cinema. The book was a plotless, hallucinogenic nightmare set in a battery chicken farm in 2033. By dint of a series of ecological disasters, eggs had become the only form of protein still safe to eat. The book's principal character was a security guard employed to protect the hens from ill-nourished thieves and predators. On publication the critics had praised the book's chillingly dystopic futuristic vision, but it was the narrator's consumption of a vast pharmacopoeia of mind-altering drugs which had guaranteed *Cock*'s enduring cult status. It was the tripped-out sequences which made the book so impossible to film. It made *Naked Lunch* look like Walt Disney. Richard remained affronted that nobody was willing to attempt to film his narcotics-addled masterpiece. It was a measure of his desperation that every time he saw Andrew he tried to persuade him to take the project on.

'You've read the book, I take it?' said Richard.

'Oh, well,' said Andrew. 'It was a long time ago.' In fact

Andrew had never actually finished any of Richard's novels. Their manifest brilliance tormented him. He could usually manage about ten pages before his eyes fogged over with envy.

'So you can see the potential?' Richard persisted.

'Doesn't the guy think that he's turned into a chicken at one point?'

Richard shook his head. 'Not a chicken. That would be illogical. It's the wrong sex. A rooster.'

'A rooster.'

'Hence, *Cock*.'

'Oh. Right. I see.'

There was an awkward pause.

'At least think about it.'

'I don't know,' said Andrew.

'Just consider it. That's all I'm asking.'

Andrew sucked on his teeth. 'All right. I'll think about it. But no promises. And of course, even if *I* think it'll work, it's unlikely that the Swedes would ever –'

'That's good enough for me.' Richard stood up. 'Champagne. My shout.'

Andrew shifted uncomfortably. 'I'm not sure you've quite –'

'I'll get two bottles, shall I? Back in a minute.'

By the time they had reached the bottom of the second bottle of champagne, Catherine had cheered up, and Richard was in a much more fulsome mood. He was talking, at inevitable length, about his recent trip to America. Andrew hadn't realised that he'd been away. He tried not to mind Richard's languidly delivered celebrity tittle-tattle: a spat between two revered poets, the sexual peccadillo of a well-known magazine editor which involved a string bag of shelled walnuts. Andrew sank into a morose stupor. Next week's rendezvous with Clara was stalking his conscience, slowly obliterating the light.

'And what did Richard bring back for you, Annabel?' asked Catherine. 'Did you get a reward for being abandoned in London?'

The atmosphere of jollity evaporated instantly.

'Actually, Cathy,' began Richard, 'that's a bit of a –'

'He forgot,' interrupted Annabel. 'A silk scarf from Takashimaya. That was all I wanted. But no.'

Richard looked exasperated. 'Do we have to talk about this now?'

Annabel ignored him. 'Just a scarf,' she said to Catherine. 'Not much, really.'

'Look,' sighed Richard, 'I'll call tomorrow and order you one.'

'That's not the *point*, Richard. It's not about spending the money. It's about spending the *time*.'

'You could have come with me. Then you could have gone to Takashimaya yourself.'

'I had *rehearsals*,' said Annabel tartly. 'For the concert.' She paused. 'You *do* remember the concert?' Richard rolled his eyes heavenwards.

'I'll get some more champagne,' said Andrew, and escaped to the bar. You could always spot the childless couples, he thought. They were less adept at hiding their emotions, unpractised at the bland, dissembling mask of domestic harmony – postponing arguments until after the kids' bedtime.

At least Richard and Annabel still *fought* with each other, he reflected as he waited to be served. The heavy shroud of resigned apathy had smothered his own marriage, extinguishing every spark of discord before the smallest risk of conflagration occurred. For years Andrew and Catherine had practised a pragmatic defeatism, each preferring to allow

55

the other small victories rather than go through the insipid rigmarole of argument and counter-argument. Anything for the quiet life. The warm, meandering discussions which used to creep on late into the night were long gone. Now they engaged in bracing exchanges of information which pertained exclusively to domestic arrangements. They discussed menus over breakfast, and updated each other on social engagements over dinner. That was all. A heavy sadness settled on Andrew's shoulders as he carried the bottle of champagne back to the table.

'I think I might go and powder my nose,' announced Catherine as he sat down.

Annabel stood up. 'I'll come with you.'

Andrew and Richard watched their wives as they crossed the wine bar together.

'So,' said Richard after a moment, 'do you want to talk about it?'

Andrew turned to look at him. 'Talk about what?'

'Come on, Andy. Something's eating away at you.'

Andrew looked at him, instantly suspicious. 'How can you tell?'

Richard's eyes glinted. 'I'm right, aren't I?'

'Of course not.'

Richard sat back. 'Oh, OK. Suit yourself.'

'Really,' said Andrew. 'Everything's fine.'

'Whatever.' Richard drained his glass of champagne.

There was a long silence.

Andrew stared at the table, willing himself to remain silent. For all of Richard Sulzman's insufferable pomposity, he could draw confidences out of Andrew as easily as turning on a tap. Richard pulled off a tricksy balance of compassionate sympathy and supercilious disinterest which somehow always promised Andrew release from the torrid ache of his secrets. All Richard had to do was ask; hypnotised, Andrew was incapable of preventing his most intimate thoughts from gushing out. It was infuriating.

Richard waited.

'Can I ask you a question?' said Andrew eventually.

'Of course.'

'In confidence.'

An infinitesimal pause. 'Sure.'

'On your trips abroad. Do you ever – have you been tempted to, ah, stray?'

Richard looked at him. 'To *stray*? What am I, a sheep?'

'You know what I mean.'

'Jesus, Andy, are you asking me if I've ever had an *affair*?'

'I suppose I am, yes.'

'When, exactly?' said Richard. 'I was married twice before, you know.'

'Well, since you met Annabel, for the sake of argument.'

'You're asking me whether I've cheated on Annabel,' said Richard flatly. 'May I ask why you want to know?'

'Let me put it another way,' said Andrew. 'Is it something that you've ever considered?'

'Well of course I've *considered* it. Who hasn't?' Richard looked over Andrew's shoulder in the direction of the toilets. 'Me, actually. At least until recently.'

'Aha.'

'You don't think I'm a shit?' said Andrew. '*I* think I'm a shit.'

'You haven't told me what you've done yet.'

'Oh, well. I haven't actually *done* anything.'

'But you feel guilty.'

Andrew nodded. 'I've never so much as *looked* at another woman before.'

'Huh,' said Richard, and then fell silent.

'Cathy deserves better,' prompted Andrew. 'Don't you think?'

'Is it anyone I know?' asked Richard, leaning forward.

Andrew shook his head. 'Someone I met through work.'

'Is she pretty?'

'Gorgeous,' said Andrew sadly.

'Doesn't help,' observed Richard.

'I don't even know anything *about* this girl. I've only met her once, for Christ's sake.'

'Maybe that's the answer,' said Richard. 'Perhaps it's not about *her* at all. You're just captivated by the novelty of it all. The thrill of transgression.'

'Imagine that. Even my *shallowness* might be superficial.' Andrew drank the last mouthful of his champagne. 'Ten years of wedded bliss,' he sighed.

'Do you love her?' asked Richard.

Andrew barked a sorrowful laugh. 'How should I know? We're still strangers.'

'I meant Catherine,' said Richard.

'Oh, *Catherine*,' breathed Andrew. Catherine, Catherine! 'Yes, of course I love her.' It was true. He loved his wife very much. A fresh shower of shame rained down.

Richard frowned. 'What is it you want? Are you looking for absolution?'

'No, not absolution,' sighed Andrew. 'I just want all this pain to go away.'

After that, both men sat in silence.

A few minutes later Catherine and Annabel slid back into their seats. Catherine brushed her hand across Andrew's shoulders as she passed behind him. Her fingertips felt like red-hot needles through his shirt.

SIX

Catherine Shaw looked around her sitting room and sighed.

The rest of the house had a coolly modern, unostentatious feel – Catherine had filled it with an ocean of Conran – but the sitting room was a painful, anachronistic aberration. When Andrew's father, Patrick, had finally admitted defeat and abandoned his beloved Rycroft, there had been no room in his hated modern bungalow for all of the ancient furniture which had populated the old, rambling house. To Catherine's dismay, Andrew had insisted on taking much of it, and their sitting room was suddenly turned into a shrine to his childhood, the antiquated exhibits curiously dislocated. There were chintz-covered settees (these were *settees* rather than *sofas*), lampshades fringed with florets of dangling velvet, and two – two! – nests of glass-topped mahogany side-tables. At least she rarely came in here any more, except to listen to Toby practise.

Catherine sat at the piano, and traced a lingering finger along the polished ivory. The black and white keys waited in regimented silence, eighty-eight soldiers of infinite possibility. In the hollow seat of the piano stool lay a thick stack of music, untouched for years.

Toby was the only one who played these days, and he did so with long-suffering affront. Catherine knew how much he hated his daily practice, but she was determined to make him persevere. When she was his age she had been similarly reluctant, unable to see the point of the endless cycles of arpeggios and scales. It was only later, discovering the facility that her well-drilled fingers had acquired, that she understood that these were the keys she needed to unlock the secrets of the instrument. Toby would realise this too, in time, and then he would be grateful. She was looking forward to watching him discover the comforting embrace of a melody. First, though, his manifest distaste for the whole affair needed to abate somewhat.

Catherine stood up. It was Tuesday, so at least there was this morning's yoga class to look forward to. Rahsaan was going to be teaching the rudimentary elements of meditation. She slung her bag over her shoulder and left the empty house. Sinead would be on her way back from the school run by now, doubtless stuck in a traffic jam somewhere. Catherine strode briskly towards the Essex Road, dodging the baby buggies which listlessly patrolled the pavement, navigated by mothers who glanced at their watches every thirty seconds, willing the day on. Their small cargoes eyed each other in silent commiseration. Unmoving lines of cars choked exhaust fumes into the summer air. Catherine thought of Florence in her airy, smoke-free nursery in Highgate. At least her daughter was spared this lonely trundle every morning.

In Catherine's eyes, Sinead's continued presence in her house stood as damning testimony to her own maternal transgressions. She had always felt ill-equipped for the role which Nature had thrust upon her. From the first time she gazed down into Toby's dark, unblinking eyes, to her dismay there had been none of the wordless joy she had been promised, no beatific starburst of pure adoration. Instead she was swamped by paralysing anxiety. At once the baby eclipsed every other facet of her life. Her curriculum vitae – all those qualifications and achievements, those carefully collected markers which define a life – was instantly erased and replaced by a single entry: *mother*. Toby became the sun around which Catherine orbited ceaselessly. During the day his needy hyperactivity demanded constant vigilance. At night, desperate for the sanctuary of sleep, Catherine lay in bed, staring into the darkness, needled continually back into consciousness by the fear of unspecified disaster unfolding in the baby's bedroom.

She wheeled Toby aimlessly up and down the pavements of north London, fighting exhaustion and loneliness. She watched numbly as the other mothers bent down and whispered softly to the bundles in their prams, radiant with maternal love. Toby bawled and crawled and ate and shat, day after changeless day, and all Catherine wanted was to escape back to her cramped, windowless office and its tottering columns of paper. She found herself yearning for the petty poison of office politics, the bitching and gossip around the coffee machine. And of course she missed her authors, her books, the plaudits and the prizes. She wondered blankly how she could have given it all up so easily, with scarcely a thought. It all seemed like an eternity ago. She couldn't remember the last time she'd read a book which didn't have cardboard pages.

Most of all, Catherine missed a life which was hers, and hers alone. Her marriage had been a process of ongoing erasure. Andrew had been the first to plunder her: she had lost her flat, then her name. But it was Toby who had done the real damage. Back then there was no hint of the thoughtful, softly-spoken child he had now become. Instead he had been rapacious and unmerciful, crashing through

Catherine's life with the careless violence of a rampaging invader. The ferocity of the attack had left her stunned and defenceless. Victory secured, father and son greedily divvied up the spoils. Catherine became communal property, her life defined by the needs of others.

And yet when her maternity leave came to an end, Catherine didn't return to work. Instead she remained at home with Toby's snot-filled wailing, trapped by the inescapable burden of maternal precedent.

Catherine's mother had sacrificed a promising academic career to raise her children, and she had always borne her martyrdom with pointedly extravagant suffering. Her resentment cast a long shadow: not wishing to be the only one to fall foul of her own mistake, she taught Catherine that mothers who pursued a career were heartless and selfish. It was a cruel legacy. Catherine was hamstrung by guilt, both by her desire to return to work and the prospect of abandoning Toby to the cold hands of strangers. Shouldn't she *want* to stay at home? Was there something wrong with her? Catherine teetered miserably on her mother's diabolical scaffold of emotional blackmail, but in the end she could not throw herself off. Instead she became complicit in the erosion of her identity, losing herself in the unending tedium of domestic chores.

When he was four years old, Toby began to attend a nearby kindergarten. Every morning Catherine watched her son trudge disconsolately off down the corridor. Her cheerful smile as she waved goodbye hid a slowly bruising heart, but her sadness never lasted long. Hours stretched ahead of her, deliciously unscheduled. For the first time, she began to consider a return to work. She made some calls. Catherine reconstructed her old professional persona, hiding her motherhood behind expensive make-up and designer suits, and went out for lunch.

Twice she was offered a job before the first course arrived.

Hesitantly she told Andrew what she was considering. He said nothing to discourage her. Catherine had some more lunches. The telephone began to ring.

Then, as she was trying to decide which position to accept, Catherine found herself pregnant again.

Florence was an accident – an unlucky statistical glitch. Andrew's sperm had had to breach barriers of latex and spermicidal cream to reach the fertile homelands of Catherine's fallopian tubes. (After Toby's birth, Catherine had been reluctant to go back on the pill, and so she and Andrew had begun to use condoms instead. For a while it lent a certain novelty to their lovemaking, although the hiatus while Andrew crouched over himself did sometimes spoil the mood. Andrew's penis was a faintly ridiculous thing anyway. As she watched it approach, packed into its red latex sheath like an exotically-spiced sausage, the milky teat quivering with lewd intent, Catherine would struggle to suppress her giggles. Once Florence was born, they abandoned their experiment with rubber. Now at least, Catherine told herself, she no longer had to worry about the inherent comedy of the scarlet prophylactic.) Ever since she had gazed disbelievingly down at the thin turquoise line which announced the arrival of Florence's tiny embryo inside her, Catherine had maintained a near-faultless masquerade of delight, but the painful cycle of despair and self-recrimination was reset to zero. Another child, another sentence of imprisonment: Catherine was hemmed in once more by her guilt. Her dream of a return to work seemed further away than ever. The disappointment knocked the fight out of her.

Soon after Florence's birth, Sinead had arrived to marshal laundry, shopping, cooking and children. Catherine languished in defeated indolence on the sofa, unable to escape her horror at what had happened. After months of baffled torpor spent staring out of the kitchen window at the unused greenhouse at the bottom of the garden, Catherine began to collect orchids. She loved the flowers' alien beauty, their beguiling otherness, but her enthusiasm was born less out of a passion for horticulture than the need for escape: alone with her orchids at the bottom of the garden, she was able to occupy a magnificently solitary life, at least for a while. She nurtured the plants from seedlings to their adult glory. The greenhouse's environment needed to be constantly monitored, the plants' food and water intake carefully regulated. Catherine attended to every detail, gratified by all that needy dependence. But flowers were all she felt equipped to care for: Catherine poured her maternal instincts into her orchids while Sinead looked after Toby and Florence. As Catherine worked amongst the bags of potting compost, her children lingered on the periphery of her consciousness, as if they were peering in through the glass, watching her. The greenhouse might have been her sanctuary, but even there she could never completely escape her guilt.

The changing room was full of well-preserved women carefully climbing into leotards. As always, Catherine had changed at home. She saw no reason to undress in public. The nakedness of strangers in the changing room made Catherine feel fourteen again. She never knew where to look. Annabel was sitting in their usual corner, flicking through a magazine.

'Hi,' said Catherine.

Annabel stood up. 'Hello, *darling*,' she said. The two women kissed each other. Catherine was always slightly nonplussed by Annabel's displays of ostentatious affection. She wasn't even entirely sure why they were friends. When Catherine first began editing Richard he was still married to his second wife, a forbidding French academic. Catherine had helped him through that divorce, and she had been invited to Richard and Annabel's wedding a year and a half later. Since then the two women had got to know each other well, but Catherine was always bemused by Annabel's apparent belief that they were best friends. Her allegiance lay with Richard, not his current wife. Still, there hadn't been much she could do to combat Annabel's determined friendliness without appearing rude. All of a sudden they were chatting on the telephone every day and going to weekly yoga classes together. Catherine wasn't quite sure how it had happened, but she was pleased that it had. Annabel was her only friend.

'So how are you?' she asked. 'Still buzzing after Friday night?'

'Not great, actually,' replied Annabel.

'Oh dear,' said Catherine, wishing that Annabel would learn to distinguish between innocuous social pleasantries and enquiries which warranted a substantive answer. 'What's happened?'

Annabel sighed. 'It's Richard.'

'Richard? What about him?'

'Well, call me paranoid, but at some point you have to start wondering when affable disorganisation becomes something more sinister.'

Catherine opened a locker and put her bag inside. 'Sinister?'

'When, for example, it becomes a convenient excuse to disappear without notice or reason.' Annabel paused. 'Look, I know I should be used to all this. After all, he goes to the States for a fortnight and I don't think twice about it. And it's probably nothing. But this afternoon we were supposed to go shopping together. You remember that squabble we had on Friday night, about the scarf from Takashimaya?' Catherine nodded. 'Richard was very sweet about it afterwards. He promised to take me to Knightsbridge for some quality time with his credit card.'

'I thought it wasn't about the money, but the time,' said Catherine, raising an eyebrow.

'He was coming *with* me. That was the point. But this morning he told me we'd have to do it another time. He suddenly remembered he had an interview with some guy from the *Observer*. It was all arranged weeks ago apparently, before the trip, and he'd forgotten about it.'

Catherine shrugged. 'Maybe he *did* forget. You know him. You said so yourself. Affable disorganisation. Blame it on an excess of flighty artistic temperament.'

Annabel chewed her lower lip. 'Maybe.' She paused. 'I'm just wondering if he's – you know.'

'Richard? Never.' Catherine frowned. 'What on earth has brought all this on?'

'Well, I don't have any incriminating evidence, if that's what you mean,' said Annabel. 'I haven't found lipstick on his collar or anything like that. It's more an absence of what used to be there.' She sighed. 'Perhaps I'm being ridiculous.'

'Can you talk to him about it?'

'Good grief. Of course I can't. Anyway, what if he said yes? What if he turned around and admitted that yes, actually, he *is* having an affair? Then what would I do?'

Catherine looked at her levelly. 'I don't know. What *would* you do?'

Annabel shook her head. 'This may be a case of ignorance being bliss.'

'Just as long as it won't drive you mad with worry.'

'That's the big question, isn't it?' said Annabel. 'Which is worse, ignorance with hope, or knowledge without?'

'Richard wouldn't. He'd have to be mad.' Catherine smiled brightly.

'He just seems so *distracted*.'

66

'Well, look,' said Catherine, 'the story's easy enough to check. Wait and see if there's an interview in the *Observer*.'

Annabel was silent for a moment. When she looked up there were tears in her eyes. 'Oh, Cathy,' she said. 'What am I going to *do*?'

Catherine stepped forward and placed a hand on Annabel's shoulder. 'Annabel, listen,' she said. 'It's going to be all right. I promise.'

Annabel's gaze settled on her. Catherine was shocked by the naked need in her eyes. 'Do you really think so?' she whispered.

'Of course. You know Richard. He's never exactly been easy to fathom. He likes to keep people guessing. Even you. But that doesn't mean that there's something going on.'

'No. No. You're right.' Annabel thought. 'Still. I'd like to know what's going through his head sometimes.'

'Hah. Wouldn't we all.'

'He never talks about his previous marriages, you know.'

'Heavens. Would you *want* him to?'

'Well, it's all *part* of him, isn't it? Those experiences have all gone into making him the man I married.' Annabel paused. 'Sometimes I wonder whether he's got something to hide. Maybe there's some dark and terrible secret about his ex-wives that he's keeping from me.'

The other women had started to file out of the changing room. 'Are you sure you don't just want to hear that he loves you more?' asked Catherine.

'Perhaps I do. Not unreasonable, is it?'

'Not in the slightest.'

They followed the crowd out into the corridor. 'By the way,' said Annabel, 'I hope you won't mind my asking, but I couldn't help noticing that lovely bracelet you were wearing on Friday night. It looked divine.' Annabel tugged at the strap of her leotard. 'Do you remember where you got it from?'

67

Catherine did not falter. 'I honestly don't,' she replied. 'I expect it was a present from Andrew. I could ask him, if you like, although I don't suppose he'll rem–'

'No, don't worry.' Annabel was silent for a moment. 'I just –' She shook her head. 'Never mind. Come on. Let's go and meditate our troubles away.'

In the studio, Rahsaan was waiting for them. He sat crossed-legged on the polished wooden floor. The sound system leaked Enya. 'Ladies,' he said. (No man had ever attended any of Catherine's yoga classes.) 'Take a mat and make yourselves comfortable.' His shaved head bobbed as he spoke. Rahsaan was wearing long orange surfing shorts and a tie-dyed T-shirt with the sleeves cut off to display the prancing lion tattooed on his right shoulder. For weeks Catherine had thought that the lion symbolised inner strength and yogic *prana*, until she spotted the letters CFC incorporated in the design, identifying Rahsaan (whose name, Annabel had told her, was actually Lee) as a follower of Chelsea Football Club. The fading blue ink of the tattoo accentuated the pellucid whiteness of Rahsaan's skin.

Annabel and Catherine collected their mats and manoeuvred themselves into the lotus position. A reverential silence descended.

As she crossed her legs and settled herself, Catherine could feel her pulse thumping. Discussing the possibility of Richard's infidelity with Annabel had given her a shameful, licentious thrill. All that dissembling excited her. She could have politely backed away from the subject, but instead she had dived in, compounding her betrayal, exhilarated by the risk.

Rahsaan got to his feet. There was a crude ostentation to his lithely pulsating physique which Catherine found repellent. '*Aham Brahma asmi*,' he said, bowing deeply towards the assembled crowd. The women bowed seriously back. 'Over recent weeks we've been looking at some of the postures and breathing controls of Hatha Yoga. This morning I'm going to introduce you to some of the preliminary elements of the Yoga of meditation.' There was a low murmur of excitement. Rahsaan continued. 'The first step in all meditation is to achieve a quiet mind. You need to turn your attention inwards in order to sink into deeper layers of consciousness. The first stage of this process is called *pratyahara*, or sense-withdrawal. To achieve this, I want you to close your eyes, and begin to breathe through your nose.'

Several minutes later, Rahsaan spoke again. His voice was softer now. 'We move on to the second stage, *dharana*. Think of a single object. Not too large, not too small. I want you to visualise it as clearly as you can, and focus all your attention on it. Concentrate on it in your mind's eye, to the exclusion of everything else.' He lapsed again into silence.

The only object which Catherine was able to visualise was Richard Sulzman's large, circumcised penis.

There was no interview with the *Observer* that afternoon, of course. Richard had telephoned Catherine yesterday, full of apologies for his behaviour on Friday night, and asked her to meet him in the Great Eastern Hotel for lunch. He had probably booked a room for afterwards. Catherine was already looking forward to the satisfying weight of his body on top of hers. There was something thrilling about Richard's solid bulk. He sometimes made her orgasm so violently that she couldn't move afterwards, as if her body had been taken apart and then hastily, messily reassembled. It could take hours before everything settled back into place and she could function normally again. The carnality of the sex was thrilling. It was raw lust, undiluted physical desire. Catherine was grateful to Richard for wanting her so directly, without equivocation or qualification. There was no need for polite preliminaries, the awkward play-acting of romance. All they wanted was the excitement of each other's touch, and perhaps the solace of a secret shared. As she sat on her yoga mat, Catherine felt a warm wetness between her legs.

'Next we seek to achieve *dhyana*, unity of the mind with the object of contemplation.' At the sound of Rahsaan's voice Catherine opened her eyes. Rahsaan was looking directly at her. The leer on his lips suggested that he knew exactly what she had been thinking about. Catherine quickly shut her eyes as the blood flooded to her face.

She didn't open them again for the rest of the class.

SEVEN

Andrew Shaw stepped out on to the sun-blasted street and glanced at his watch. His date with Clara was now only thirty minutes away.

The last four days had been a largely sleepless hundred-hour orgy of self-recrimination. Andrew had even got as far as crafting a casually apologetic e-mail – can't make it, something's cropped up, terribly sorry, *you know how it is*. His finger had hovered anxiously over the mouse, ready to click on the Send button, but in the end he had deleted it, still unsent. He told himself that to back out now would somehow make matters worse – his gutless betrayal compounded by a gutless evasion – but there was another reason why he was unwilling to cancel the lunch. It was the memory of Clara's cheek against his at the end of that first evening, lingering a fraction too long. That exquisite pause! – propriety shattered. He could still feel her breath on his skin, whispering silent promise.

Andrew set off down Frith Street, surreptitiously watching his reflection in every shop window. The sun beat down on his back. He turned right on to Old Compton Street and continued westwards. The closer Andrew got to his destination, the more slowly he went. Soon he was creeping forwards with the toe-curling stealth of the irredeemably guilty.

Finally he subsided to an ungainly slouch in front of the restaurant he had chosen for lunch. It had booths, perfect camouflage for this sort of thing. Andrew peered at the menu, wrinkling up his nose in manifest boredom as he did so. His heart was roaring. He wondered fleetingly what Catherine was doing. He yawned unconvincingly and with a haunted glance over his shoulder, stole inside.

Twenty-five minutes later, Andrew had finished a large whisky and was silently cursing himself for his abject idiocy.

Of course Clara wasn't going to come.

Well, he told himself, at least this little indignity had been inflicted in the privacy of his own restaurant booth. Nobody else ever needed to know about it. Cautious relief spread through him, sharpened by a twist of regret. He began to peer idly at the menu. Just as he was starting to look forward to a guilt-free lunch, a guilt-free afternoon, and a guilt-free life, Clara appeared at the end of the booth. She was wearing a blue silk shirt with perhaps one button too many undone, and a beige linen skirt which ended well above the knee. She looked stupendous.

'Hello,' she said, flashing a smile. 'Sorry I'm so late.'

'Are you? Hadn't noticed.' Andrew scrambled to his feet and kissed her cheek. Intoxicating scent filled his nostrils. She sat down opposite him. They looked at each other for a moment.

'Good to see you again,' she said pleasantly.

Andrew's armpits immediately prickled with sweat. It was one thing to type sweet nothings on a computer, quite another to deliver them winningly across a table. A waiter had appeared at their table, pen poised and eyebrow cocked.

72

'Do you want a drink?' said Andrew.

Clara turned to the waiter. 'A glass of very cold champagne.'

'And another whisky,' called Andrew as the waiter drifted off.

Clara laced her long, elegant fingers together and tilted her head to one side. 'So, Andrew. How's work?'

'Work?' said Andrew hollowly. 'Work's all right.'

'I love your show,' said Clara. 'Brilliant television. So – compelling.'

Andrew wasn't sure whether Clara was being extraordinarily naïve or extraordinarily cynical. He took a deep breath. 'Well –'

'And it must be quite something, actually *owning* the company.'

Andrew shifted uncomfortably, aware that it would probably be a tactical own-goal to mention the Swedes at this point. 'Remind me what it is you do again?' he said.

'I'm a researcher for the BBC. Which is fine, you know, for the moment.'

'You have other plans?'

'Of course I do.' Of course she did. Andrew could see the flames of naked ambition dancing behind her eyes.

'Well.' He swallowed. 'Perhaps we could discuss them.'

Clara smiled at him. 'I admire you, Andrew, I really do. Look at you. You're talented, *very* successful, a tremendously busy man, and yet –' she lowered her eyes demurely '– you still make time for people like *me*.'

Andrew coughed. 'Really, you mustn't –'

'I can't think of many people in your position who would be selfless enough to help someone just setting out on their career. Especially since you don't even *know* me very well.'

'Have you eaten here before?'

'I'm just grateful,' said Clara, 'that there are still a few good people who aren't always thinking of themselves.'

Andrew buried his head in the menu. 'The seafood is supposed to be excellent,' he croaked.

To his relief, the drinks arrived. Clara raised her glass towards him. They clinked discreetly. She took a sip of her champagne. 'So, anyway. I'm fascinated to hear more about those things you mentioned in your e-mail.'

He looked at her uncertainly. 'Those *things*?'

'All those new projects.'

'Oh,' said Andrew. '*Those* things.' He had hoped that Clara would have forgotten about last week's ridiculous e-mail.

'It all sounds so *interesting*,' said Clara. 'And tremendously brave. Those documentaries especially!'

'It's all very much in the early stages of development,' said Andrew weakly. 'If that. More sort of *pre*-development, really. We haven't even got close to the drawing board yet.'

Clara leaned back and delivered a peal of delighted laughter. Her hand inched closer to his across the tablecloth. 'I do hope there might be an opportunity for someone like me in your new plans,' she said softly.

'Yes, well. The thing is, Clara –'

'I really would be most *terribly* grateful.' Clara looked him directly in the eye. As their gazes locked, her fingertips brushed lightly over his cuticles. She performed a slow, unambiguous blink.

Andrew was struggling to remember exactly what sort of drivel he had spouted in his e-mail when suddenly a plan floated into his head, fully-formed and without apparent flaw. He quickly circumnavigated the idea. It seemed watertight. He leaned back into his banquette and looked hungrily into Clara's eyes, suppressing the bilious gurgling of his

74

conscience. 'As a matter of fact, Clara, there *is* one particular project which you might be interested in.'

She looked at him. 'Go on.'

'Do you know Richard Sulzman?'

'Of course I do. That is, I know *of* him.'

'Richard Sulzman,' Andrew told her, 'is one of my best friends.'

Clara's eyes, remarkably, grew a little wider. '*No*.'

He pushed on. 'Have you read *Cock*?'

'Of course.'

'You probably know that nobody has ever committed *Cock* to film.' Andrew paused. 'Between you and me, Richard has been trying to persuade me to take the project on for years. I've always refused, no matter how hard he begs.'

'Good heavens, *why*?' breathed Clara.

'Because it's an impossible job. I worry that I won't be able to do justice to his genius.' Andrew managed to force these words out without choking on them. 'The – *richness* of his vision may be beyond me.'

Clara pshawed excitedly.

Andrew kept wielding the trowel. 'Anyway, that's all just by way of background, really. Because the thing is, I think I may be having something of a change of heart. And I must admit, now I'm very tempted. After all, you know what they say. Nothing ventured.'

Clara leaned forwards. 'So you're thinking –?'

Andrew put up his hands. Reel her in. 'Oh, it's very early days.' He took a sip of his drink. 'Tell me honestly, though,' he said, lowering his voice, 'do you think I'm mad for even considering it?'

'Oh, *no*. Not at all.' Clara tossed her hair. 'I think it's a wonderful idea.'

Andrew took a deep breath. 'Well, right now what I need

most of all is an executive producer. Someone to oversee the entire project. A big ideas person.'

'Andrew,' said Clara softly, 'I *know* what an executive producer does.'

'Of course you do. Of course you do.'

Clara rested her chin on her hands and gazed at him for a few moments.

Andrew cleared his throat and somehow managed to speak. 'Are you interested?'

There was a long pause. Clara stared down at the table-cloth. 'Do you know what?' she said. 'The strangest thing.'

'What?' asked Andrew, suddenly worried.

'I've completely lost my appetite.'

He swallowed. 'Your –?'

'Shall we go somewhere else? Let's forget the food.'

'Somewhere else,' repeated Andrew.

'Right.'

There was a long silence.

'Where exactly do you want to go?' croaked Andrew.

'Where do you think? To a hotel, of course.'

Andrew blinked. 'A hotel.'

She smiled at him. 'I told you I was going to be grateful.'

Too fast, too fast, shrieked Andrew's brain. 'Look, Clara, before we go any further, there's something I probably should have mentioned before. And please don't think I'm a complete shit.' He paused. 'The thing is, I'm married.'

Clara burst into laughter.

'What's so funny?' he asked stiffly.

'I *know* you're married, Andrew.'

He blinked. 'You do? How?'

'It's written all over your face. You're *oozing* furtiveness. I can almost *see* the guilt wafting off you.'

'And it doesn't bother you?'

She looked at him.

76

'OK,' he said weakly, 'so it doesn't bother you.'

'Can we go now?' asked Clara.

Andrew was frozen to his seat. 'The thing is,' he began, 'my secretary –'

'Call her.' Clara produced a tiny mobile phone and thrust it into his hand. Helpless, Andrew reluctantly prodded Petrushka's direct line into the keypad.

'Ah, Petrushka?' Andrew looked across the table at Clara. She winked back. 'It's me. Yes. Listen, I've got caught up in a – in a meeting. You're going to have to clear my diary for this afternoon and rearrange for later this week. OK? Good.' He numbly handed the phone back to Clara.

'The whole afternoon?' she said archly.

'So. Here we are again.'

'Here we are.' She looked around. 'Nice place.'

'I got you your usual. Hope you approve.'

Catherine picked up the proffered glass and took a long drink. 'Oh yes,' she sighed. 'I approve. That's a proper drink.'

'The preprandial cocktail,' mused Richard. 'A wondrous thing.'

'It kept the British Empire going pretty much single-handedly towards the end,' remarked Catherine, holding her glass up to the light.

'OK,' conceded Richard, 'maybe not quite so wondrous.'

'Excuse me,' said Catherine. 'No need to play the Brit-baiting Yank with me, thank you very much. It might work with Andrew, but I know you too well. I'm immune to your little games.'

Richard grinned ruefully. 'Spoilsport.'

Catherine realised that they hadn't kissed each other hello. Hardly necessary, she supposed, given why they were there.

'I saw Annabel this morning,' she said. 'At yoga. We talked about you.'

Richard spread his large hands and shrugged. 'What else is there to talk about, really?'

Catherine smiled sadly. She was not proud of her affair. It wasn't a victimless crime, she knew. There were other people involved. She was aware of the dangers of collateral damage. Up until now she had erected a maze of emotional walls to keep her conflicting loyalties at a manageable distance. Her affair with Richard and her friendship with Annabel had been separated by a fortification of wilful dispassion, but after this morning's conversation in the changing room, Catherine's roles as lover and friend were threatening to collide. She could not escape the memory of Annabel's eyes, desperate to believe her reassuring lies.

'Actually,' she said, 'there's something you should know.'

He eyed her coolly. 'Uh-huh.'

'Annabel is getting suspicious.'

'Suspicious?'

'About you. She actually asked me this morning whether I thought you were having an affair. Asked *me*. Obviously I told her it was nonsense.'

Richard said nothing.

'I just thought you should know,' said Catherine. 'Oh, and by the way, she's going to be looking out for an interview in the *Observer*. What a terrible excuse *that* was, if you don't mind my saying so.'

'That was no excuse,' said Richard. 'I'm meeting the guy after this.'

'Oh.' Catherine faltered a little. So there would be no gleeful malingering, then, no lying about ordering room service all afternoon.

'Are you all right?' asked Richard.

She bit her lip. 'I'm fine.'

'You seem a bit – I don't know.'

Catherine sighed. 'To be honest, it was odd, listening to

78

Annabel talk about you this morning. I didn't like it much.'

Richard peered into his glass, as if he were searching for his next line. 'I already know about Annabel,' he said eventually.

'You do? How?'

'She's my *wife*, Cathy. I'm not a complete brick. I can tell when something is bothering her.'

'Oh,' said Catherine.

There was a pause. All around them people were murmuring, their heads close together. Richard looked about uneasily. Finally, reluctantly, his eyes settled back on her.

'Catherine, listen. I'm sorry about this. But we have to stop.'

'Stop?'

'Our affair.'

'Well, yes –'

'I loved it, and I wish it could be otherwise, but it's over.'

Catherine shook her head. 'No.'

Richard gently put his hand over hers. 'It's nothing to –'

She pulled away. 'Stop it.'

'Stop what?'

'This nonsense. You can't just *dismiss* me like some naughty schoolgirl.'

'That's not what I'm doing,' murmured Richard.

Catherine recognised the look of grim determination on Richard's face and was paralysed by dismal longing. 'That's *exactly* what you're doing,' she said.

'Come on, Cathy. It's for the best, surely you can see that.'

'No, I can't, actually. I can't see that at all. Explain to me why it's for the *best*.'

'I just think we were getting too – I don't know.' Richard shifted in his seat. 'Take last Friday. Outside the Union Chapel.'

79

'What about it?'

'You seemed so *angry*.'

'I wasn't *angry*. I was disappointed, that's all.'

'You just seemed so – Christ. I hate to say it.'

She knew then that the game was lost. 'Say it.'

'You seemed so *needy*. There. You seemed so goddamned needy.'

There was a pause.

'Not my role?' said Catherine quietly.

Richard shrugged. 'I get needy at home.'

'And this was just a bit of fun?'

'It was an *affair*, Cathy. It was *supposed* to be fun.'

Catherine couldn't answer.

'Then there's Annabel,' continued Richard. 'And Andrew.'

'Richard, for God's sake. Whatever you do, don't pretend that you give a damn about *Andrew*.'

'All I'm saying is that we're both married to other people. And if we carry on then someone is going to get hurt.'

'It's a little late for a crisis of conscience, wouldn't you say?'

'Maybe,' conceded Richard. 'But watching Annabel worry herself sick has made me reconsider things. I don't want to hurt her any more.'

'And that's it? No polite discussion, no considered debate?'

Richard looked away. 'I guess not.'

'You guess not. Well, bully for you. You guess not.'

'Don't hate me for trying to do the right thing.'

'Oh, *please*,' snorted Catherine. 'Do you really think I'm going to swallow your hypocritical bullshit? I know you too well. You could at least have the courtesy to be honest, Richard. Why can't you admit it? You're just frightened of getting caught.'

Richard exhaled heavily. 'Maybe. But don't hate me for that, either. I'm just trying to –'

'Oh, Richard, I don't hate you,' said Catherine, hating him with every mournful bone in her body.

They looked at each other.

'So what happens now?' she asked after a long silence.

'What do you mean?'

'Are we supposed to go our separate ways and just forget all this ever happened?'

'Shit, Cathy, I don't know. I suppose so, yes.'

'You suppose so.'

'Obviously we'll still see each other all the time. But just not, well. Like that.'

'No. Not like that.'

'Just good friends,' said Richard with a small smile.

'But that was all we ever *were*,' said Catherine sadly, putting her empty glass down on the bar. She blinked back a treacherous tear, and walked away.

Clara kicked off her shoes and looked around the room. She crossed the carpet and opened the minibar. 'Excellent,' she said, peering inside. She turned around and brandished two quarter-sized bottles of Moët. 'One each,' she said with a grin.

Andrew closed the door behind him. 'Great,' he said limply. He was in desperate need of another drink. He had just handed a thick bundle of notes, fresh from the cash machine, to a smirking receptionist, and could still feel his face burning up with shame. He might have guessed that Clara would choose this hotel. It had recently opened amidst great fanfare, celebrated both for its high-concept design and high-concept prices.

Clara popped the corks. 'Here.' She walked towards him, an open bottle in each hand. 'Cheers.'

They clinked, and Andrew took a long drink of champagne. The bubbles flew up his nose. He gazed mutely at Clara's long, lithe body, astounded to find himself there, about to do this thing. 'Look,' he said, 'I wouldn't want you to think that the only reason I mentioned the executive producer job is because – because of this.'

'Oh no, of course not,' replied Clara seriously.

Andrew took another swig of champagne. 'Because obviously I'd never do that.'

'It's OK, Andrew,' said Clara.

'It's –?'

'Look, I like you, and you like me.' Clara smiled at him. 'You're doing me a favour with this job, and I'm grateful. You're a nice man. You're also married. Big deal. I'm sure you have your reasons for doing this. Now, if you'll excuse me, I'd like to go and freshen up a little.' She raised her bottle once more in salute and then went into the bathroom, closing the door behind her.

A minute later, Andrew heard the sound of running water. He went over to the enormous window which took up one entire wall of the room. The motionless traffic on the street below stewed in silent fury. The city's usual cacophony was absorbed by the vast expanse of glass, cocooning guests in detached silence. Andrew wondered what he was doing here, hoisted up high and alone and remote from the world he knew.

Finally Andrew saw the flaw in his brilliant plan: his promise of a job on a non-existent project like *Cock* was a lie too far. A warning light had begun to flash inside his head: his conscience was dangerously overloaded. Bulging with lies and deceit, impending meltdown beckoned. With quiet despair he suddenly understood that he was not going to be able to go through with this.

He crept across the room and put his ear up to the bathroom door. Clara was humming quietly to herself. There were some gentle splashes: she was in the bath. Andrew tiptoed to the bedroom door and let himself out.

* * *

Catherine walked back from Liverpool Street, a grim hike through Shoreditch and Hoxton. She skirted the battered fringes of cheerless housing estates, their concrete ramparts overrun with a forest of satellite dishes. The deserted streets shimmered with lethargic menace in the blistering glare of the sun.

She walked quickly, fuelled by bruised pride and indignation. It had not taken long for her sorrow to be replaced with anger.

Catherine didn't love Richard Sulzman, nothing complicated like that. But her affair had been the last, tenuous link to her abandoned career, an alternative partnership with the author she missed the most. Behind its illicit thrill and physical rewards had lain the hope that something of her old life remained – something to which she might one day return. Now Richard had severed that last, fragile connection. She had been cast adrift with nothing left to hope for.

By the time she arrived home it was mid-afternoon. She opened the front door and stood for a moment in the hallway, listening to the silence. Sinead would be on her way to collect the children from school. Catherine went upstairs and lay on the bed. She stared at the ceiling, the heavy weight of accumulated disappointments pressing down on her chest, pinning her in place.

When Sinead arrived home with the children, Catherine made a briefly smiling appearance and then fled to the greenhouse, unable to face the cheerful, uncaring chaos of her family. She busied herself amongst her orchids, seeking comfort in the unthinking ritual of chores. She worked diligently, bent over her pots, afraid to look up and consider the view.

A few hours later Sinead stuck her head around the greenhouse door. 'Mrs S? I need to get ready for tonight.'

'Tonight?' said Catherine.

'It's Tuesday,' Sinead reminded her.

'Oh,' murmured Catherine. 'Your night off. Of course.'

'The children are fed,' said Sinead. 'Florence is just waiting for her bath.'

'Her bath. Yes.' With a sigh, Catherine put down her trowel.

Ten minutes later, Catherine sat on the toilet and numbly watched as Florence sat in the bath and splashed and sang. Her happy, off-key delivery echoed sweetly off the bathroom walls.

Sinead put her head around the door and flicked a straggle of hair out of her face. Her eyes were freshly scalloped by ferocious slashes of purple and black make-up. As usual, she was wearing her oversized leather biker's jacket, despite the warm summer's evening. 'Right, then,' she announced, 'I'm off.'

This second abandonment of the day was suddenly more than Catherine could bear. Before she could stop herself, she began to cry, quietly at first, and then with dazzling intensity. Her chest rose and fell as she struggled for breath. Her body shook with the physical effort of producing the tiny, stinging tears. Catherine felt as if she were going to die of regret. Both Florence and Sinead looked at her, appalled.

'Sorry,' gasped Catherine between sobs. 'Sorry –'

At the sight of her mother's tears, Florence began to cry as well. Sinead pulled off her jacket and moved forward as Catherine sank to her knees, hiding her face in her hands.

'Why don't you go and have a lie down?' said Sinead neutrally as she lifted Florence out of the bath and began to rub her dry. 'I'll put Florence to bed.'

Catherine looked up. 'Oh, Sinead, would you?' She paused.

'I'm sorry about this. It's been a difficult day. I'm awfully tired.'

Sinead's face remained inscrutable. 'That's all right,' she said.

Catherine found herself unable to bear Sinead's laconic sympathy. 'Oh, but you were on your way out,' she cried. 'You must go!'

'No, don't worry,' said Sinead. 'You take a moment.'

'Thank you, Sinead,' said Catherine meekly. She retreated to the bedroom and listened through the door as Sinead cajoled Florence into bed. She was bitterly disappointed with herself. There was no excuse, not for that. But Sinead's departure for an evening of freedom and pubs and other carefree pleasures made Catherine's loneliness suddenly too much to bear.

Sinead finally left an hour later, and only then did Catherine dare emerge from her bedroom. Florence was asleep. Toby was playing with his Gameboy. She listened at his bedroom door to the squall of electronic blips, punctuated by an occasional sigh.

Andrew still hadn't arrived home from work. The clock edged slowly forwards.

Andrew drifted aimlessly through the streets. He perspired with self-loathing. To his dismay, there was no glow of self-congratulation at his craven escape from the hotel, no fillip of self-righteousness at a good deed done – or even a bad deed avoided. For he knew the real reason for his hasty escape from the hotel room: he had been terrified.

Realising that Petrushka was not expecting him to return for the rest of the day, he had performed a slow and solitary tour of Soho pubs, drinking himself into sorrowful numbness. It had been a long afternoon. Clara frolicked nakedly in his imagination. His body and soul frothed deliriously: lust and guilt clawed at each other's throats. By early evening, Andrew had been wired, lifted up to a state of transcendental horniness. The possibility of discreet frottage with the woman standing in front of him at the bar made him dizzy with desire. The barmaids' ruby-red porn-star nails curled lubriciously around the erect handles of the beer pumps. Girls lifted cigarettes to their lips with filthy, tantalising deliberation. The chalked-up menu on the pub blackboard transmogrified into an orgy of stick figures. His packet of dry roasted peanuts became a mammoth condom wrapper. The thought of Clara in the hotel room flayed him unforgivingly, drink after drink.

Andrew was dazzled by regret and relief.

Drunk and lonely, he descended into broody introspection. A barb of disappointment skewered him. Guilt, regret, fear: these, he realised sadly, were second-rate emotions, strictly the domain of the little guy. Even his lust was of a squalid, undiscriminating variety. And there was nothing he could do to redeem himself now. Guilt had trailed him around for too long. It had stalked him remorselessly, breathing hotly down his neck, as close and attentive as a lover. Finally he had turned and embraced it, danced with all its shades of regret and pain. He became defined by the coruscating poison which slithered along his veins at night, eroding sleep. He lay awake, blinking in the darkness, wired by remorse.

But Clara? Clara was peanuts. In the grand circus of Andrew Shaw's culpability, Clara was just a side-show.

Andrew had never told Catherine about the book he had written. He knew that the humiliation of her cheerfully charitable response would be too much to bear. The fact was, however much Andrew adored Catherine, the noxious legacy of his own thwarted literary ambitions prevented him from applauding her professional achievements. He would listen in icy silence as she enthused about every new young author she worked with, while envy gnawed viciously away at him. He knew it wasn't Catherine's fault. But to Andrew the successes of her authors – Richard Sulzman in particular – were simply painful reminders of everything that he had failed to achieve himself.

So when Catherine decided not to return to work after her first maternity leave, he was secretly delighted. They soon settled into a new, improved routine. Andrew became the intrepid hunter-gatherer, returning home each evening with news from the outside world. Catherine played along, doing the wifely, stay-at-home bit. It was all highly satisfactory, until, four years on, Catherine told him that she was finally considering a return to work.

The resurgence of her sparkling career, of course, would mean a return to the bad old days of Andrew's jealousy and inferiority complex. There was also the prospect of Catherine being pulled back into Richard Sulzman's sinister orbit. Tolerating Richard's obnoxious behaviour at dinner parties was one thing, but Andrew never wanted to compete with him for Catherine's attention again. He was already coming a poor second to Toby. Husbands, he knew, ranked well behind sons and superstar novelists. And after four years of having *his* media career discussed over dinner, he did not want to be eclipsed once again by Catherine's success.

It was the prospect of all this which had caused him to drink the best part of two bottles of wine on the night when he had stayed at home to babysit Toby while Catherine attended, as Richard Sulzman's guest, a glitzy book award ceremony at the Dorchester Hotel. It was the prospect of all this which had prompted his drunken rummage in Catherine's underwear drawer. And it was the prospect of all this which had driven the needle through the centre of each foil packet.

Soon afterwards Andrew had fallen into an inebriated stupor on the bed. He did not hear Catherine return from the party. When he awoke the following morning, he was still drunk. The subsequent hangover entirely erased his memory of the previous evening.

It was only when, two months later, Catherine breathlessly announced that she was pregnant that he remembered what he had done. A bomb detonated inside him. The emotional shrapnel was still flying now.

Andrew was nearly destroyed by guilt. He watched Catherine's swelling stomach in horror. It was a constant, torrefying reminder of his crime. Catherine's obvious pleasure at the pregnancy did not alleviate his shame even a fraction. The brutal unilateralism of what he had done chilled him. It had been an act of inhuman selfishness, an unspeakable betrayal. He silently promised his unborn child that he would find ways to atone for his transgression. He would love this new baby more than he had ever loved anything, ever. He would claw his way back to redemption by the unwavering hugeness of his devotion.

But as he stood in the maternity ward and felt the weight of new human life in his arms, he felt no heart-stopping rush of adoration for his new daughter. The burden of what he had done was suddenly insupportable, eclipsing everything else: all Andrew could feel, all he had ever been able to feel whenever he looked at Florence, was a terrible, paralysing, unending guilt. And so, rather than becoming the doting father that he had promised, Andrew had beaten a retreat to the chill detachment of an older generation. He went into self-imposed exile and became the patrician enforcer, benign but remote. He learned to define his children by nothing more than the logistical consequences of their existence: babysitters, holiday destinations, school fees, Sinead. He hovered on the fringes of their young lives, looking on in muted bewilderment and filled with a huge, obliterating sadness.

Finally Andrew stumbled into a taxi. As he watched the city's lights flash past, memories of his mother and wife and children were shuffled together with other dimly recalled episodes of opportunities missed and challenges feebly ducked. His drunken brain began dealing out the whole pack, one by one.

When he arrived home, it was almost midnight. All the lights were off. He went downstairs to the kitchen and poured himself a large glass of whisky. As he slumped at the kitchen table, Sinead appeared at the door. She let out a yelp as she saw him.

'Oh, Mr S,' she whispered. 'I didn't –'

'Hello, Sinead. Where've you been?'

'Tuesday's my night off,' said Sinead defensively.

'Oh,' sighed Andrew. 'Did you do something nice?'

Sinead burst into tears.

Andrew climbed to his feet and stood awkwardly next to her. Sinead hid her face in her hands as she cried. Andrew coughed. 'Is it –?'

'It's my boyfriend,' sobbed Sinead.

Andrew struck a hastily-agreed bargain between conscience and soul to write off the majority of the day's crimes if he could offer a little sympathy to this poor girl. When her sobs showed no sign of relenting, he prompted: 'Your boyfriend –?'

'My *ex*-boyfriend.'

'Oh dear,' said Andrew. 'What's happened?'

Sinead threw herself into a chair. 'He's a musician? Plays in pubs and stuff.' Andrew nodded encouragingly, trying his best to focus on what she was saying. 'Well tonight, right, he's doing this gig at a pub in Camden? And I was late, wasn't I? Mrs S was in a bit of a state earlier and asked me to stay around to help her with the children. So anyway, I finally get to the pub and when I walk in there's Pete with his tongue in some tart's ear and I say to him What do you think you're doing? and he says to me Look if you don't get here on time what do you expect me to do? Sit around and wait for you? And I say Well yes actually that is *exactly* what I expect you to do and he laughs and says Well sorry but this is rock and roll and if you're not here on time then that's your look-out Oh really I said So that's it, is it? and he laughs again and says That's it sorry babe now if you'll excuse me I'm busy and then he just turns around and carries on slobbering over this bitch, pardon my French, as if I'm not even there.'

Andrew adopted an expression of sympathetic concern as he tried to decipher the story, whose comprehensibility was compromised by innumerable alcoholic elisions and a marked strengthening of Sinead's accent. 'Right,' he said eventually.

'And he's a bastard and I know he's a bastard and you'll probably tell me that I'm better off without him and there are plenty more fish in the sea and a lot more pebbles on the beach and all the usual crap because that's always what everyone says isn't it but actually Pete's the only bloke I've met since I've been in London who's nice or rather who I thought was nice and I know this is sad because he's obviously a prick but I actually miss him already and what am I going to do now on my Tuesdays?'

'Look, do you want some whisky?' asked Andrew.

Sinead looked up at him. 'Thanks, Mr S. That would be grand.' As Andrew put a glass down in front of her she stared at it for a moment and then drank half of it in one gulp.

'Steady on,' said Andrew. 'That's good stuff, you know. Single malt.'

Sinead gave him a look somewhere between pity and contempt. 'It's *Scottish*,' she said. Wordlessly she drained her glass and poured herself another large slug without waiting to be asked. Andrew watched her with interest. She was a funny one, Sinead. Silent waters and all that. She took another gargantuan mouthful of whisky. 'How am I *ever* going to find anyone else?' she moaned.

'You will, you'll see,' yawned Andrew. He wanted to rest his head on the table. It felt full of lead. It had been a long day. 'Pretty thing like you.'

Sinead looked up. 'Really? Do you think I'm pretty?'

Andrew burped. 'Of course.'

'Do you know, Mr S,' said Sinead, scratching her head, 'I never really realised what a very nice man you are.'

'Oh, really,' said Andrew. He waved a hand in front of his face, shooing the compliment away.

'No, honest,' insisted Sinead. 'You are. Very nice. You're kind, and you're quite fit, really, for a, you know, for an older man.'

Andrew frowned. 'Quite fit?' he said, unsure whether he'd heard correctly. He hadn't done any exercise in years.

'You know.' Sinead edged her chair fractionally closer to his. 'Quite *attractive*.'

A few minutes later, Sinead was straddled across Andrew's lap, rubbing the groin of her jeans against Andrew's crotch. She held his face in her hands. Her tongue filled his mouth.

Rather to his own surprise, Andrew was kissing Sinead back.

EIGHT

Andrew opened the door, impossibly slowly.

The door squeaked on its hinges as he advanced into the darkened bedroom with the cautious, over-compensating deliberation of someone who knows that they have had too much to drink. Catherine lay beneath the duvet, not moving. Andrew closed the door behind him. He remained motionless for a few seconds, and then began to tiptoe towards the bed. Catherine could hear his laboured breathing as he approached. She caught the sour reek of whisky on his breath.

There was a thud, followed by a short grunt. Catherine switched on her bedside lamp. Andrew was bending down, clutching his shin.

'Where the hell have you been?' she demanded.

'Cathy,' gasped Andrew. 'I've just banged my –'

'Where have you *been*?'

'Did I wake you up?'

'Yes,' she lied.

'Sorry.' Andrew sat down on the bed, his back to her, and rubbed his ankle.

'So. Where were you?'

'Just out.'

93

'Who with?'

'Oh, you know. Some of the guys from work. Last-minute thing.' Andrew paused. 'Damian's birthday.'

'You might have called.'

'Thoughtless of me,' agreed Andrew.

'Very.'

There was a silence. 'I'm going to have a shower,' said Andrew heavily, and disappeared into the *en suite* bathroom. As Catherine settled back into the sheets she heard Sinead's lonely footsteps on the stairs, on her way up to bed. A moment later, the shower's sibilant whisper filled the room. Catherine turned over to look at the bedside clock. It was past midnight, the boundaries of a new day already breached. She sighed as she switched off the light. Sleep felt a million miles away. She returned to her memories.

Mozart, Brahms, Chopin – these were the names which illuminated her youth.

Catherine had been a gifted pianist – talented enough to be offered a place at the Guildhall School of Music and Drama. In her final year there, she was asked to accompany another student in a recital of the *Dichterliebe*, Robert Schumann's setting of sixteen poems by Heinrich Heine. The song cycle charted the progress of an infatuation, from blossoming hope and happiness to bitter disappointment and despair. The singer's name was Daniel Woodman. Rehearsals were to take place at an address in Hampstead rather than the usual college practice rooms. Catherine made her way there at the appointed time. The door was opened by an unshaven young man in a pair of dirty jeans and a white shirt, half unbuttoned. He gazed at her for a moment.

You must be Catherine, he said. She nodded. I'm Daniel, he said. Come in.

She followed him down a corridor to a large studio. The

sun flooded through a quartet of skylights. The walls were painted white. In the middle of the room stood an upright piano. There was no other furniture.

Interesting place, said Catherine, finally finding her voice.

Not mine, unfortunately, said Daniel Woodman. It's my uncle's. He's an artist. Don't worry, the piano's decent. Do you want some coffee?

Catherine smiled. Coffee would be good, she said.

She followed him into the small kitchen and watched as he prepared cups, milk, and sugar. As they waited for the kettle to boil they began to discuss the Schumann. I should make one thing clear from the outset, said Daniel. You are not, repeat *not*, an accompanist.

No? said Catherine.

He shook his head. We're collaborators. Piano and voice, voice and piano. Both parts are equally important. Actually, forget collaborators, he said, waving a coffee spoon at her. What we are is *co-conspirators*. He grinned. How does that sound?

That sounds perfect, Catherine told him.

For the next three days, in that dazzlingly bright room, a delicious alchemy took place. The composer's songs were pulled off the page and given life. Note by note, bar by bar, music coalesced into performance. Catherine and Daniel moulded the piece into something which was theirs alone.

Daniel performed with thrilling expressiveness. Catherine believed every word he sang. She listened to his voice and simply wanted to cry. Her excitement grew as the days passed. Each note was a firecracker beneath her fingers. Her journeys home were made in a state of delicious exhaustion. As the train made its slow progress southwards, her head remained in the cool, light-filled room.

The creative process was a scintillating, addictive high.

Catherine and Daniel drank deep of Schumann's cup, revelling in the emotional intensity of the *Dichterliebe*. Their voyage towards the heart of the songs created a sharply accelerated intimacy. The music left them raw, bruised, and elated, and they had no one to turn to but each other.

The kiss came at the end of the third day. It was the most natural thing in the world.

They only knew each other in that room. Reluctant to quit it now, they found a blanket and spread it out next to the piano. They lay there, side by side, fully clothed, ecstatic. The world beyond the white walls faded away.

Neither felt the hardness of the wooden floor beneath them.

He held her all night. By the time they fell asleep, just as the first glow of the approaching dawn washed across the skylights, everything had changed, for ever.

The next morning, and every morning which followed, Catherine woke up blinking in disbelief. At the start of each new day she had to reacquaint herself with the astonishing news that she had fallen in love. The information never lost its capacity to surprise her. It was simply there, gloriously true. A constellation of infinite pinpoints of happiness exploded along the length of her body, across the expanse of her soul.

Catherine's passion recast everything in a new light. Objects were defined solely by their role in her love affair. The soiled trains which belched their way beneath the city now held the sweet promise of a journey to Daniel's flat. The piano was no longer simply a musical instrument; it was the fuse which had ignited their romance. And the music which Catherine had known for so long suddenly acquired a brilliant new dimension. Every note was framed in a stunning new context. Love! Imagine! Catherine was no longer simply a mirror which reflected the composer's spirit. Now she could draw the music deep into herself and expel it again through her fingers, refracting it through her own passion. The music poured out of the piano, shimmering with Catherine's new ardour.

Two weeks after the recital, they borrowed a van. On a bright autumn day, with the help of two friends, they laughingly wrestled Catherine's piano out of her student digs and into Daniel's flat in Tufnell Park. Then they sealed themselves away, alone with their happiness, and each other. At night they watched old movies, Hollywood's hymns to the myth of grand romance. As the orchestra swelled and the on-screen lovers fell into each other's arms, Catherine and Daniel sat dazed on the sofa. Their own affair shone all the more sweetly in the glittering reflection of all that beautiful schmaltz: nobody was writing a script for them.

Music was everywhere, of course. Catherine played, Daniel sang. They performed everything from Beethoven to Bacharach, Schubert to Sinatra. She wanted to fling her arms around him and never let go.

Catherine was sharply surprised by the ferocity of her longing, the undimming desire which inflamed her. Both her past and her future were redrawn by his existence. She dreamed of all the years together that were still, deliciously, to come; and soon it was impossible to conceive of a time when she had not known him.

And then.

All those old films should have warned her, she could see that now. Once the camera stopped rolling and the crew packed up, what were the odds on those mismatched celluloid couples staying the distance? There were no happy endings in Hollywood. There were just happy beginnings.

Catherine could not identify the precise moment when the first aching shadow of disquiet crept across her. Little by little, though, she sensed a cooling from across the room. All of a sudden Daniel was no longer so enraptured with the story of them. The broad grin which could unlock her at fifty paces was replaced by a polite, tight-lipped smile. The eyes drifted away more readily now, caught by other distractions. She could feel their nest of intimacy being weakened by every insidious tug from outside.

He began to stay out late. She remained in the flat, vast and empty without him, and waited in solitary terror. She sat at the piano and played for hours, crashing angrily through piece after piece, not hearing a note. Finally she would collapse into the empty bed, dreading the acrid twist of her dreams.

Then, finally, one night he did not come home at all. Catherine had stayed awake until the morning, determined not to be defeated by the terrified riot of her imagination. The following day she crawled around the flat, bug-eyed with exhaustion, praying for him to come home safely. There was bound to be a simple explanation, she told herself, ignoring the chest-tightening fear which was squeezing the hope out of her.

Daniel finally returned in the middle of the afternoon. It took two days for him to destroy her completely.

For forty-eight miserable hours he slowly demolished Catherine with a battery of blustered excuses and evasive responses. Each furtive parry undid her a fraction more. Things had changed, he said. Perhaps it was time to move on.

Again and again and again she asked: but *why*?

It was Daniel's inability to provide a satisfactory answer

98

to this question which had annihilated her. Catherine floundered helplessly in her ignorance. She shook her head in furious disbelief, wanting to hammer her fists against him. You're making a *mistake*, she cried.

Perhaps you should go, he said.

A week later, the piano came home. The same friends, the same van, but this time the journey was made without laughter, in the cold February rain.

Alone once more, Catherine became memorialist-in-chief of her own love affair. By sparing himself from the discomfort of confession, Daniel Woodman had condemned her to the agony of ignorance, and she sought relief from her pain in the anaesthetic of distorted remembrance. She picked through her memories, discarding those which did not quite measure up to the heady delirium she wished to preserve. Gradually her months with Daniel coalesced into untouchable legend, a time of perfect, ineffable happiness. She buried herself in her story with delicious, sorrowful regret. A head of dark curls half a carriage away could still make Catherine's intestines cavort in nervous anticipation, but she had no wish to see Daniel again. She needed him to remain as she had chosen to remember him. A confrontation now could only imperil her memories, and their honeyed pain was the oxygen of her dreams.

Catherine was a fine pianist, but there were others who were better. She knew that there would be no garlanded professional career for her, and so after graduation she turned away from music and its cargo of bitter memories. Instead she applied for a position as a junior editor in a publishing house. There she immersed herself in books, each new novel a cleansing sea of words. She learned to hone other people's stories, rather than her own. Within four years she had become one of the company's most successful young editors.

And life went on. Catherine met new people. She embarked on relationships, but they rarely lasted for long. It wasn't Daniel she missed, but the blistering eruption of passion which he had ignited within her. Nothing else compared. Every new romantic masquerade was doomed to failure, cast into shadow by the brilliance of her memories.

Andrew Shaw was attractive, witty, and charming. Catherine liked him very much. They went out for a lot of dinners, and spent one or two nights a week in each other's beds. As she undressed and slipped into his arms, Catherine told herself that this was better than night after night of loneliness. There had been weekends in Lisbon and Dublin, ten days in Bermuda. Sometimes, as she hurried from the office to meet him in front of cinemas and theatres, she caught herself smiling at the prospect of seeing him again. As time passed they cultivated a shiny patina of togetherness. Clothes migrated between the flat she shared in Fulham and his Docklands loft. Invitations soon came addressed to them both.

Andrew adored her, she knew. And even though there was no crippling, lung-busting desire, no terrified certainty that life would end without him, she found herself loving him back, in her own quiet, grateful way. Catherine remembered the first time he had tried to cook for her. The roast chicken had emerged from the oven, extremities blackened and flesh still wetly pink. She had never forgotten the look in his eyes as he watched the uncooked blood seep on to the carving board. His disappointment was nearly unbearable. She had wanted to hold him tightly, to stroke his hair and soothe away his distress.

Then one evening Andrew had clumsily fished a small

black box out of his pocket and pushed it across the table towards her. As she gazed down at the trio of diamonds which crowned the engagement ring, Catherine felt obliged to give him an answer straight away. To ask for time to think it over seemed incalculably mean, and to say no seemed incalculably ungrateful. All that effort, all that devotion! So she had said yes, and then she had begun to cry.

There was never any question that she would change her mind; Catherine knew that it would destroy Andrew completely. Instead she concentrated on preparations for the wedding, and her hearty industry eventually smothered the faint chorus of misgiving which still lingered on within her. She learned to count her blessings. Andrew was a good man. By the time she found herself walking into the church on her father's arm, she had convinced herself that this was what she wanted.

Everything had gone well enough at first, until that disastrous trip to the opera. During the interval Andrew had made some fatuous remark about sitting in the Gods, and suddenly Catherine found herself swamped by disappointment. The weight of her compromise suddenly threatened to crush her: there she was, married to a man who complained about cheap opera seats! She was appalled. And so her tears had fallen through the second half of the performance and all the way home, as Catherine had quietly mourned.

It was after this first breach of her defences that her memories of Daniel Woodman had returned to haunt her. She was suddenly crucified by the absence of passion in her new marriage. Catherine hid her disappointment behind a veil of exaggerated hysteria. The most banal sentiment was liable to trigger a fresh cascade of tears as she lamented the drab emotional landscape which now surrounded her. She didn't love Andrew any less; she simply didn't love him as much as she should have.

She retreated to the piano, seeking solace. Andrew liked to listen to her play. He thought that she was playing for him. In the end, she always returned to the same tune, a song from the Schumann cycle. She played the accompaniment as Daniel Woodman's voice rang out inside her head:

> *When I hear the sound of the song*
> *That my beloved sang,*
> *My bosom is near to bursting*
> *With the savage strain of sorrow.*

Andrew nodded approvingly as he listened. He didn't know that he was only hearing half the tune. He was deaf to the melody, unaware of the real story.

Catherine had been three months pregnant with Toby when Rosa announced that she was dying. She had come out with it, just like that, one weekend in Wiltshire. Lung cancer. Patrick had stood behind her, his hand resting gently on her shoulder. Andrew was nearly destroyed by grief. The news had swarmed around them like a vast cloud of insects, defying comprehension and obliterating the sun.

Rosa, of course, was stoical about the whole thing. It was left to the rest of them to stagger blindly through their sorrow, trying to make sense of it all. Andrew and Patrick had retreated to the bottom of the garden to chop down a tree. Their axes flew through the cold afternoon air. Catherine stood at the sitting room window and watched them work. Patrick's brow was a jagged crease of fury. Andrew wore an unyielding mask of pure terror.

Rosa came up behind her. 'They'll survive, you'll see,' she said.

Catherine continued to look out of the window, saying nothing.

'Patrick's strong,' continued Rosa. 'If nothing else he'll be driven on by his anger.'

'His anger?'

'He blames me,' explained Rosa. 'Not unreasonably, I suppose. I rather wish I could have got something other than *lung* cancer, to be honest. Now I shall have to bear Patrick's wounded affront until I shuffle off.'

'Does he really blame you?' asked Catherine.

Rosa nodded. 'Of course he does. But not as much as he blames himself. I'm afraid this has all rather spoiled his grand plan.'

'What grand plan?'

'Patrick has been plotting my spiritual salvation for years, Cathy. It's his obsession. Well, that and cricket. He prays for my soul, you know. Every day.' Rosa gave her a small smile. 'He knows I'm a lost cause, but that's never stopped him trying. I suppose he feels he has a duty not to give up. Typical Christian. Carrying on defiantly in the face of all common sense. I think he's been trying to finagle a pass for me, up there on the right hand of the Almighty, or wherever it is. Anyway. The point is, whatever timetable he was pursuing has gone out of the window. And now he feels guilty.'

'But that's ridiculous.'

'Isn't it? I'm not sure whom he thinks is being punished. Me, for being an unbeliever, or him, for not trying hard enough to save my soul.' Rosa sat down on the arm of the sofa. 'At any rate, he's very angry about it.'

'And you?' asked Catherine. 'Are you angry?'

Rosa thought. 'No. Not angry. I'm sorry, though.' She looked at Catherine and smiled. 'I was having so much *fun*.'

The two women stood in silence for a moment, watching their husbands.

'And Andrew?' said Catherine eventually. 'Is he strong?'

Rosa looked out of the window and watched her son for a moment. 'What do you think?'

'He adores you.'

'No, sweet Catherine, he adores *you*.'

Catherine looked down.

'You know what these doctors' prognoses are like,' said Rosa quietly. 'About as reliable as weather forecasts. Six weeks, six months, tomorrow. Whatever. Fat lot of use it all is. All I know for sure is that soon I won't be able to keep my eye on you any more.'

'We'll be fine.' Catherine patted her stomach.

'Not you plural. You singular.' Rosa pointed at her. 'My eye on *you*.'

Catherine turned towards her. 'On me? What do you mean?'

'I'm not blind, Cathy,' said Rosa. 'You might be able to pull the wool over Andrew's eyes, but you can't fool an old woman like me.'

'Rosa –'

'You're keeping secrets.'

Catherine stared at her.

'Andrew thinks you're wonderful. And he thinks you're happy. He's too blinkered by love to see the sadness in your eyes.' Rosa pulled on her cigarette. 'I'm fond of you, really I am, but right now all I care about is that Andrew is going to be all right. I don't have much time left to shilly-shally about, so you'll excuse the blunt approach.' She was calm, determined. 'I want you to promise me something.'

'All right,' said Catherine.

Rosa looked searchingly into her eyes. 'For God's sake, Cathy, please. Whatever it is, *let go*.'

Without another word she turned and walked out of the room.

*　*　*

104

That evening they had driven back to London, pursued down the motorway by a ferocious storm. The only sound in the car was the rhythmic sashay of the windscreen wipers. Andrew's eyes cast listlessly into the middle distance as he drove, as if he were searching for something in the darkness which might make sense of his mother's illness. The cancer was proliferating, cell by painful cell, a slow erosion of life. Catherine watched him in silence, and knew that Rosa was right. This frightened man and his child growing inside her – this was her future now. There was nothing to be gained by looking back now.

Back in London, she walked into the sitting room and sat down at the piano. She gazed at the keys in front of her. There were too many memories stored in their monochrome tranquillity. She closed the piano lid.

She had not played a note since.

NINE

Catherine was woken by an urgent tug on the duvet. She opened her eyes. Sunshine was creeping around the edges of the bedroom curtains, casting the room in a warm half-light. Toby stood next to the bed in his pyjamas, looking worried.

'Toby?' she mumbled. 'What is it?'

'It's Sinead,' said Toby.

Catherine propped herself up on an elbow. 'What about her?'

'She's gone.'

'Gone where?'

'I don't know. She's just gone.'

Catherine threw back the duvet and staggered upstairs to Sinead's bedroom. The room was empty.

Andrew appeared at the door, yawning. 'What's going on?'

'Sinead's gone,' Toby told him.

'What do you mean, she's gone?'

'She's left,' said Catherine flatly.

'Oh Christ. Oh no.' Andrew looked stricken. 'Did she leave a note?' He looked around him.

'I can't see one,' said Catherine. She shook her head. 'How could she just leave without a word? Something must have happened.'

'I'll go and check downstairs,' said Andrew, and disappeared.

Catherine sat down on the edge of Sinead's bed. First Richard, now Sinead. Another desertion. What had she done to deserve this?

'Mum?' whispered Toby. 'Has Sinead gone for ever?'

'I don't know, darling. But it rather looks like it.'

Toby flung his arms around Catherine and burst into tears. She held him tightly, shocked. Toby clung to her as his small body heaved. The sound of his high-pitched sobs filled the empty bedroom.

'Why didn't she say *goodbye*?' he choked.

Catherine stroked his hair. 'I don't know, Toby. I don't know.'

Toby looked at his mother. 'Did she not love us, then?'

'Oh, darling, of *course* she did. I'm sure she'll be in touch and then she'll explain everything.' Catherine stood up. 'Tell you what. Why don't you go downstairs and help Daddy look for a note?'

'OK,' sniffed Toby.

'I'll go and wake up Florence, and then we'll see what's what.'

When Catherine arrived downstairs a few minutes later with Florence lagging sleepily in her arms, Toby looked up. 'There was no note,' he reported.

'Oh dear,' said Catherine.

Andrew was standing in the middle of the kitchen with his hands on his hips, looking distracted. He glanced at the kitchen clock. 'Look, I know it's difficult, but I should really be getting –'

'Oh, *go*,' sighed Catherine, putting Florence down.

'Cathy,' said Andrew softly. 'I've got to go to *work*.'

Catherine felt a twinge of guilt at her unthinking volley of petty acrimony. 'You're right,' she said after a moment. 'I'm sorry. It's just that this is the last thing I need. Of course you must go.'

'Sure you'll be all right?' asked Andrew.

'Oh, we'll be fine.'

'Right,' said Andrew. 'Good. OK. Well, I'll get cracking, then.' He disappeared back up the stairs.

Catherine contemplated the kitchen, flummoxed. 'Florence, darling, come here and have some breakfast.'

'Where's Sinead?' asked Florence as she meandered towards the kitchen table.

'She's *gone*,' said Toby blackly.

'We *think*,' added Catherine, shaking cereal into two bowls. She was craving a large cup of strong coffee.

Florence did not seem unduly bothered by Sinead's sudden disappearance. She accepted her bowl of cereal from her mother, unperturbed by this breach of protocol. 'What else does Sinead give you for breakfast?' Catherine asked Toby.

Toby thought carefully. 'Ice-cream,' he said after a moment.

'*Really*,' said Catherine.

'Sometimes,' said Toby, crestfallen.

'What about apple juice?'

'Oh yes,' said Toby. 'I suppose. That too.'

Catherine poured two glasses of juice and tried to calculate the implications of Sinead's disappearance. It was a logistical disaster, that much was obvious. There were piles of clothes to be ironed, the horror of the school run beckoned, and a long list of grocery shopping was tacked on to the kitchen notice board. The children were still in their pyjamas. She glanced at the clock, and sighed.

'So, Toby, is anything exciting happening at school these days?' she asked.

Toby finished his mouthful before replying. His pyjamas were covered with pictures of a dark-haired boy wearing glasses and a wizard's hat. The boy looked a bit like Toby, only less serious. 'It's the dress rehearsal of the school play this afternoon,' he said.

'The school play?'

'There's always a play,' explained Toby, 'at the end of every summer term.'

'At the end of – gosh, Toby, when does term actually *end*?'

Toby looked at her. 'Friday,' he said.

'Friday!' cried Catherine.

'You are *coming* to the play, aren't you?' said Toby after a moment.

'Oh yes, of course,' said Catherine. She paused. 'What, er, what is it that you're actually –?'

'I'm assistant stage manager,' said Toby gravely.

Catherine clasped her hands together. 'How *wonderful*.'

'It's a very important job,' Toby told her.

'Goodness, I can imagine.'

'I have prop lists,' said Toby. 'I'm in charge of checking that everything's in the right place.'

'That's a big responsibility,' said Catherine, suddenly besotted with her son. 'What's the play?'

'*James and the Giant Peach.*'

'Well, I can't wait,' said Catherine, still reeling from the news that term was due to end in two days.

Florence had managed to ferry approximately half of the contents of her bowl into her mouth. Her face was a mashed collage of yellow and white. Soggy flakes of cereal hung precariously from her cheeks.

'Florence?' said Catherine. 'Have you finished?'

By way of reply, Florence lowered her head into the bowl, anointing her fringe with milk.

'Oh, *Florence*,' sighed Catherine.

'She always does that,' said Toby.

'Right, well, I'll get her cleaned up. You go upstairs and get dressed. I want you back down here in your uniform in ten minutes.'

Toby climbed down from his chair without a word. As he traipsed out of the room, Andrew appeared at the kitchen door, dressed for work. Toby and Andrew passed without acknowledging each other's existence.

'Everything all right?' asked Andrew.

Catherine sighed. 'Florence has just baptised herself with milk.'

'Yes, she always does that,' said Andrew.

Catherine blinked. How was it that she was the only one in this family who was unaware of her daughter's peculiar breakfast habits? 'If Sinead really has gone, from now on you'll need to get home earlier than you did last night,' she said, as neutrally as she could.

'Don't worry,' said Andrew. 'I'll call the agency today. We can find a replacement within a week. Maybe next time we'll get someone with a bit more, I don't know. Zip.'

'No,' said Catherine. 'That's all right.'

Andrew frowned. 'What do you mean?'

'We don't need a replacement. I can manage.' Catherine listened to herself, horrified.

Andrew looked at her. 'You can manage,' he repeated.

'No need to sound so doubtful.'

'No, it's not that, it's just that I never exp–'

'After all, they're *my* children.'

'Of course they are. I just assumed –'

'Well perhaps you should start assuming a little less, then,' said Catherine tartly. It had been Andrew's assumption that she *needed* help which had prompted her impulsive outburst in the first place. She was already wishing that she had kept her mouth shut.

110

Andrew looked at his watch. 'I really have to go.' He looked baffled, anxious to escape.

'Daddy!' shouted Florence. 'Kiss!' She flung her arms out towards Andrew. Andrew looked at her breakfast-spattered face and waved at her apologetically. He turned and fled.

'Right then,' said Catherine, picking Florence up. 'Let's go and get you ready, shall we?' Catherine climbed the stairs to her daughter's bedroom. Perhaps, she thought, this wouldn't be so bad after all.

Fifty minutes later, trapped on the Holloway Road, Catherine had revised her earlier, optimistic prognosis. The line of immobile traffic shimmered in a choked haze of sunlight and carbon monoxide. Angry indicator lights blinked as motorists tried to change lanes, angling in vain for a way out of the impasse. The violence of a thousand cranked-up car radios was seeping into the clotted atmosphere. In the back seat, Florence and Toby, crazed by boredom, were within moments of killing each other. Catherine kept one eye on the dash-board clock. They were already late. Her life had suddenly been hijacked by the capricious whims of faceless school administrators.

Catherine was doing her best to remain calm. So far she hadn't shouted at the children. She was willing herself into a Zen-like trance, repeating her yogic breathing exercises as she inched the car forward, concentrating on the movement of her feet on the pedals as she changed from neutral into first gear and back again. Toby anxiously pointed out the time every thirty seconds or so, which was failing to improve Catherine's mood.

When they finally reached Highgate, the coffee shops and cosy estate-agent windows made it seem like a Home Counties market town after the exhaust-drenched squalor they had left behind at Archway. Here there was another, more exclusive rush hour: the place was bumper to bumper with bungalow-sized Range Rovers on the school run. As Catherine approached the gates of Toby's school, he leaned forward.

'You don't have to come in, Mummy,' he told her.

She twisted around in her seat. 'Why not?'

'Lots of the boys are just dropped off at the gates.' The look of supplication on her son's face bruised her.

'All right then,' she said, pulling up at the curb. 'How about here?'

'Fine,' said Toby as he unhooked his seat belt.

'Have a nice day,' called Catherine sadly.

Toby opened the door. 'OK,' he said.

'I'll pick you up at the usual time,' said Catherine.

Toby shook his head. 'I've got the dress rehearsal, remember?'

'Oh, of course. When should I come?'

'Don't worry. Finlay Burton's mum is going to drop me off afterwards.'

'I see,' said Catherine. Who was Finlay Burton? she wondered. More pertinently, who was Finlay Burton's mother? And when had this been arranged? There was a twist of unease in her stomach. She pulled out into the traffic and watched Toby in her rear-view mirror as he turned and walked into the school. 'Right,' she said to Florence, the sadness catching in her throat. 'Your turn now, darling.'

'Hooray!' chirruped Florence, not very diplomatically.

Five minutes later, Florence was dragging Catherine into her nursery. Mother and daughter were greeted in an empty corridor by a grey-haired lady who bent down and fondly patted Florence's hair. Florence gazed up at her in unabashed adoration.

'Daphne!' shouted Florence.

'Hello, Florence,' said the woman. 'You're a wee bit late

112

today, aren't you?' She looked up at Catherine. 'Hello Mrs Shaw. We haven't seen you for a long time.'

Catherine smiled through the accusation. 'It *has* been a while,' she agreed pleasantly.

'No Sinead today?'

'Sinead's gone,' said Florence.

Catherine shrugged to show that this news was not something which bothered her unduly. 'That's right, Daph–'

'Mrs Perkins,' corrected the woman.

'Ah, so, yes,' faltered Catherine, blinking, 'Mrs Perkins. Sinead has left us.'

'Oh well.' The woman delivered a humourless smile. 'These people are always replaceable, aren't they? Not like mothers.'

Bitch, thought Catherine. 'Actually, I'll be looking after the children myself from now on.' She blinked. There! She'd said it again!

'Well, come on, little one,' said Mrs Perkins, as if she hadn't heard. 'Let's go and have some fun, shall we?' She took Florence's hand and led her off down the corridor. Florence walked away from her mother without saying goodbye. She didn't look back.

Catherine stood abandoned in the middle of the corridor.

It was just before six o'clock in the morning in New York.

In Beijing, it was early evening. People would be getting on their bicycles to go home. In Wellington the pubs would soon be closing.

Andrew Shaw's finger idly roamed the world.

Catherine had given Andrew his International Executive Clock the Christmas after they were married. Beneath the digital display was a copper-coloured map of the world, the different time zones demarcated by irregular vertical lines. Touch any zone, and the correct time in that part of the world was displayed. Andrew didn't consult the clock often. To have

113

all that information literally at his fingertips was a torment. Just knowing what time it was in other parts of the world reminded him how often he longed to be somewhere else.

Still, sometimes it could be a useful escape mechanism. With the twitch of his finger Andrew could be waking up on a beach in Phuket or indulging in bacchanalian *après-ski* in Colorado. Right now he had taken refuge in an elegant Parisian café by the banks of the Seine, where the bells of Notre Dame would shortly be chiming noon. A waiter had just delivered a small, steaming coffee to his table. A group of pretty girls sashayed past. The belles of Notre Dame. One of them smiled at him. He winked back. In Paris the sun was shining, and all was well with the world.

'Are you winking at me?' asked Joel.

'Of course not,' said Andrew.

'You *were*. You were winking at me.'

'Something in my eye, that's all.' Andrew performed another wink, slow and deliberate this time, and inserted the tip of his forefinger into his eye socket for good measure. The French girl had disappeared down the pavement, never to be seen again. He suppressed a small sigh.

'OK, so what do you think?' Joel was looking at him expectantly.

There was a pause.

'What do I think?' said Andrew.

'I suppose you're going to say it's crazy.'

Andrew had no idea what Joel was talking about. 'Why do you suppose that?' he asked carefully.

Joel shrugged. 'I don't know. This is a bit mad, even by Swedish standards.'

Andrew deciphered the clue. 'This is Stockholm's idea?'

Joel nodded. 'Freddie's very keen.'

'Then I don't see that we realistically have a choice, do we?'

'I suppose not,' agreed Joel.

'That's settled, then.' Andrew's eyes drifted back to his clock. In Rio de Janeiro people were just sitting down to breakfast.

There was another, longer, pause.

'Andrew,' said Joel, 'are you all right?'

Of course, Andrew was far from all right. He was being stalked by the memory of the previous evening.

After several minutes of determined dry humping, Sinead had grabbed Andrew's hand and placed it on her chest. Andrew's fingers had instinctively closed around the flesh of her breast. Sinead had let out a small hiss at his touch.

Up to that point Andrew's responses had been animal-istic, unthinking. His sexual frustration and drunkenness had combined to bypass all reason, logic and decency, and had turned him into a rampant, slobbering beast. For some reason, though, Sinead's hiss had broken the spell. As if waking from a dream, Andrew was appalled to discover the au pair riding him like a bucking bronco, his hand on her tit and her tongue half-way down his throat. With a muffled shriek (Sinead's tongue was still *in situ*) he heaved himself off his chair, sending her sprawling across the kitchen floor. Without another word he fled upstairs.

In the shower he had masturbated furiously, a desperate act of self-defence. His ejaculation was pleasureless, but it had at least finally banished the priapic demons that had been tormenting him all afternoon. Christ, he had thought, as he watched the strings of sperm slither across the shower floor towards the plughole. *Sinead*.

Finally Andrew had crawled into bed. He lay beneath the duvet and stared wide-eyed into the darkness.

* * *

115

Unsurprisingly, the whole episode had ratcheted up his guilt index to an all-time high. If Clara represented a crime imagined but never committed, Sinead was the reverse. Those first few moments of unthinking carnality crucified him. The discovery of Sinead's subsequent disappearance this morning had actually increased his remorse, something which up until that point he had believed impossible. The poor girl had obviously been emotionally vulnerable, perhaps even a little unhinged. Andrew imagined her wandering along a deserted railway line as dawn broke over the city, her clothes in tatters, dazed and defenceless. Around the next corner lurked a predatory posse of – well, it didn't really matter, did it? The point was, Sinead was doomed – and it was all his fault.

Mixed in with this new font of guilt was anxiety about what she might do next, in the event that she survived the deserted railway line scenario. She was just *out there*, unpredictable and beyond his control. As Andrew's imagination began to froth with paranoia, Sinead metamorphosed into a vengeful psychopath, bent on retribution at any price. He knew he could never prevent her from telling Catherine about the night before, if she were so minded. All he could usefully do was to prepare his denial, and so he had spent the morning practising his indignant refutation of Sinead's allegations, struggling to achieve the right balance of quiet hurt (that Catherine would believe such a thing even for a moment!) and self-righteous anger (that Sinead would try to destroy their marriage with her spiteful lies!). So far his efforts had all borne the hollow ring of guilt. When Joel had knocked on his door fifteen minutes earlier, he had decided to give himself a break and began gazing at his map of the world instead, tuning out Joel's chatter.

Joel was looking at him now, a concerned frown on his face.

'Well?' he said.

'I'm fine,' sighed Andrew.

'You don't look it,' said Joel. 'You look awful.'

'I have a small hangover,' explained Andrew. (His hangover was monstrous.)

Joel looked unconvinced. 'I'm not talking about how you feel physically. More, you know, spiritually.'

'"More, you know, spiritually"?'

'You look done in. You look *beaten*.'

Andrew closed his eyes for a moment. Even someone as intuitively dim as Joel could occasionally fluke a direct hit. 'Really, I'm fine,' he said. The last thing he wanted to do was to share his problems with Joel. The benign pseudo-holistic twaddle which would follow would be intolerable. Andrew was in no mood to be enjoined to hug a tree. 'Thanks, anyway.'

'Well, OK, then,' said Joel, standing up.

'The thing is, Joel, I'm incredibly depressed.'

Joel sat down.

Andrew stared at the ceiling for a long time. 'Do you ever just look at your life and wonder what went wrong?'

Joel looked blankly at Andrew. There was an awkward pause.

'Er, yes?' said Joel eventually.

'Oh, God, what a relief. Me too, all the time. All the bloody time. My life, my family, my job, my marriage –'

'Your job?' said Joel.

'– sometimes none of it seems to make sense. It's strange, because I daresay a lot of people would take one look at me and think, well, what's he got to complain about? But it's not the external stuff that's important, is it? It's how you feel – inside.'

'And how *do* you feel – *inside*?' asked Joel.

Joel, thought Andrew, had been watching too much *Tilly!*

'Dead,' he answered. 'I feel dead. Dead and bemused. And tired. And very pissed off.'

'And *beaten*?' asked Joel hopefully.

'I suppose so. Beaten. Yes. My God. Beaten. Beaten by life.' Andrew slumped back in his chair. 'What a mess.'

'Can I make a suggestion?' said Joel.

'Please do.'

'You've lost your way, haven't you?'

Andrew frowned. 'You call that a suggestion?'

Joel smiled with his usual infuriating equanimity, and stood up. He walked around the desk and began to massage Andrew's shoulders with firm, rhythmic squeezes. Andrew sat frozen in his chair, horrified. 'Wow,' whispered Joel, bending down and breathing into Andrew's ear. 'Boy, you are tense. *Molto, molto* tense.'

'Yes, well,' muttered Andrew. 'It's been a difficult time.'

'So anyway,' said Joel. 'Here's what I think. I reckon you're going through a bit of a crisis.'

Brilliant, thought Andrew.

'It happens to the best of us,' continued Joel. 'We lose sight of our inner selves. We forget *who we are*. And do you know what you need to do?'

'No, Joel,' sighed Andrew. 'What do I need to do?'

'You need to reacquaint yourself with your spiritual essence. And once you've done that, you must free your soul, follow your heart, and unleash the caged animal within.' As he spoke, Joel's fingers increased their pressure on Andrew's neck. Andrew hated to admit it, but it felt wonderful.

'The caged animal within?' he said.

'I'm speaking metaphorically,' explained Joel.

'Yes, thank you, Joel,' said Andrew stiffly, 'I realise that. But what does the caged animal *signify*?'

Joel thought for a moment. 'It's the *real you*.'

118

'The real me.'

'It's you before life got its claws into you. Before you got lost along the way, confused by all the shit. The old you, with all your hopes and dreams intact.'

To Andrew's disquiet, Joel's gobbledegook was starting to make a sort of sense. 'And exactly how does one go about unleashing the caged animal?' he asked.

Joel shrugged. 'Search me.'

Andrew twisted around to face him. 'You don't *know*?'

'Afraid not,' said Joel cheerfully, taking his hands off Andrew's shoulders and walking back around the table.

Andrew was struggling to overcome a surge of disappointment. 'Oh. I see.'

'Everyone has their own path to follow,' said Joel as he crossed the room.

'Their own path,' muttered Andrew.

Joel turned at the door. 'And we'll do this thing on Friday, if that's all right with you.'

'This thing?'

'The Swedish thing.' Joel winked and tapped his finger against the side of his head.

'The Swedish thing,' said Andrew. 'Right.' Joel disappeared.

The telephone rang.

'Richard Sulzman for you,' said Petrushka.

There was a pause as Andrew stared at the damp patch on the wall opposite his desk, bleakly contemplating his life.

'Andrew? Shall I put him through?'

'No, Petrushka, I really don't think I can stomach his patronising –'

'*Andy*.'

'Richard,' exclaimed Andrew. 'What a nice surprise. How are you?'

'I'm good. I'm doing good.' A pause. 'How you doing?'

119

Andrew's nose wrinkled. 'Yes, I, too, am doing good, thanks awfully for asking.'

'Listen,' said Richard, 'are you doing anything tomorrow lunch time?'

'Tomorrow lunch time? I don't think so. Why?'

'I wanted to ask you for a drink.'

'A drink?'

'You know, wet thing, usually comes in a glass.'

Andrew frowned. 'Any particular reason?'

'Yeah, a very particular reason. I want to talk to you about something.'

'Oh yes? About what?'

'I'll tell you tomorrow.'

Andrew thought. 'Is this about *Cock*?'

'It's not, no.'

There was a pause.

'Is it about –?'

'Sorry, I'm not biting. You'll have to wait until tomorrow. If you can make it, of course.'

To his annoyance, Andrew's interest had been piqued by Richard's little cloak and dagger act. 'Tomorrow would be OK.'

'See you at the Three Horseshoes, one o'clock?'

'One o'clock.'

'Great. And Andy?'

'What?'

'Do me a favour? Don't tell Catherine you're coming.' Richard hung up.

Andrew stared into space, lost in thought.

What could Richard possibly want to talk to him about? And why would he not want Catherine to know about their meeting?

One of the more unnerving aspects of Catherine's friendship with Richard was that the two of them never disagreed about anything, ever. All of Andrew's attempts to uncover a subject of discord had met with failure: Catherine and Richard presented a united front on every topic. They supported each other's opinions and argued each other's points; anyone brave enough to take them on rarely emerged with their dignity intact. (By contrast, in public Catherine automatically took issue with everything Andrew said, as if matrimonial agreement on any subject were socially obnoxious.)

But Richard's request for discretion suggested that perhaps a chink had appeared in their usually impenetrable armour of familiarity. He was keeping secrets from Catherine! Andrew's mind fermented in delicious conjecture. What was the old bastard up to?

Of course, Andrew had no intention of doing as Richard had asked. He was going to tell Catherine everything as soon as he got home.

Back from Highgate, Catherine stood in the middle of the kitchen and stared at the pile of unironed clothes which was balancing precariously on the top of the washing machine. There was also the cleaning to do. And the supermarket run. All before she picked Florence up from the nursery. She glanced at her watch. We could always have a take-away this evening, she thought. And the cleaning could wait until tomorrow. Catherine felt her resolve wobble. Perhaps, she thought, a new au pair wouldn't be such a bad idea, after all. Or at least a cleaning lady, someone to come in once or twice a week.

With a sigh, Catherine went to the fridge. It was nearly empty. The bare shelves hummed in arctic accusation. She took out the last remaining pot of yoghurt and peeled back its lid. As she ate, the wordless anxiety which had been plaguing her since the previous afternoon suddenly threatened to swamp her.

Catherine's world suddenly felt unbearably fragile. It

121

seemed that her affair with Richard had performed a more complex function than she had previously realised. It hadn't just been an exercise in furtive thrill-seeking. It had also been a buttress against her past.

She finished her yoghurt and sat staring at the empty plastic pot. Poor Andrew, she thought. Throughout their marriage – that very public waltz performed under the watchful eyes of family, friends and society at large – Catherine's private world had been a lonely dance on an empty stage.

Rosa's plea from all those years ago echoed still: *Let go.*

She had done her best. She had found ways to survive. Toby had once explained to Catherine that most of his magic tricks did not depend on clever mechanical devices. Instead they relied upon a simpler ruse: distracting the audience at the critical moment so that the magician's subterfuge went unnoticed. Misdirection, it was called in the trade. Catherine understood the concept well. Her affair with Richard had performed the same sneaky function. Along with the petty thievery and the yoga and the orchids, it had been a means of pulling her eyes away from the insipid spectacle that her life had become. Catherine had allowed herself to be seduced by her own conjuring trick, but without Richard to thrill her, she doubted whether she would be able to sustain the illusion. The spectred presence of Daniel Woodman had already begun to loom once more in her imagination. Catherine did not want to smash herself on the rocks of her memories. She did not want to revisit all that. That was why she needed to make Richard change his mind.

She went upstairs to the bedroom.

A while later, Catherine put down her pen.

Richard –
A letter? You're probably thinking. Well, yes. You may call

122

*it old-fashioned; I call it self-defence. It's the only way I'm
going to be able to put my thoughts straight and get them
out without any interruptions from you (forgive me).*

*Please, Richard, rethink your decision. Let's begin again.
I promise that I won't be needy, if that's what you're worried
about. I'm willing to consider any terms or conditions you
think are necessary. That's all just detail. What matters is
that we get to maul each other into ecstatic submission every
once in a while.*

I long to touch

She lay on the bed and stared at the unfinished sentence.
She resisted the temptation to scrawl pages and pages of
pornography. She wanted to remind Richard how mind-
blowing the sex was, how they each performed and applauded
acts which had no place in their usual matrimonial reper-
toires, but such titillating lewdness lacked subtlety. Richard
was an elusive prey. He would need to be caressed and
finessed back into her embrace.

Catherine was lost in thought, considering tactics, when
the doorbell rang. She hid the unfinished letter and hurried
downstairs. She peered through the spy-hole. After a
moment's hesitation, she opened the door.

'Annabel,' she said.

'Cathy. You're here. Thank God.'

'Is everything all right?'

'Can I come in?' Annabel stepped through the door and
threw her arms around Catherine, burying her face in the
folds of her top. Then she began to cry, her long sobs heavy
with pain.

Cautiously Catherine's arm crept around Annabel's shoulders. 'Annabel? What is it? What's happened?'

Annabel's grip tightened. The echo of her choked tears
filled the hallway. Finally she said, 'It's Richard.'

Catherine's stomach tightened. 'Richard? What about him?'

'Give me a cup of coffee first.'

Five minutes later they sat at the kitchen table. Annabel's tears had finally abated. Her eyes were bloodshot, heavy. 'Remember all that stuff we talked about yesterday at the gym?' she said.

Catherine nodded, suddenly terrified.

'Well, last night he arrived home, fixed us both a drink, and then told me everything.'

'Everything?' whispered Catherine.

Annabel nodded, not looking at her.

Catherine felt a tide of nausea rip through her. Here was the collateral damage she had been dreading for so long. 'Look, Annabel,' she began, 'I can ex–'

'It's been going on for a year. A whole *year*.' A single tear fell from Annabel's cheek. 'And to think I'd only just begun to suspect him!'

Catherine looked at her. 'He didn't tell you who?'

'No, he didn't tell me who. And I didn't ask. Frankly, I'd rather not know.'

'Oh, Annabel,' said Catherine, dizzy with relief, 'I'm so *sorry*.'

'Anyway, he says he's ended it.' At this Annabel began to cry again.

Catherine looked on, appalled. Each fresh tear which spilled from Annabel's brimming eyes ramped up the storm of self-hate roaring inside her, because she knew that this changed nothing. She still wanted Richard back. She would hurt Annabel some more.

'You think he was telling the truth?' she asked. 'About ending it?'

Annabel wiped her eyes. 'As a matter of fact I do, yes. After all, he volunteered the information. Why would he admit it and then carry on anyway? It doesn't make any sense.'

124

Catherine sat there blinking, fatally punctured.

Annabel was right. Richard knew that the first person his wife would run to for comfort was Catherine. He was sending her a message. His confession was the clearest signal he could have given that he was never going to change his mind. He was very deliberately burning this particular bridge. Catherine's hopes evaporated in an instant. There would be no reconciliation, not now.

'Really Annabel,' she whispered, devastated, 'I don't know what to say.'

'Don't say anything. Not to Andrew, and certainly not to Richard.'

Catherine closed her eyes for a moment in the effort to produce words. 'What are you going to do now?'

Annabel sniffed. 'I honestly don't know. Wait and see, I suppose.'

'You're not – well, you're not going to throw him out, or anything like that?'

There was a long silence.

'Cathy, darling,' said Annabel, 'I adore him.'

Catherine was too surprised to speak.

Annabel saw the look on her face and stood up. 'I should probably go.'

'No, that's absurd. Stay. As long as you like.'

Annabel shook her head. She wiped her face on her sleeve and smiled at Catherine. Her eyes were full of pain. 'I'll go.'

The two women walked slowly to the front door. Annabel turned to her. 'Sorry again. Such a burden.'

'Don't be ridiculous.'

'Thanks for listening.'

'I'm just so sorry,' said Catherine.

Annabel turned and set off down the pavement. Catherine closed the front door and collapsed to the floor in a cloudburst of tears.

TEN

Andrew Shaw stepped out on to the pavement, grateful for the breeze which caressed his shoulders. London was melting, caught in a stultifying heat wave. The humidity had slowed the city to a syrupy crawl. Of course, Andrew's office had no air-conditioning.

It was time for his afternoon coffee. Petrushka usually sent some minion from downstairs to fetch it for him, but Andrew had offered to go himself, hoping that the fresh air would chase away what remained of his hangover. He looked upwards into the blue-white sky and experienced a momentary flash of freedom. Sinead, Clara and Catherine all receded for a blissful moment. He set off in the direction of Wardour Street.

As he stood in the queue at Starbucks, Andrew looked at the menu behind the counter. There was, he realised for the first time, no Small, Medium and Large. Instead there was Tall (what sort of diabolically twisted universe was this, where *Small* became *Tall*?), Grande, and Venti™. A Venti™-sized cup appeared to be a small bucket. Andrew stared at the menu, wondering whether he should try something other than his usual cappuccino. But when the green-aproned assistant (*barista*, indeed!) asked for his order, he heard himself ask for his usual, pedestrian cappuccino. He handed over his money, defeated by his own timidity. For Christ's sake. What hope was there for him, really, if he didn't even have the courage to try a new sort of coffee? He took his drink to an empty armchair, feeling obsolete, inadequately equipped to deal with modern life.

Then an old memory floated through the air.

The way you wear your hat
The way you sip your tea
The memory of all that
No, they can't take that away from me

Andrew recognised the voice at once. It was Lady Day – Billie Holiday, Rosa's favourite.

And then suddenly there he was, aged seven or eight, watching from the door as his mother dragged Patrick across the sitting room to one of Billie Holiday's records, turned up too loud. Rosa's laughter peeled through the house as Patrick followed her cautiously through the forest of chintz, worried about knocking something over. It was early afternoon; perhaps they had been drinking over lunch. A cigarette dangled from one side of Rosa's mouth as she danced. Warm sunlight fell through the windows. It caught the halo of smoke which surrounded her, and cast her in dramatic silhouette.

The way you haunt my dreams!

It was the same old story – Rosa leading the charge, Patrick stumbling along behind, Andrew watching silently from the sidelines. Her spirit was always too much for either of them – even now, long after she had gone. They had never been able to compete.

When Andrew began bringing girlfriends home, he used to watch with quiet horror as they all fell in love with his mother. Rosa showed none of the muted suspicion which parents were supposed to exhibit on such occasions. Instead she would take each girl aside at the earliest opportunity, offer her a cigarette and tell her a string of filthy jokes.

Andrew came to dread those weekends. He would spin in a frenzied confusion of hilarity and mortification. The journeys back to London were worse. Rosa was the only topic of conversation. Andrew would listen in silent resignation to every new rhapsodic tribute. It was usually soon afterwards that he began to detect the faintest glimmer of disappointment behind his girlfriends' eyes – disappointment, Andrew knew, that he was not more like his mother.

Of all his girlfriends, only Catherine had seemed impervious to Rosa's charms. She had responded warmly enough to her overtures, of course, but there had been none of the wide-eyed infatuation which Andrew had come to expect. Catherine failed to mention his mother once during the drive back along the M4. For that alone, he knew he would adore her for ever.

Rosa had a favourite saying, her own secular litany. It was a quotation of Walter Pater's: 'To burn always with this hard, gemlike flame, to maintain this ecstasy, is success in life.' Well, that was Rosa all right. She was always at full tilt, always burning.

Billie Holiday warmed him with old memories.

He decided to go shopping.

'Here we are, Florence. Home at last.' Catherine opened the back door of the car and released the safety mechanism on Florence's car seat. Florence slithered out of the seat to freedom.

'Stay on the pavement, please,' called Catherine. She closed the car door and opened her handbag to look for her house keys. At the nursery Florence had thrown her arms around her mother and given her an ostentatious kiss. Catherine had had to resist turning towards the other mothers to perform a small curtsey. Florence had sung cheerful nonsense all the way back home. It had all been rather delightful, and Catherine had even managed to forget about Richard for a while. As she stepped up to the front door, she saw an envelope sticking half-way out of the letter box. She pulled it out. On it was scrawled: SHINAID. Catherine turned the envelope over, frowning.

Behind her there was a heart-tightening shriek of brakes and the howl of skidding rubber. Even before she turned around, Catherine had already begun to scream.

Florence was in the middle of the road, in the arms of a young man. They were standing a foot or so in front of the fender of a dirty white van. Catherine could see the driver of the van shouting silently through the windscreen, unbuckling his seat belt as he did so. It took a second for Catherine to process the information presented to her. As she looked at her daughter, safe in the arms of a stranger, Catherine glimpsed a whole different life, streaking away from her now, a life where the last sixty seconds had played a little differently – a life of eternal regret. As this alternative future sliced viscerally through her, she let out a low moan.

She stood frozen by the front door. All she could think was that it should have been *her* who had saved Florence, not a passing stranger. Wasn't there some sort of mystical maternal radar for emergencies like this? Catherine remembered reading stories of mothers finding reserves of superhuman strength to lift collapsed cars off their children. An overwhelming sense of disappointment swept through her.

There was no hidden extra gear of motherhood, no turbocharged state of grace for her.

'What do you think you're doing?' shouted the driver, climbing out of his van. He advanced on the man who was holding Florence. 'Bloody hell. I could have killed that little girl.'

'She's not *mine*, mate,' said the stranger. 'I just saw her run into the road.' Florence's eyes were as wide as saucers. She was clinging tightly on to the man's neck. She didn't look in Catherine's direction.

'Excuse me,' Catherine finally shook herself out of her shock, 'if you have to shout at anyone, you should shout at me.' She pointed at Florence. 'That's my daughter. I'm responsible for her, not this gentleman.'

The two men both turned to look at her.

'Would you both like to come in for a cup of tea?' asked Catherine, unsure what else to say. 'I'm so sorry to have caused you such trouble.' At this, to her disappointment, she began to cry.

'Nah, I've got to get on,' said the driver, glancing at his watch.

'Tea sounds good to me, though,' said the other man, looking at Florence and tickling her under the chin. 'What's your name, sunshine?'

'Cat!' said Florence.

'Well, hello, Cat,' said the man. 'My name's Gabriel.'

'I'm sorry. You mustn't think –'

'It's all right. Really.'

'But what if you hadn't –'

Catherine couldn't finish the sentence. The man handed her another tissue from the box on the table. She took it wordlessly.

'Lovely tea,' he said after a moment. He lounged easily

in his chair, looking around him with interest. His jeans were torn at the knees, his hair pulled back into an untidy pony-tail. His T-shirt was emblazoned with a single word. The word was: KINKY.

There was a pause.

'Look, it could have happened to anyone,' said the man.

'Yes, but it happened to *me*.' Catherine dabbed at her eyes. 'It *always* happens to me. I can't do anything right.' She hated to weep in front of this stranger, but there was no stopping her now. Florence was playing quietly in the garden with her Tonka truck.

'My God,' cried Catherine, 'I owe you *everything*.' She stared at the man in bewilderment. 'If you hadn't been there, if you hadn't seen the van, if you hadn't jumped out in front of the van to pick her up –' She stopped. 'How can I ever repay you?'

The man turned and looked out at the garden. Florence sat with her back to the house, lost in her own world. 'Forget about it,' he said. 'I just did what anyone else would have done.'

'No.' Catherine shook her head. 'You saved my daughter's life. I want to thank you.'

He smiled. 'Really. It's all right.'

'I just wish –' Catherine subsided into silence.

'I should go,' said the man, looking at his watch.

Catherine stared at him. 'So soon?'

'I'm already late.'

'Look,' said Catherine, 'at least let me give you something to remember us by.'

The man looked awkward. 'Really, there's no need –'

'How about a photograph?' said Catherine. 'Of Florence.'

'All right. A photograph would be OK. Thanks.'

Catherine stood up. 'I'll go and find one. Shan't be a minute.' She went up to the spare bedroom and rummaged through the drawer where the family photos were kept. She chose one taken earlier that summer – Florence sitting at a small table in the garden, eating a sandwich. She was grinning at the camera, her face a chaotic palette of strawberry jam and breadcrumbs. Catherine was about to turn to go downstairs when she stopped. What was she doing, giving a photograph of her two-year-old daughter to a stranger? Her gratitude was suddenly eclipsed by a maelstrom of suspicion. She imagined Florence and her jam sandwich proliferating across cyberspace, triggering a cyclone of depravity. After a moment's hesitation she continued back down the stairs, shaking her head. This stranger was no pervert. He had just saved Florence's life, for heaven's sake. So much for gratitude. Catherine blushed.

'Here it is,' she said as she walked back into the kitchen. 'She's a bit of a mess, but since that's pretty much her usual state, I didn't think –'

Catherine stopped.

The man had disappeared.

She ran into the garden, bottling up the scream which was filling her lungs.

Florence, though, was still playing happily by the climbing frame. Catherine watched her, shaken by the terrified pumping of her heart. After a moment, she turned and walked slowly through the rest of the house. The man was not there. He had vanished.

Catherine returned to the garden.

Why would he leave without saying goodbye?

Catherine leaned against the side of the climbing frame, perplexed. Surely she would have heard the front door shut behind him. It didn't make any sense. He had appeared out of nowhere, and now he had vaporised in the same way, like a ghost.

* * *

132

Andrew arrived back in the office in the middle of the afternoon, clutching a brace of shopping bags. He closed the door of his room and put his telephone on divert. He unpacked the Sony Discman from its box and pulled out a compact disc from another plastic bag. Billie Holiday, her head tilted to one side and a sad smile twisted on her lips, gazed past him. A flower was pinned in her hair and a pearl necklace hung at her throat. At first the Cellophane wrapping refused to yield to his clumsy fingers.

Finally, he opened the silver jaw of the Discman and inserted the disc. He pushed the tiny earphones into his ears and pressed the Play button. There was a hushed sigh as the compact disc started to spin.

Lady Day began her quietly bruising hymn to the glories of romance. Every word, every syllable, was drenched with pathos. She sang with a terrible, forlorn knowingness:

> *For nobody else*
> *Gave me a thrill*
> *With all your faults*
> *I love you still*

It had to be you – *but I already know how much you'll hurt me*, whispered the silence at the end of each line. Her performance was wistful and elusive, a coil of smoke floating away into the night. Lester Young's saxophone and Sweets Edison's trumpet punctuated her mellifluous lament with sympathetic sighs. Billie Holiday, that vision of deranged elegance: the white gardenia in her hair, the needle tracks along her arms. Every note she sang laid her soul bare. The sweet tragedy of a love affair! Her plaintive cry was cracked with naked emotion. Lady Day, Rosa liked to say, only sang the *truth*.

When the music subsided languorously into silence, Andrew hit the Pause button and stared into space.

He listened to the tune again and again. Each time Andrew felt as if he were being exquisitely mugged. Note by note, the light-fingered musicians gently robbed him of his worries. The notes spilled sweetly into his head, a gentle tornado. Every jazzed crotchet, every elided syllable of Lady Day's soft lament, took him back to the last time he had heard this song, on that cold afternoon, as it floated across the Wiltshire countryside.

Before the ceremony, Patrick and Catherine stood in the kitchen at Rycroft and spoke quietly to each other while Andrew wandered through the bedrooms of the old house. Rosa was everywhere; his childhood had revolved around her, utterly dependent on the fact of her *being*. But now the completeness of her final absence bowled in through the door behind him, smashing his memories into baffling fragments. Andrew looked around him blankly, his childhood suddenly erased.

Rosa had had plenty of time to plan the funeral arrangements. She had left comprehensive instructions as to how her body should be disposed of and her memory celebrated. There was no ambiguous escape route down which Patrick and Andrew could flee towards propriety and good taste. Her body was to be cremated and her ashes scattered amongst the stones at Avebury in a pagan ritual of her own devising, with the strictest condition that there should not be the slightest whiff of religion, not so much as a hint of the possibility of an afterlife. So it was that a crowd of about thirty people had gathered in the twilight to listen to the peculiar ceremony which Rosa had concocted for herself. Catherine, eight months pregnant, had stood patiently throughout, hands folded protectively over her swollen stomach. Patrick and Andrew haltingly recited Rosa's selection of poems and readings. It had been her last riposte, a final shake of the fist at Patrick's unwavering faith. That was Rosa all over, of course: she was never going to cede any quarter, not even in death. Andrew had never forgotten the pain in Patrick's eyes as he stumbled through a reading from Kahlil Gibran, rather than a reassuring passage from the Gospel. For the finale Andrew had lifted the tape machine high above his head as Billie Holiday sang 'It Had to be You', one last time.

Her voice was stolen by the wind.

That evening, when Andrew returned home, the house was quiet. He climbed the stairs, wondering whether Sinead had returned to exact her revenge for his behaviour the night before. Catherine was in Florence's bedroom, reading her a story. He put his head around the door.

'Daddy!' cried Florence.

'Hello, Daddy,' said Catherine drily.

Andrew studied her expression. 'Any sign of you know who?'

Catherine shook her head. 'Not a thing.'

'Oh.' He expelled a breath, which he had apparently been holding for some time. 'How did you get on otherwise?' he asked. 'Everything all right?'

'Well, we're all still in one piece, if that's what you mean.'

'Anything I can do to help?' he said.

'Go and see what Toby is up to,' suggested Catherine. 'And then pour me a large glass of wine.'

Andrew nodded. 'What's for supper?'

'Pizza.'

'Pizza? Really?'

She looked at him. 'Do you have a problem with pizza?'

'No, of course not,' said Andrew. 'But we usually have pizza on Sun–'

'Of course if you prefer you can always choose a recipe

yourself, pop down to the supermarket to buy the ingredients, and then cook the damn thing.'

'Jesus, Catherine, pizza's fine.'

'I'm just saying,' said Catherine, flashing him a thin smile before returning to the book. Florence listened to her read with rapt attention, sucking her thumb. Neither looked up at him. Andrew watched for a moment and went down the corridor. He knocked on Toby's door and stepped inside without waiting for an answer.

Toby was kneeling next to his bed, an array of silk handkerchiefs and coloured balls spread out on the duvet in front of him. By his pillow lay a plastic magic wand, its white tips chipped from endless spell-casting. He turned towards Andrew, affronted.

'*Daddy*,' he complained. 'You can't just *come in*. I'm practising.'

Wasn't anybody pleased to see him? 'I just thought I'd come and say hello,' said Andrew.

'Daddy,' said Toby suddenly, 'do you know what would be brilliant?'

Andrew's eyes narrowed. 'What?'

'It would be *brilliant*,' said Toby, 'if I could have a gun.'

'A toy gun,' said Andrew.

'Well, yes, obviously a *toy* gun,' sighed Toby, apparently not for the first time.

'Come on, Toby, we've talked about this a million times. You know what Mummy thinks about guns.'

'But that's the point,' wheedled Toby. 'I'm not asking Mummy. I'm asking *you*.'

Andrew held up his hands. 'Mummy's the one you need to talk to, you know that. She wears the trousers.'

'The thing is,' said Toby after a moment, 'I sort of said that I'd get one.'

'You sort of said? Who did you sort of say that to?'

136

'James Macintyre.'

Andrew crossed his arms. 'Well that wasn't very clever, was it?'

'Yes, but I thought,–'

'You'll just have to go back and tell James Macintyre that you were wrong,' said Andrew, annoyed that he had allowed himself to get drawn into this. He had always avoided confrontation with his children by maintaining that their lives were governed exclusively by maternal diktat. This had the additional advantage of allowing him to blame all unpopular decisions on Catherine. It occurred to Andrew that this was precisely why Toby had brought the matter up with him. His son was learning how to work the system.

'But he'll laugh at me if I don't,' said Toby.

'That'll teach you to tell lies, then, won't it?'

'*You* just told a lie,' said Toby accusingly.

'I did no such thing.'

'You *did*.'

'Toby, I won't have you – all right, then, what did I say?'

'You said that Mummy wears the trousers.'

'And?'

Toby crossed his arms. 'She hardly *ever* wears trousers.'

'Oh, Toby. That wasn't a *lie*.'

'But it wasn't true, was it?'

'Well, no, it might not have been strictly *true*. But that doesn't make it a lie.'

Toby frowned. 'Why not?'

It was, Andrew recognised, a legitimate question. 'It's just an expression. It doesn't mean anything.'

'That's another lie,' said Toby.

'Well, yes, all right, of course it means *something*,' said Andrew irritably. 'But it's got nothing to do with trousers.' Toby's face was a concertina of bemused concentration. Andrew pressed on, demoralised by his son's pedantic literalness. 'It's about who's in charge. If you're in charge, then people say you're wearing the trousers. Even if you're not *actually* wearing trousers.'

Toby watched his father, his eyes full of distrust. 'So, OK, what about when you said that we've discussed guns a million times?' he demanded. 'Because that's not true either, is it?'

'No, it's not,' agreed Andrew.

'So was that an *expression* as well?'

Andrew looked sourly at his son. 'Not really, Toby, no. I was exaggerating. To make a point.'

'And that isn't a lie either?'

Andrew was beginning to feel a twitch of annoyance at his son's efforts to make him look like a hypocrite. 'Look, can we please drop this?'

Toby sank sullenly on to his bed. 'James Macintyre's dad says that you should never shit a shitter.'

There was a pause.

'And do you,' asked Andrew, 'have the remotest idea what that means?'

'Not really,' admitted Toby.

'I don't like it when you argue with me, Toby, and I certainly don't like it when you use words you don't understand. You should bear that in mind next time you want to pick a fight.'

'I wasn't picking a fight,' mumbled Toby.

'Yes you were,' said Andrew.

'No I wasn't,' said Toby.

'You're doing it again,' said Andrew.

'That is *so* unfair,' said Toby after a moment.

Andrew looked at his son. 'James Macintyre's dad was right about one thing, Toby,' he said. 'You should never shit a shitter.'

He closed the bedroom door and escaped.

* * *

When Catherine went down to the kitchen, Andrew was sitting at the table, an open bottle of wine and two glasses in front of him. She picked up her glass and took a large mouthful. The wine was wonderfully cold.

'How's Toby?' she asked.

'God, Cathy, I don't know. How *is* he?'

She looked at him. 'Didn't you just speak to him?'

'I suppose I did. When did he become so fractious and pissy?'

'Pissy?'

'Answering back, picking arguments, that sort of thing.'

'Well, he's a boy. It's what they do.'

'Tell me it's just a phase he's going through.'

'It's just a phase he's going through.'

'Thank heavens.'

'The thing is, Andrew, it's one phase after another. It never ends. It never, ever, ends.' Catherine moved to the French windows and gazed out at the garden. 'Did you know that Toby is the assistant stage manager in his school play?'

'Really?' said Andrew.

'It's on Friday,' she said. 'Four o'clock. Do you think you could make it? I think we should both be there. Supporting parents. You know.'

'But if he's just a stage manager we won't even see him, will we?'

'I suppose not.'

'So what's the point? It's not as if we'll say, "Well done Toby, that looked like a *really well stage-managed play*," is it?'

Catherine took a swallow of wine. 'He's seven years old, Andrew. That's *exactly* what we'll say.'

Andrew sighed. 'All right. Friday at four should be fine.' He poured some more wine into their glasses. 'So how was your day?' he asked. 'Anything interesting happen?'

Catherine had already decided not to tell Andrew about Annabel's tearful appearance on their doorstep that morning. He would be titillated by the gossip of Richard's infidelity, but she could not bring herself to deliver the additional news that Richard had ended the affair – information which Catherine was still doing her best to ignore. She certainly didn't want to listen to Andrew's gleeful speculation about who Richard's mistress was.

'Interesting?' she said. 'Round here? What do you think?'

Nor would she tell him about Florence's rescue from the path of the speeding van. Guilt trapped the words in her throat. She was already struggling under such a presumption of ineptitude that she didn't want to provide Andrew with any evidence to support his case.

Besides, the sudden appearance and disappearance of the stranger who had saved Florence's life had unnerved Catherine more than she cared to admit. She had been pondering the episode all afternoon, struggling to make sense of it. The problem was the infinite combination of factors which had led the man to be walking down that particular road, on that particular day, at that particular time. His presence there seemed so unfathomably *random*. What if he'd stopped at some point along the way to tie his shoelace? What if there'd been a delay on the Tube? Then he would have been that much further up the street. Then all their futures would have been utterly different. Catherine was having difficulty coming to terms with the fact that the continued existence of life as she knew it depended on such incalculably slender odds.

'Can I ask you a question?' she said.

'Of course.'

'Don't think I'm going mad.'

'OK,' said Andrew.

Catherine stared at the table. 'Do you ever think about Fate?'

'Fate?'

'You know. Predestination, that sort of thing.'

'Heavens.' Andrew pulled a face. 'No. Sorry.'

'You never get the feeling that some things were just meant to be?'

'Not really.'

There was a pause. 'You don't think there's some grander scheme of things which we don't understand?'

'Personally, no. Although millions do. It's called religion.'

'Oh no,' said Catherine quickly. 'I'm not suggesting anything like that.' She paused. 'It's just that sometimes things *happen*, you know. Coincidences, lucky breaks, whatever you call them. And when you look back, you realise that every event is caused by an infinite number of other events, most of them completely random, and then you begin to realise that the chances of things happening as they do are actually infinitesimally tiny. Then you can't help but wonder whether things are really as random as they seem.'

There was a long silence.

'But it sounds ridiculous to you,' concluded Catherine.

'Look,' Andrew sighed, 'I'm my mother's son, Cathy. I'm genetically programmed to scoff at the idea that there's someone up there who's looking after us all, pulling strings. But I wish I *could* believe it. Religious conviction must be a wonderful thing if you can pull it off, don't you think? I mean, I envy my father. His faith is astonishing. It's what gives him his infuriating *serenity*. He genuinely believes that he knows why we're all here. And he's not even scared of death. How amazing must *that* be? He's got this wonderful life. All he cares about is Jesus and cricket.'

'I'm not *talking* about religion,' said Catherine anxiously.

'Of course you are,' scoffed Andrew. 'What sort of "grander scheme of things" do you have in mind, if not that?'

Catherine was silent.

'That reminds me,' said Andrew. 'He's coming to stay this weekend, isn't he?'

'Patrick? This weekend?'

Andrew nodded. 'He's going to the test match.'

'My God. You're right. I'd completely forgotten.'

Andrew emptied his glass. 'It'll give you a chance to ask him about all this stuff. He's the expert, after all, not me.'

'Please stop saying that,' begged Catherine. She didn't like Andrew's teasing her about religion. She was an atheist. Of course she was; she had been for years. Religion had no place in their lives. Catherine and Andrew occupied a secure comfort zone of cynicism, floating coolly above the spiritual fray. They practised benign condescension towards those who mortgaged their destinies in this world on the off chance of salvation in the next. But how, then, to explain this peculiar disquiet? Catherine could not escape the vague suspicion that perhaps, somehow, the stranger's appearance that afternoon hadn't simply been a question of luck.

'Oh, by the way,' said Andrew, 'something strange happened today. Richard Sulzman called me.'

Catherine didn't blink. 'What did he want?'

'That was the funny thing. He wouldn't say on the phone. He asked me to meet him for a drink tomorrow lunch time.'

Catherine stared at her glass. 'Huh,' she mumbled.

'You haven't heard the best bit,' said Andrew. 'Get this. He asked me *not to tell you*. What do you think about that?'

Catherine looked at him. 'He said that?'

'I think he's got a guilty secret he doesn't want you to know about.'

This made no sense at all. What game was Richard playing? Surely he wasn't going on some sort of confession *spree*? First Annabel, then Andrew. Catherine tried to remain calm, to focus on what Andrew was saying. 'Why would he care what *I* think?' she asked eventually.

'Come on, Cathy. It's *you*. Of course he's going to worry.'

'Richard doesn't especially care what *anyone* thinks of him,' said Catherine. 'It's one of the benefits of unassailable self-belief.'

Andrew grunted. 'Arrogance is another name for it.'

She looked at him. 'You really don't like him, do you?'

'Who, Richard?' Andrew snorted. 'Whatever gave you that idea?'

'In that case, perhaps you should cancel.' Catherine spread her fingers carefully across the table top. Her tone was light, untroubled. 'Do yourself a favour. Expose yourself to as little Richard Sulzman as possible.'

'You *must* be joking,' said Andrew. 'I wouldn't miss this for the world. Richard's got a secret.' He rubbed his hands together. 'Can't think why he wants to share it with *me*, though. Guilty complex, perhaps.'

'What do you mean?' asked Catherine, her heart lurching.

'Anyway, that's his decision.' Andrew hadn't heard her. 'Tomorrow I shall have some high-grade gossip to trade.'

'Don't you think you're being rather unpleasant?' asked Catherine.

'Probably,' agreed Andrew. 'But it's about time. I've taken enough bullshit from *him* over the years.'

'For God's sake, Andrew.'

'There's no need to defend him,' said Andrew. 'We don't even know what he's done yet.'

'I'm not *defending* him,' retorted Catherine. 'I'm just saying –'

'Oh, don't worry, I know what you're *saying*,' said Andrew, his good cheer vanished.

They looked at each other in silence across the kitchen table.

143

ELEVEN

Catherine stepped inside the gates of the old cemetery. All around her a violent battle between nature and death was being waged. An untamed forest rioted between the graves. Ivy strangled generations of tombstones in its sprawling grip. She walked around the periphery of the cemetery. There was a barely suppressed menace behind the lurking chaos of the tombs. On the eastern side of the graveyard the only noise was a chorus of invisible birds and the distant machine-gunning of a workman's drill. Catherine read faded epitaphs as she went. Everywhere there were hopeful declarations of faith. *Gone to a Better Place. At Peace With the Lord.*

In front of a tombstone which said simply, *In Loving Memory of Little Roy*, Catherine began to cry, her heart punctured by the quiet tragedy of this century-old loss. She sat down on a wooden bench, arrested by her small display of naked emotion.

She had hardly slept the previous night. Instead she had lain awake worrying about what Richard Sulzman was going to say to Andrew over their lunch today. Her marriage, she saw, was at Richard's mercy. Married adulterers remained

144

discreet thanks to the nuclear deterrent principle of Mutually Assured Destruction: you couldn't destroy another's marriage without ruining your own. But now Richard had gone ahead and detonated his own bomb, which meant he had nothing left to lose. Catherine squirmed with apprehension. Even if he didn't tell Andrew about her infidelity today, there was always tomorrow. And the next day. She looked at the wild dilapidation which surrounded her, contemplating the possible disintegration of her family.

True, her marriage had never been a passionate love affair. But what Andrew and Catherine had was a track record, a *history* – ten years of familiarity and fondness. They had put in the time, and for all her regrets, she suddenly realised that she could not bear to see everything unravel now. A gust of guilt swept through her, chilling her bones. She had hidden behind a thicket of half-truths and silence from the start. But Andrew had put his head down and trudged onwards without complaint, always loyal, always patient. The skewed imbalance of their needs and desires was all that they had.

Then there were the children. Catherine imagined new, broken lives for them – two bedrooms, two homes, the forlorn shuttling between bitter parents. And one day they would learn that this was *all her fault*. Catherine did not know whether she would be able to survive their disappointment.

She stared up at the cloudless sky. There was nothing she could do but wait and see what Richard said.

And then there was this other thing: yesterday, Florence's life had been *saved*.

To Catherine's disquiet, she had been unable to answer Andrew's question last night: what grander scheme of things *had* she meant, if not religion? An alien kernel of doubt had been planted inside her as a result. And so, after dropping the children off at school, she had driven to Highgate

Cemetery. It was a tentative step away from her resolutely secular world, a cautious toe in the water of piety. She looked around her and sighed, unsure what she had been hoping to achieve amidst this sea of death and remembrance. There was never going to be a stunning moment of revelation, not here. The cemetery was just a testament to human mortality, and the boundless optimism of those who remained to grieve. Nothing more.

Catherine gazed out over the graves in front of her. A stone angel stood on top of a nearby moss-covered memorial.

All of a sudden, she felt a flash of white heat across her shoulder blades. She stared at the angel, her heart thumping. *Gabriel.*

The stranger's name had been Gabriel.

There was a knock on the door. Andrew put his hands behind his head and yawned. 'Come in,' he called. It had been a quiet morning. He was pleased to have something to take his mind off the slow trudge of minutes and hours before his drink with Richard at lunch time.

The door opened and Joel peered in.

'Joel,' said Andrew, disappointed. 'It's you.'

'There's somebody here to see you,' said Joel. 'I met her on the stairs.'

Andrew sat up, immediately cautious. '*Her?*' It was Sinead, he knew at once – here to deliver her blackmail demands.

'We had a little chat on the way up, actually,' said Joel. He looked at Andrew. 'You've been a naughty boy, haven't you?'

Andrew swallowed, his fears confirmed. 'Listen, Joel, promise you won't say anything to –'

'Anyway,' said Joel, 'here she is.' He opened the door.

'Oh my God,' said Andrew.

'Hello, Andrew,' said Clara. 'Surprised to see me?'

'Don't mind if I stay, do you?' said Joel, shutting the door behind them both.

'What – well, what are you doing here?' stammered Andrew.

'I came round,' said Clara, 'to discuss plans.'

'Plans?' said Andrew.

'Plans,' she agreed. 'For the project we discussed.' Her voice hardened. 'Only I've just discovered that your Chief Executive here knows absolutely nothing about it.'

Andrew shifted uncomfortably in his chair. 'Well,' he said. 'That's right. He doesn't.'

'But I thought you'd cleared all this with your Board,' said Clara furiously.

Andrew blinked in disbelief. Why would Clara imagine that his offer still stood after his disappearance from the hotel? 'No,' he replied carefully, 'what I *said* was –'

'When were you going to share this with the rest of us, Andrew?' interrupted Joel tightly. 'A film? A *film*? What do you think Freddie's going to say?'

'Who's Freddie?' demanded Clara.

'Don't worry about *Freddie*,' said Andrew.

'Freddie Larssen,' said Joel. 'He's the Corporate Development Officer of our parent company in Stockholm.'

Andrew closed his eyes.

'Your what?' growled Clara.

'Our parent company,' said Joel. 'What has this got to do with –'

'Do you not even *own* this pile of shit, then?' said Clara, turning on Andrew.

'Not any more, no,' he admitted. 'We sold this pile of shit a few years ago.'

'I don't believe this,' said Clara.

'I'm sorry,' said Joel. 'Exactly what –'

'Did you mean a single word of what you said?' snapped Clara.

'Of course I did,' said Andrew. 'But I think you must have misunderstood the precise status of –'

'Excuse me,' snorted Clara. 'I didn't misunderstand a damn *thing*.'

'But I never said it was definitely going to happen,' protested Andrew.

There was a moment's silence.

'And you owe me money,' said Clara.

Andrew blinked. 'What for?'

'The champagne from the minibar,' hissed Clara.

'Minibar?' said Joel.

'Those hotel prices are bloody steep.'

'*Hotel* prices?' said Joel.

Clara glared at Andrew. 'The very least you could have done was to pay the sodding bill.'

Andrew glanced at Joel. He laced his fingers together and looked over them at Clara. 'I really have no idea what you're talking about,' he said.

There was a moment's silence.

'Bastard,' said Clara flatly. Without another word she stood up and stormed out of the room, slamming the door behind her.

Finally Joel spoke. 'A *film*, Andrew? Have you gone stark, raving mad?'

Andrew put his head in his hands. 'Quite possibly,' he murmured.

This was ridiculous.

Surely.

Catherine changed gears as she approached the round-about at Archway. She was a rational, intelligent person, she told herself. She was a rational, intelligent person living at

148

the beginning of the twenty-first century in full possession of all her faculties. So she was not – *she simply could not be* – the sort of person who believed in angels.

A blue car raced around the intersection, skipping a red light and cutting dangerously across her before disappearing up Highgate Hill in a howl of burning rubber. Catherine swore loudly at the car as she braked hard to avoid it. The first word she had uttered in more than an hour was five letters long, and spectacularly vulgar. The oppressive sanctity of the graveyard retreated a little. She swore again, and then filled the car with a long string of obscenities. Soon Catherine was yelling expletives, barking filth at the windscreen. The vulgarity was exhilarating. The violence of the words momentarily scorched away the revelation in the cemetery, but when she finally subsided into silence, her disquiet returned.

An *angel*?

Back in the house, Catherine switched on the iron, hoping to escape her worries in a squall of domestic industry.

She began to iron one of Andrew's shirts. Thirty minutes later she held it up to examine her work. A three-inch crease scythed across the right chest panel. Catherine sighed. She knew that Andrew would never notice the effort she had gone to. Shirts got ironed by someone who was not him; he didn't especially care who. She tried to flatten the crease into submission, and then attacked the next shirt, wielding the iron with a more reckless abandon. She soon stopped worrying about eradicating each tiny crease. It was easy enough to ignore small imperfections. That had been the story of her marriage, she thought. A lot of glossing over had been required.

The telephone rang. Catherine crossed the room quickly. 'Hello?'

'Hello, Catherine. It's me.'

'Mum. How funny. I was going to call you today.'

'Really.'

'No,' said Catherine, 'I *was*.'

'And here I am. How extraordinary.'

'Please don't,' said Catherine.

'Please don't what?'

'That whole sarcasm thing.'

'I don't know what you're talking about.'

'Yes, Mother, you know *exactly* what I'm talking about.'

'No, I don't.'

There was a pause.

'All right,' sighed Catherine, 'have it your own way.'

'Yes, well, that's what you always do, isn't it?' Her mother had an extraordinary gift for these emotional brawls, always the aggressor, yet also somehow the eternal victim. 'So anyway,' she said, skipping away from the blow she had just landed, 'did you have something in particular you wanted to say?'

'Well, we have one piece of news, I suppose. Sinead's left us.'

'She has? Why?'

'Well, that's the funny thing. We don't know. She just disappeared. We woke up yesterday morning and she had gone, without leaving a note.'

'Oh well. I'm sure it'll be easy enough to get a replacement.'

'Actually,' said Catherine, 'from now on I'm going to look after the kids myself.'

There was a pause.

'Are you sure?' said her mother eventually.

'Hang on,' said Catherine. 'I was under the impression that this is what you think I should have been doing all along. You know, being the attentive mother, the good housewife, all that stuff.'

'Well, yes, but do you really think you'll be able to cope on your own?'

'I don't know,' admitted Catherine. 'But I'm going to try.'

'All right,' said her mother. 'Good for you, I suppose.'

'Tell you what, Mum. You can help me, actually. Do you remember what you used to do with us during the school holidays? How did you keep us from all killing each other? School ends this week and I need something to keep the kids occupied.'

Her mother was silent for a moment. 'You always liked Scrabble when you were small,' she said.

'Scrabble. You do remember, do you, that your grand-daughter is two years old?'

There was a wounded silence. 'Perhaps I should go,' said her mother.

'Don't be silly,' said Catherine. 'There's no need to –'

'If you won't listen to my suggestions with even a modicum of grace, Catherine, then perhaps you shouldn't ask for them in the first place.'

Catherine sighed. 'I'm sorry. I didn't –'

'Anyway, you're obviously busy.'

'I'm just doing the ironing.'

'The ironing.' Apprehensive disbelief.

'So, at least wish me luck,' joked Catherine.

'Good luck,' said her mother. She had never sounded more serious.

As Catherine walked back to the ironing board she caught the acrid smell of burning cotton. With a small cry, she ran forward and snatched the forgotten iron from Andrew's shirt. Its charred silhouette remained. She peeled the ruined shirt off the board. It was a double-cuffed affair with a cutaway collar. It was Andrew's favourite.

* * *

151

The pavement outside the pub was bristling with groups of lunch-time drinkers. They loitered in the sunshine, each posse huddled tightly in on itself to repel unwanted invaders. Andrew pushed his way through the crowds and stepped inside. Soho pubs were too noisy, too busy, too smoky. He battled irritably through the lager-fuelled scrum towards Richard Sulzman, who was standing by the bar, waving at him.

'I got you a pint,' said Richard. Like every other American Andrew had ever met, he was unable to say the word 'pint' without adding an ironic inflection to demonstrate how quaint, how very *English*, it was.

'Thanks,' said Andrew, and took a long drink.

'I love English pubs,' said Richard, looking around him in satisfaction. 'So much *atmosphere*.'

'Atmosphere?' said Andrew. 'Is that what you call it? I feel like a sardine.'

'So anyway,' said Richard pleasantly, 'how are things?'

Andrew put his glass down on the bar. He had suffered a morning of silent reproach and dark-eyed suspicion from Joel following Clara's visit. Not wishing to incriminate himself further, Andrew had maintained a lofty silence, refusing to explain about *Cock* or Clara's references to hotel minibars. And of course there was the small matter of the missing au pair. Andrew was becoming convinced that he would next see Sinead on the television news as her body was pulled out of the Regent's Canal. Over Richard's shoulder Andrew saw a group of people whispering and pointing in their direction. 'You really don't want to know,' he said.

'OK,' said Richard. 'How's Cathy?'

'Is that why you dragged me out for a clandestine drink? To ask me how my wife is?'

Richard waved this suggestion away. 'It's called small talk.'

'Small talk.'

'You know, the polite exchange of inconsequential information.'

'You consider my wife's well-being to be inconsequential?'

'Perhaps I've confused you. Would it help if we talked about the weather instead?'

'Catherine's fine,' said Andrew flatly. 'As far as I can tell.'

'As far as you can tell?'

Andrew shrugged. 'You know.'

'Ah.' Richard nodded. 'The mysterious ways of women. More opaque than the polish on their fingernails.'

'Ten years together and I still have absolutely no idea what's going through her head,' sighed Andrew. 'Take last night, for example. Without any warning she asked me whether I thought there was a God.'

'Excuse me? Are we talking about the same woman?' asked Richard. 'Catherine Shaw? As in, Atheist Catherine?'

'Atheist Catherine. The very same.'

Richard frowned. 'That *is* strange.'

'I mean, what am I supposed to think? There was no explanation, nothing,' mused Andrew. 'Just these vague thoughts about Fate and destiny and grand, cosmic schemes that we can't understand. It was very peculiar.'

'Keeps you on your toes, though,' said Richard.

Andrew grunted. 'It just made me realise how little I know her.'

'Come on,' scoffed Richard. 'How much do you think you really know anyone? We all keep secrets, even from our loved ones.'

'You think?'

'Sure. Nobody's *completely* honest. It's a masquerade.' He paused. 'This wouldn't have anything to do with that girl, would it?'

'Which girl?' said Andrew.

153

'My God, how many are there? The one you mentioned last Friday. You know, from work.'

'Oh, Clara. Actually, that's all ancient history now, I'm pleased to say.'

'What happened?'

'Nothing,' said Andrew. 'Nothing at all.'

'Huh,' said Richard. 'Bad luck.'

Andrew was too tired to explain. 'Yes, well,' he muttered.

'Christ, Andy, cheer *up*. There's no point moping about it.'

'I'm *not* moping.'

'Look. You've had a knock-back. OK. But you've got to keep going. You're being faced with the age-old question. Is the glass half-empty, or half-full? Is life an adventure, or a joyless marathon? Will it be relished, or merely endured?'

'It doesn't feel like an adventure *or* a marathon to me,' said Andrew.

'No?'

Andrew looked around the pub. 'Don't you ever get the feeling that real life is something that just happens to other people?'

'Explain.'

'Well, I just feel as if I'm standing on the sidelines while the rest of the world marches off into the fray. None of the interesting stuff ever happens to *me*.'

'Everyone feels like that from time to time,' said Richard.

'Oh, come off it,' scoffed Andrew. 'Not you, surely.'

'Especially me. I earn my living on the sidelines. Spectating is my job. I watch, I study, I observe.'

'Yes, but you're *part* of it all at the same time.'

'I am?' Richard's eyebrows jitterbugged in amusement. 'How do you know?'

'You must be. Surely you wouldn't be –' Andrew struggled for the right, begrudging formulation '– as successful as you are, if you hadn't *lived*.'

154

'Oh yeah,' agreed Richard, yawning, 'I've got a PhD from the university of life, all that bullshit. But my stories? I make them up, Andy, I don't *live* them. Jesus, I spend all day at home sitting in front of my typewriter. What sort of lonely, boring life do you suppose *that* is?'

Andrew was silent.

'So look, you're not alone. We all worry that everyone else is having more fun.' Richard finished his beer in one long swallow and put the empty glass back down on the bar. 'You know, it wouldn't hurt you to look on the bright side for once. You've got a nice wife, a good job, a big house. You've got two beautiful, healthy kids. Which is two more than I've got.'

Andrew looked at him. 'Do you ever regret not having kids?'

Richard looked at his shoes. 'I've always said that my books are my children, but you know what? They never visit. They never call.'

There was a pause. Andrew signalled to the barman for two more drinks.

'Shall I tell you what your problem is?' said Richard.

'Who says I have a problem?'

'Sciamachy. That's your problem.'

This, of course, was a classic Sulzman trick. Every so often Richard dropped words into his conversation which no ordinary person could reasonably be expected to understand. Rather than admit their ignorance, most people struggled on and dug themselves into an ever-deepening hole of misunderstanding until Richard administered the coup de grace and exposed both their lexicographical shortcomings and, worse, their efforts to hide them. He enjoyed inflicting these small humiliations on others. It was a cruel sport. It was also a way of reminding everyone exactly who the acclaimed multi-million-selling novelist was.

Andrew had been caught out by this stunt once before. At a dinner party a couple of years ago, Richard had begun talking to him about anagnorisis in modern drama. Andrew had thought they were discussing a fear of word puzzles.

'Sciamachy?' he said.

'The fighting of imaginary opponents,' explained Richard, hiding his disappointment. 'Futile combat. Shadow boxing.'

'You're saying I'm making all this up?'

Richard shrugged. 'Perhaps you're seeing opponents where in fact there are friends. Not everyone is against you.'

'You asked me out for a drink to tell me how to live my life and teach me new words? Thanks, Richard. I'm touched.'

'Well, no. That wasn't actually why I asked you out for a drink. That's just a little extra free service I provide for my friends. You know, life coach and vocabulary enhancer.'

'So why *are* we here? You said there was something you wanted to tell me.'

Richard nodded. 'There is.'

Andrew crossed his arms. 'Something you don't want Catherine to know about.'

There was a pause. 'Not especially,' agreed Richard. 'Although I said that more for your sake than mine.'

'OK.'

Richard stared into his drink for a moment. 'The thing is, Andy – well. The thing is, this is going to be difficult.'

Andrew looked at Richard. All traces of humour had vanished from his face. 'Difficult,' said Andrew.

'It's about Catherine,' said Richard.

'All right.'

'You know what I was saying earlier? About how we all keep secrets from each other?'

156

'For God's sake, Richard, spit it out. What is it?'

Richard raised his eyes to meet Andrew's. 'We think Catherine is a thief.'

TWELVE

'This is ridiculous.'

'You're upset, obviously.'

'Upset? You think I'm *upset*?'

'This sort of thing must come as a shock.'

'I'll tell you what comes as a shock, Richard. What comes as a *shock* is the fact that *you*, you of all people, could even consider such a thing.'

'Andy. Please understand. I'm not *accusing* her.'

'No?'

'I'm telling you because we're worried. We think Cathy might need help.'

'Help?'

'We think she needs to talk to someone. A psychiatrist.'

'Great. So now my wife is not only a thief, but she's going nuts as well.'

'The first step to solving any problem is admitting that you *have* a problem.'

'Oh, Jesus. Spare me.'

'This hasn't been easy for us either, you know. We love Cathy. You know that. We both do. But we don't know what else to do. I mean, put yourself in my shoes.'

'I'll tell you what, Richard. If I were in *your* shoes, I wouldn't be so quick to jump to insane conclusions. I wouldn't be so quick to start making these sort of ridiculous accusations about other people, especially people you claim to be so very fond of. Whatever happened until innocent until proven guilty, for Christ's sake? So Cathy was wearing a bracelet that looks like one of Annabel's. Big deal. Big *fucking* deal.'

'It didn't look like one of Annabel's. It *was* one of Annabel's.'

'How do you know? How can you be so completely sure? Did you see it?'

'No I didn't, not personally. It was –'

'Well then.'

'Annabel saw it, though. She'd know it better than me.'

'Well, maybe they just both bought the same bracelet. Can't be beyond the realms of possibility, surely?'

'Actually, yes. It was a one-off piece, you see. A friend of mine on Long Island made it. Annabel thought she must have lost it. We've been through the house twice over the last six months. Forensic sweeps, the works. And nothing.'

'Until it magically appears on Catherine's wrist.'

'I know it sounds crazy, but Annabel was *sure*.'

'Annabel was sure. So I'm just supposed to accept this.'

'Why would she make something like this up?'

'Question goes both ways. Because let me ask you this. To establish, what do they call it, guilt beyond reasonable doubt, then you have to establish motive, and opportunity, and all that other stuff. Correct? And there you're in trouble. I mean, have you stopped for a second to ask *why* Cathy would ever do such a thing?'

'That's why we think she might need help. These sorts of pathologies are notoriously hard to –'

159

'OK, that's enough. Pathologies? Jesus *Christ*, Richard. This is lunacy.'

'It's hard to come to terms with, I know.'

'Listen. Until you can tell me the how and the why, I don't want to hear another word about this.'

'Shit, Andy, the how and the why?'

'Because otherwise it's all bullshit. Just bullshit.'

'Look, I'm just trying to help. I thought you should know about it. We don't want to see something awful happen to her.'

'That sounds like a threat.'

'A threat?'

'Are you going to report her to the police?'

'No, of course not. Who do you think we are?'

'So. All right, then. What exactly do you want *me* to do about it?'

'All I'm asking is that you take a look for this bracelet. We just want the damn thing back. What you choose to do about Catherine is your decision. She's your wife.'

'But you think what?'

'There are things you can do to address this sort of thing. It's an illness. It can be cured.'

'You don't think there's the slightest chance, just the remotest possibility, that Annabel might actually be *wrong* about this?'

'Don't be angry. We're only trying to help. Where are you going?'

'Back to my office. I have work to do.'

'What about the bracelet?'

'The how and the why, Richard. The how and the why.'

Andrew walked back through Soho, unable to feel the pavement beneath his feet.

* * *

'Mummy?'

'Florence, have you got your seat belt on?'

'Cat!'

Catherine swivelled in her seat. 'Let me see.'

'Mummy.'

'Cat! Cat! Cat!'

'Very good, Florence. Could you do some other animals, do you think?'

'*Mummy.*'

'What is it, Toby?'

Her son's eyes were large in the rear-view mirror. 'Has Sinead come back?'

'No, darling, she hasn't,' said Catherine as she pulled out into the afternoon traffic.

'Oh.' Toby looked out of the window.

'Don't worry. Everything will be fine. I promise.'

'Do you think she was very unhappy?' Toby's voice was tiny.

Catherine tried to fathom the provenance of her son's morose sensibility. Had she squeezed all the fun out of him before his eighth birthday? A lurching guilt gripped her. 'Gosh, Toby, I don't know.'

'I don't think she'll ever come back now,' he said.

There was a pause. 'Perhaps you're right,' said Catherine quietly. She was still appalled at her family's naked need of Sinead. Their domestic machine was already faltering towards awkward dislocation without her, but Catherine would never take her back now, no matter how much her children begged. That sort of needy dependence was right-fully *hers*. 'We'll muddle on well enough without her, you'll see.'

They drove for a while in silence. The traffic crawled along the Holloway Road impossibly slowly. Skeletal cyclists in wraparound sunglasses and garish Lycra tops flashed past

161

on either side of the car as they weaved through the stagnant river of fume-belching vehicles.

Catherine tapped the steering wheel anxiously. Andrew hadn't called her. As the afternoon had drawn on, she had become increasingly apprehensive. If Richard had given him some irresistible gossip – something, in other words, which did not concern *her* – he would have been unable to wait until the evening to share it. His silence was growing more ominous by the minute.

She looked in the rear-view mirror. Florence was staring out of the window, her eyes big and blank. Catherine thought again about the mysterious stranger who had snatched her out of the way of the speeding van. An *angel*? The idea lingered, naggingly persistent. Perhaps Andrew had been right last night, after all. This wasn't about Fate. This was about *God*.

Catherine had gone to church as a child, because that was what one did back then, but the Almighty had always been a slightly bothersome presence, beadily watching her every move. It had been a tremendous relief when she had finally managed to extricate herself from her beliefs. But now He was back, camped outside Catherine's ramparts. She was under siege. She wondered whether she had really witnessed her own personal miracle. It seemed ridiculous, but she couldn't just dismiss the whole episode as a tremendous slice of luck.

She no longer knew what to think. Last time she had looked, the Holloway Road didn't lead to Damascus.

Half an hour later Catherine parked outside the house, and Florence and Toby clambered out of the car. 'Come here, you wonderful children,' she cried. 'Give your mum a big hug.' She pulled Toby towards her. She held him tightly until his body went limp in defeat. After a moment, a reluctant arm sneaked around her waist. Florence was squawking with delight. She clung on to Catherine's other arm with a bruising grip, her small fingers poking brutishly into her mother's skin. Catherine squatted on the pavement, holding her children. She felt the afternoon sun on her back, and wondered whether things would ever be quite the same again.

'How lovely!' she sighed. At this signal, Toby stepped away. A familiar blast of emotion cracked across Catherine's chest. She stood up and herded the children into the house, her heart a quiet furnace of love and regret. Inside, the answer machine stared implacably back at her. Andrew still hadn't called. A stiletto of apprehension twisted deep within her.

She realised that she needed to cultivate a more focused defence against Richard's confession. It was unthinkable, quite unthinkable, that any of this should change. Catherine came to a decision. No matter what Andrew had learned over lunch, tonight she would present him with a picture of family life so warm and satisfying and perfect that he would immediately forgive her everything. She would barricade her family behind a wall of domestic bliss. She would play the perfect wife and mother. She would cook something wonderful. Then what? She remembered her mother's strange suggestion that they all play Scrabble together. Well, why not? She smiled. Scrabble, then. A family game of Scrabble. Andrew would like that.

And if all went well, perhaps later on they could go upstairs together.

Yes, Andrew would like that.

When Andrew arrived home that evening, a chicken casserole was simmering gently in the oven. Catherine dropped two ice cubes into a gin and tonic as he appeared at the kitchen door. She turned towards him and flashed a smile.

'*Hi.*'

'Hi,' said Andrew. He looked tired.

'Got you a drink,' she said, holding it out to him.

Andrew took the proffered glass. 'Thanks.'

There was a pause.

'Florence is asleep,' said Catherine. 'Toby's upstairs.'

Andrew took a large mouthful of drink. He closed his eyes as he swallowed.

'So go on, then,' prompted Catherine, unable to stop herself.

Andrew looked at her warily. 'Go on then what?'

'Don't *tease* me, Andrew. You know what I'm talking about.' She could feel her heart thumping. 'How was your drink with Richard?'

'It was weird,' said Andrew after a moment. 'He taught me a new word and lectured me on how I should be living my life.'

Catherine stared at him. 'That was it?'

'Pretty much.'

She felt light-headed. 'Doesn't sound terribly secret.'

'It wasn't.'

'Did Richard say *why* he didn't want me to know about it?'

'Oh.' Andrew stared into his glass. 'Well, there was one other thing, but I'm not supposed to tell you.'

There was a long silence. 'You will, though.'

'Yes. I will.' Andrew nodded heavily. 'Here's the thing. Richard and Annabel are planning a surprise birthday party for you.'

Catherine leaned against the kitchen counter.

'They've booked a venue and everything. Richard wanted to ask me about guest lists, that sort of thing. And of course it's my job to get you there without raising your suspicions. But I've blown that already, haven't I? I never could keep a secret from you.'

'A party,' breathed Catherine.

'Promise you won't let on that you know,' said Andrew. 'Richard will be furious if he realises you've twigged.'

Catherine shook her head. A day's tortured conjecture, all for this.

'I can't quite believe it,' she said.

'Yes, well,' said Andrew. 'Just be sure not to say anything to either of them.'

'When is all this fixed for?'

'Look, I've already said too much. Let's at least keep some of it a surprise.'

Catherine nodded. 'Yes, yes, of course.' She beamed at him. 'Let's do that.'

A party!

'I'm doing chicken casserole for supper,' said Catherine.

'Sounds good.'

'With tarragon.'

'Tarragon. Great.'

'I said Toby could stay up. We can all eat together.'

'Oh. OK.'

'Then I thought we could have a nice game of Scrabble. The three of us.'

There was a long silence.

'Andrew?'

'Scrabble?' said Andrew.

'Is that a problem?'

'Why do you want to play *Scrabble*, for heaven's sake?'

'I thought it would be fun,' said Catherine faintly.

'Fun,' echoed Andrew. 'You thought Scrabble would be *fun*.'

'For all the family.'

'What's the occasion?' asked Andrew.

'No occasion. I just thought it would be nice, that's all.'

Toby appeared at the kitchen door. He looked at his father. 'Hello, Daddy.'

'Hello Toby,' said Andrew.

There was a sticky pause.

Catherine smiled. 'Hey, Toby. How would you like to play Scrabble after supper?'

Toby's face was an inscrutable knot. 'Scrabble?' he said.

'Doesn't that sound like fun?'

'With you two?'

'Who else? Yes, with us two.'

'But you'll *thrash* me,' said Toby.

Catherine laughed. 'Of course we won't.'

'You will,' grumbled Toby.

'You'll get to stay up late,' said Catherine.

'How late?' demanded Toby.

'Not *too* late,' sighed Andrew.

Father and son exchanged looks.

'So what do you say?' said Catherine.

Toby looked at his parents in bemusement. Why, asked his eyes, are you asking my opinion, when all three of us know that it has absolutely no bearing on the outcome of anything? 'All right,' he said bravely.

'Great!' exclaimed Catherine, clapping her hands together. 'That's settled, then. Scrabble it is. Now, why don't you men lay the table, and I'll get dinner out of the oven.'

Five minutes later they sat in silence around the kitchen table, prodding at Catherine's casserole. The chicken was dreadfully overcooked. Elbows shuttled back and forth industriously. The accompanying sauce was emulsifying before their eyes into separate puddles of unappetising gloop.

'It's been a while since you've cooked,' remarked Andrew.

'You'd better get used to it,' said Catherine. 'With Sinead gone, it's down to me now.'

'Are you *sure* she's not coming back?' asked Toby, staring at his plate.

* * *

166

Catherine cleared away the still half-full plates. Supper had been a disaster, but she didn't care. Her marriage was safe. And Richard and Annabel were planning a party for her!

'Right then,' she said as she stacked the dirty dishes by the sink. 'Shall we get cracking?' The Scrabble box lay on the kitchen counter. 'Here we are,' said Catherine as she distributed the small wooden shelves. 'I'll score, shall I? Toby, why don't you go first?'

Toby reluctantly delved his small hand into the bag of tiles. His face screwed up in concentration as he stared at his letters. Catherine smiled at Andrew, who looked at her as if he were trying to remember where he had seen her before. After several minutes, Toby picked up three tiles and cautiously placed them on the board.

P A T

Oh dear, thought Catherine.

'Not very good, is it?' said Toby.

'Nonsense,' breezed Catherine determinedly. 'It's great.'

'Only five points,' said Toby sadly.

'No, it's a double word score, so you score ten. How about that? Straight into double figures.'

Toby brightened slightly.

'Your turn,' said Andrew to Catherine. She looked at her tiles. The letters before her remained resolutely chaotic, refusing to coalesce into words. Toby was gnawing his fingernails. Catherine understood that the most important thing was not to score more than ten. Finally she took one tile.

P A T H

'There,' she said. 'Nine points.'

After a moment, Andrew lay down four tiles.

Catherine looked at the board, so angry she could hardly speak. 'Crumbs, Andrew. Sixteen. And on a triple word score.'

'Forty-eight,' said Andrew.

'Wow,' said Toby, stricken.

'Isn't this fun?' asked Catherine.

Andrew took a long drink.

A few minutes passed in absolute silence. Catherine tried to pretend that this was exactly what she had been hoping for, this comfortable companionship around the table, but she was too preoccupied by the aura of noble defeat which her son had already adopted.

Finally Toby deposited a collection of tiles on the board and with painful deliberation arranged them into:

P A T H E T I C
              N
              G
              R
              Y

Was he trying to tell them something? wondered Catherine. She added up the score. 'Ten again,' she said.

Toby's face fell. 'I'm still miles behind Daddy,' he sighed.

Catherine had an idea. 'Have you got an "A"?' she asked. Toby looked at his remaining tiles and nodded. 'Here, then.' Catherine took the extra letter and rearranged the board.

A P A T H E T I C
N
G
R
Y

'Twenty-six points!' exclaimed Catherine. 'There you are. You'll catch up in no time.' She looked at the board. The sum of their efforts: Angry and Apathetic.

'What does APATHETIC mean?' asked Toby.

'It's when you don't care about something,' said Catherine. 'Rather like Daddy at the moment.'

'If he doesn't know what the word means, do you think he should be allowed to have it?' asked Andrew.

'Of course he can!' barked Catherine.

Andrew held up his hands.

After a few turns, the board looked like this:

```
                Z
                E
          P E N
                I
                T
    A P A T H E T I C
    D I N     E     R
    G         X     E
    R         A     E
    Y         N O W
```

The scores were: Toby – fifty-one (TREE and NOW being his other contributions), Catherine – eighteen (DIN and PEN the lowest scoring words she had been able to come up with), Andrew – one hundred and twelve (having followed APATHETIC with ZENITH on a double word score and

169

TEXAN, the X landing on a triple letter score). Catherine
languished in last place with long-suffering sacrifice. It was
her turn. She realised that, rather brilliantly, she could do
JONQUIL on a double word score. She did a quick calcu-
lation. Forty-six points. Forty-six points! Just as she was
picking up her tiles, Toby emitted a long sigh. Catherine put
her tiles back down.

```
                Z
                E
        P       N
        I               L
        T               O
      A P A T H E T I C
  D I N       E       R K
      G       X       E
      R       A       E
      Y       N O W
```

'LOCK,' she sighed.

'Ten points,' said Andrew.

'Well done, Mummy,' said Toby kindly.

'You're still *way* ahead of me,' Catherine told him.

'Daddy's still winning, though,' said Toby, glancing at his
father with a mixture of resentment and awe.

'Yes, well, perhaps not for much longer,' said Catherine,
giving Andrew's ankle a light tap beneath the table.

Andrew remained oblivious. 'How about this?' he said.
'GLAZED.'

```
      G L A Z E D
              E
          P E N
              I
              T         O
      A P A T H E T I C
      D I N   E   R   K
          G   X   E
          R   A   E
          Y   N O W
```

'Seventeen,' said Andrew, 'on a double word score. Makes thirty-four.'

'*See?*' said Toby.

'Oh, for God's sake,' snapped Catherine. Andrew was now on one hundred and forty-six. Catherine had a self-righteous twenty-eight. This was all rather unfair, she thought.

Suddenly Toby started to giggle uncontrollably. Without saying a word, he picked up two tiles and lay them down carefully, scarcely able to suppress his glee.

Catherine and Andrew stared at the board.

```
      G L A Z E D
              E
          P E N I S
              I
              T         O
      A P A T H E T I C
      D I N   E   R   K
          G   X   E
          R   A   E
          Y   N O W
```

'Penis,' said Andrew, his voice remote.

'*Toby*,' said Catherine, aghast.

Toby beamed at his parents. 'James Macintyre says that Henry Rosenthal doesn't have one.'

Catherine stared numbly at the tiles, the treacherous agglomeration of letters which seemed to be spelling the end of her son's innocence. She was unable to speak.

'They cut his off when he was a baby,' explained Toby.

'Oh God,' said Catherine.

'How many points is that?' asked Toby, peering at the board in evident satisfaction.

'None,' replied Catherine immediately. 'It's not allowed.'

'Why not?'

'It just isn't.'

'It's not a *swear* word,' said Toby.

'Since when were you an expert on swear words, Toby Shaw?'

'I'm just saying, it's not a swear word. It's a proper word.'

'No,' said Catherine, 'it *isn't*.'

Toby blinked. 'I bet it's in the dictionary.'

'Look,' said Catherine after a brief review of her options. 'I won't have you answering back to me.'

Toby's face crumpled. 'But –'

'Any more of this and you'll go straight to bed.'

'But I only –'

'Right, that's it,' interrupted Catherine, standing up and pushing her fingers through the tiles on the board, destroying the matrix of words, obliterating the evidence of her paltry twenty-eight points. She was disturbed to discover this childish act of wilful demolition oddly cathartic. She mussed the tiles some more. 'What a shame. We were having a perfectly nice game up until then.' This spectacular lie was allowed to pass unchallenged.

Catherine, Andrew and Toby sat facing each other across the mess of jumbled letters, now robbed of all meaning. None of them said a word.

THIRTEEN

Early the next morning, Andrew climbed out of bed, blinking with ragged exhaustion. Catherine slept on, undisturbed. He gathered his clothes and took them into the bathroom. He showered quickly and dressed.

Minutes later, as he tiptoed across the darkened bedroom floor, he saw Catherine's jewellery box sitting on her dressing table. He crept over and gingerly opened the top drawer. Catherine's earrings winked back at him in the half-light, tiny knots of glamour. Each sat next to its twin, an exotic collection of miniature butterfly wings. In the drawer below there was a glimmering knot of necklaces – gold, silver, pearls. But no bracelet.

'Andrew?' Catherine was staring at him, propped up on one elbow. 'What are you doing?'

He quickly shut the box and turned to face her. There were still two more drawers which he hadn't yet opened. 'Early start, that's all. Didn't want to wake you.'

'What time is it?' she yawned.

He glanced at his watch. 'It's a quarter past six.'

Catherine's head hit the pillow with a defeated thump. 'Are you feeling all right?'

'Yes,' he said neutrally. He paused. 'I thought I'd walk to work this morning.'

Catherine stared at the ceiling in silence as Andrew stepped out of the bedroom.

In the kitchen, he sipped his coffee and stared numbly around the room, dazzled by the armoury of clever culinary devices on display.

Andrew had always been proud of all this ostentatious gastronomic sophistication, but all of a sudden the gleaming appliances had begun to jeer caustically at him. *Is this what you always wanted?* The poverty of his ambition shamed him. The dark shadow of disquiet tightened its embrace.

If I leave, he thought, I won't be able to use the electric juicer any more.

He opened the front door and escaped the silent house. Andrew's bit of the block, his slab of north London real estate, had finally betrayed him. It was no longer a refuge, no longer a source of quiet satisfaction. Every brick, every hard-earned fixture and fitting, now sat heavy with silent reproach. Andrew could hardly breathe in his own home.

Is this what you always wanted?

The streets were eerily quiet. Trees cast tiny islands of shade on to the empty pavements; there was not a whisper of a breeze. It was going to be another scorching day. Andrew crossed the intersection at Angel and continued southwards. He walked past the angular brickwork and obliquely tinted glass of Sadler's Wells. Gaudy posters, pulsating rhumbas of colour, announced the arrival in town of a Brazilian circus troop.

Andrew walked on, numbly fighting the urge to sit down on the pavement and burst into tears. The boundaries of his existence had suddenly been redrawn, and he found himself yearning for the unburdened ignorance he had left behind.

As the previous evening had unfolded in all its excruciating awkwardness, Richard's accusation had echoed poisonously on inside his head. Catherine, a thief? He had watched her as she served up her inedible chicken casserole, chattering lightly as she passed the plates around the table. He had watched her as she cajoled them through that terrible game of Scrabble. The determined cheerfulness of her voice rang on, hollow and laced with deceit.

We all keep secrets, even from our loved ones.

As he had walked back from the pub the previous afternoon, Andrew was paralysed by the realisation that he no longer knew whether Catherine was capable of stealing from her friends.

He hadn't looked in her jewellery box because Richard had asked him to. He had looked because he no longer knew who his wife was.

Little by little Catherine had retreated, quietly burying herself in the unshifting sands of their day-to-day existence, beyond his reach. Her distancing had been as imperceptible as the creep of the hour hand on a clock – movement was only discernible if you looked away for a time. Andrew had looked away, but for too long. Now he found himself separated from her by a vast, obscuring emptiness. His suicidal dalliances with Clara and Sinead began to make a terrible sense. Perhaps he had subconsciously abandoned hope of ever getting the old, spirited Catherine back, and now his libido was propelling him, kamikaze-like, into one final act of wanton destruction – compassionate killing and suicide neatly rolled into one.

We all keep secrets. We all lie.

He had even lied last night. Catherine had leaped on his story of the surprise party with unquestioning alacrity – relief, almost. And tonight, he thought, I shall come home and search the rest of her jewellery box. Another deception, another betrayal.

176

His heart filled with sorrow.

There was nothing left for him here.

If I leave, he thought, I won't be able to use the electric juicer any more.

In the months before Toby's birth, Andrew had often gone alone to visit his parents for the weekend. Catherine had stayed in London, drained and exhausted by the baby growing inside her.

By then the cancer was rampaging across his mother's stricken body. When the weather was warm, Andrew wheeled her slowly around the garden. That year the flowerbeds bloomed in untended chaos. Andrew sat by Rosa's bedside, reading out newspaper reviews of plays she would never see and books she would never read. She lay silently back on her pillows as if she had been disastrously punctured. Downstairs, Patrick worked in the kitchen, preparing the next meal. The remote thud of the knife on the chopping board, the quiet zing of steel on steel: this became the sound-track of those cheerless days. Patrick prepared Rosa's meals with scrupulous attention, cooking every dish as if it were her last.

After Rosa had slipped into exhausted oblivion, Andrew and his father sat downstairs and danced the sad waltz of distant memories. Patrick told story after story, each one assiduously collated, arranged, and rehearsed. Rosa dominated every episode, of course. It had been her spirit, her large heart, which had propelled their happy little trio on towards each new happiness. And she was leaving them.

On Sunday mornings, Patrick trudged to church, and Rosa cajoled Andrew into retelling the anecdotes which his father had recounted the previous evening. She listened with a faraway look in her eyes, smiling through her pain.

'Why do you get *me* to retell these stories?' Andrew asked

her one morning. 'I'm sure I get half of them wrong. The two of you should share them together.'

There was a long pause.

'Your father and I need different things from those stories now, Andrew,' sighed Rosa. 'He sees them as a survival mechanism, but for me they're just entertainment. You get less precious about these things in my condition. All I want is to enjoy them one last time.' She paused. 'If we started to rake over these stories together, he would start crying for me, and I would start crying for him. We'd both be in tears, and where's the good in that? I haven't got time for any more sadness.'

Andrew nodded, overcome by his parents' predicament, as they bleakly waited for the end together. Even the strongest marriages finally fall into incommunicable sorrow. He thought of Catherine, and wondered if they would suffer the same lonely fate of unbridgeable silence.

Now here they were, unable to speak to each other.

Catherine stood thoughtfully in front of the long mirror. Her frock lay in a forgotten heap on the floor; her bra hung off the end of the bed. The nightdress, rescued from the sultry rainbow of forgotten silk at the back of her wardrobe, sheathed her in diaphanous glamour, fabulously alluring. She twisted this way and that, enjoying the smoothness of silk on her skin. Her eyes roamed across her body in quiet satisfaction.

She had been given a second chance. Her marriage was safe, at least for now, and she intended to do everything she could to rescue it. Last night's exercise in familial bliss hadn't exactly been an unqualified success, but at least it was a start. She was still angry with Toby for spelling PENIS, and Andrew's insensitive pig-headedness hadn't helped, but she was most disappointed with herself for her petulant over-reaction which had ruined the game.

178

In the end, there had been no sex. In bed Andrew had turned over and switched off his light before she had finished brushing her teeth. Tonight, though. Catherine tugged at the lace hem of the nightdress. She wanted to signal a new beginning for their marriage. She wanted to show Andrew that she was grateful. That she loved him. That she was sorry.

Tonight she would perform her act of atonement.

Andrew arrived at the Trident offices clutching his cappuccino. Joel was sitting at Petrushka's desk on the landing outside his office. He appeared to be looking through Andrew's diary.

'Joel?' said Andrew. 'What are you doing?'

Joel's head snapped backwards as if an invisible pugilist had just delivered a deft uppercut to his chin. 'Ah, Andrew. I didn't get the chance to remind you –'

'Whatever it is,' said Andrew, turning away from him, 'let me drink my coffee first, all right?' As he pushed open his door the whiff of cigarette smoke hit his nostrils. A man was standing by the window, gazing out across the rooftops. He casually flicked an inch of ash on to the carpet, and spoke without turning around. 'I thought I told you, Joel, no interruptions.'

'*Damian*?'

Damian turned slowly around to face him. 'Andrew. What can I do for you?'

'I beg your pardon?'

'Is that for me?' Damian stepped forward and took Andrew's coffee out of his hand. He pulled off the plastic lid and gazed down into the cup. 'Next time give me cinnamon rather than cocoa, OK? Just a light sprinkle, though.'

Andrew blinked. 'What do you –'

179

'You really should do something about decorating this office,' said Damian. 'It's a bit bloody pokey, isn't it?' He took a swig of Andrew's coffee.

'Damian,' said Andrew, 'would you please tell me what you're doing in my office?'

The door opened and Joel crept in. 'Andrew? I can explain.'

'Oh, *good*,' said Andrew. 'Because I'm less than –'

'This is the Staff Displacement Scheme.'

'The what?'

'The Staff Displacement Scheme,' said Joel. 'For one day per predetermined period, everyone swaps jobs.'

'Dear God,' said Andrew. 'Tell me you're joking.'

'Didn't you read my memo?'

'Your – no, Joel, I must have missed it.' Andrew never read Joel's memos.

'The Staff Displacement Scheme is designed to enhance employee community and interdepartmental understanding,' explained Joel. 'By assuming the responsibilities of one of your colleagues for a day, you develop a greater understanding of their functions, thereby enhancing mutual respect and facilitating future staff interaction.'

'Look, would you mind having this conversation somewhere else?' said Damian irritably. 'I'm trying to *think*.'

'Joel,' said Andrew, 'have you gone *completely* mad?'

'Freddie's very keen on it,' said Joel.

'I don't *care*,' snapped Andrew. 'Why can't he try out his hare-brained schemes on someone else for a change? We're not a colony of corporate guinea pigs, Joel. We have a business to run.' He sighed. '*Staff Displacement Scheme*, indeed. Good grief.'

'You said it was a great idea,' said Joel, hurt.

'Did I? When?'

'Wednesday morning.'

So this was what Joel had been prattling on about while

180

Andrew was enjoying his Parisian cup of coffee. Andrew sighed. 'Damian is being me for the day, is that it?'

Joel nodded. Andrew could see his fingers twitching, as if he were desperate to administer a consolatory back massage.

'Do I go and sit in Damian's office, then?'

'Ah, no. Petrushka's being Damian today.'

'Don't tell me that's what you were – Joel, are you being *Petrushka*?'

'I am,' said Joel, dignified.

Andrew laughed. 'You poor sod. Has Damian got you popping out for a sandwich yet?'

Joel wore a pained look on his face. 'I don't think you're taking this in quite the spirit that it's –'

'Sometimes, Joel, you amaze me, you really do.' Andrew shook his head. 'All right, then, I shall graciously submit to this ridiculous folly. I don't suppose it can do too much harm, if it's just for a day. Where am I supposed to be working then?'

Joel coughed. 'It's not really up to me to tell you,' he said. 'I'm just the Creative Director's personal assistant.'

At this, Damian walked towards them, his eyes glinting. 'Should I –?'

Joel bowed. 'Please.'

'Right, you,' said Damian, jabbing a finger in Andrew's chest. 'Stop pratting about in my office and haul your arse down to the post room.'

Catherine got dressed and hid the nightdress under her pillow, ready for tonight. On the bed lay a paperback Bible, rescued from the dusty oblivion of a high bookshelf. She sat down and opened it at random. She read for a few minutes in silence. The words circulated inside her head, reassuringly benign.

It seemed ridiculous, that her faith should return after all this time. But no matter how much Catherine tried to tell herself otherwise, a small flame had been ignited inside her. It burned steadily, barely flickering in the gusts of her wilful scepticism. She was slowly becoming used to its warmth. It gave her strength, this hope that she wasn't alone. And it was surely no coincidence, that this spiritual reawakening should happen just as she was rediscovering the appeal of faithful matrimony. All that enjoyable sinning with Richard was behind her now. Just as well, really. She felt a guilty pang of regret. The fact was, no matter how much she wanted it otherwise, her marriage still carried the same old freight of compromise and disappointment. Catherine sighed, wondering if she should ask for some help. She closed the Bible and knelt gingerly down by the side of the bed. She rested her elbows on the duvet and put her hands together. Her fingers pointed to the ceiling. She shut her eyes. *Dear Lord*, she began.

She stopped, horribly self-conscious.

It's been a while since we last spoke. Now, about Andrew –

Something was pushed through the letterbox downstairs. Catherine opened her eyes. *Sorry, more later*, she thought, grateful for the distraction of the just-arrived post. *Amen, amen*, she whispered as she went downstairs. What did Amen actually mean? Signing off now. Over and out. Praise be. It was good value for its four letters – huge and warm, bursting with its two long, sanctified syllables. More of a sigh, really. Ahh, men.

A cheaply-printed brochure for home-delivered pizza lay on the doormat. Catherine guiltily picked it up. Rather than return upstairs to continue with her prayers, she went down to the kitchen and opened the newspaper. After skimming the usual cocktail of death, scandal and misery, she

182

turned to the arts section. She read a brace of film reviews, and then, for the first time in years, she started to read the classical music listings for the forthcoming week in London.

Her eyes scanned the columns of print. *Fidelio* at the Opera House, *Don Giovanni* at the ENO. A Bach mass, some Prokofiev at the Barbican. The inevitable early music festival. Then she saw it. Singing a programme of Hugo Wolf's Lieder, texts by Mörike and Goethe. One in a series of free lunch-time concerts in Bloomsbury. The name swam in front of Catherine's eyes.

Andrew's day passed in a whirl of unceasing activity. From the cramped post room in the basement, chore after chore rained down upon him without respite. He ferried stacks of photocopies to the print shop and back. He shuttled across central London, delivering packages and running errands. *I'm no delivery boy, you know*, he wanted to tell the yawning receptionists. They looked away as they pointed to the box where he had to sign.

Half-way through the afternoon, Andrew sat down for the first time. His nerves were frayed, his patience eroded, his energy spent. Still, he was grateful for the distraction of a full day's work. He slumped into an orange plastic chair and eyed the piles of correspondence which he had to put into envelopes, run through the franking machine, and take to the Post Office before closing time. He looked around the small windowless room. Jason, the post room's present incumbent, was something of an amateur pornographer. He had cut photographs of half-naked women out of newspapers and had attached them to the walls with a staple gun. The staple gun sat on a nearby shelf. It was grey and heavy. Andrew imagined pressing it up against Damian's forehead and squeezing the trigger.

Joel stuck his head around the door. 'Andrew,' he said. 'Having a break, eh? Lucky you.'

'What's Jason doing today?' asked Andrew.

'Head of legal.'

'Are you *sure* this is such a good idea?'

'Listen,' said Joel, ignoring Andrew's question with exactly the same degree of contempt which Petrushka would employ if Jason were to broach the subject of management strategy with her, 'I just wanted to see how it was all going.'

Andrew shook his head. 'Never again.'

'Oh.' Joel looked disappointed. 'Most people are finding the Staff Displacement Scheme to be a positive experience.'

'Most people,' Andrew pointed out, 'are not stuck in a hole like this while an insufferable moron ponces about in their office. To say nothing of the charming wall-to-wall nipple and tit effect that Jason's created in here.'

'Well, OK,' said Joel. 'I'll stick your comments in the report.'

'What report?'

'I have to write a report for Freddie. Tell him how the day went.'

'In that case, you can tell him from me that this is an outrageous idea. His stupid scheme has made me a laughing stock.'

'I think you're missing the point,' said Joel. 'You're the big guy, now. From now on everyone will see you as a boss who isn't afraid to muck in and get his hands dirty. They'll stop thinking you're such a prima donna.'

Andrew looked at him. 'People think I'm a prima donna?'

Joel swallowed. 'No,' he said.

'Me,' said Andrew flatly. 'They think *I'm* a prima donna.'

'But *now*,' continued Joel hastily, 'you'll be the hands-on, people person.'

'The hands-on, people person,' sighed Andrew. 'Fabulous.'

There was a pause. Joel took a step into the room. 'Forgive me for mentioning this, Andrew,' he said, 'but I can't help noticing that lately you seem to have become rather – *negative*.'

'Negative? Really?'

'And aggressive.'

Andrew resisted the urge to pummel Joel's head against the wall. 'You'd probably be feeling quite negative and aggressive if you'd had the day I've had,' he said.

Joel looked at his watch. 'Well, not much longer to go.'

'I've still got all this post to do,' complained Andrew.

'Well, before you get started on that, Damian needs a tall, skinny latte and a wholemeal cinnamon muffin.' A moment later Joel took a deft step backwards, thereby narrowly avoiding the staple gun which was hurtling through the air towards his head.

She remained at the table for longer than she knew. The thirteen letters shimmered beneath the heat of her gaze. They dissolved into a blizzard of memories and then crashed crisply back into focus, again and again, a tiny cycle of violence.

Catherine ran her hands through her hair and stared at the newspaper in front of her. The letters acquired a quiet luminosity on the page. They glowed amidst the cold, grey sea of newsprint. Catherine's eyes devoured their truth: all this time Daniel Woodman had been living, breathing, and singing. The idea struck her as profoundly shocking. For Catherine, he had died the day she closed the door to his flat for the last time, and struggled home through the wind-chilled rain. Since then he had inhabited the soft-focus dreamscape of those winter months, a roguishly bestubbled Peter Pan, immune to the inevitable trudge of time. Now, though, the intervening years rushed up in ambush. Daniel would not have escaped the surreptitious creep of days. Unprotected by her memories, time would have taken its toll. A million questions exploded across her consciousness, a fireworks display of dazzling ignorance. The Daniel Woodman of today – there! on the page! – was a stranger. She continued to stare at his name. Finally she got unsteadily to her feet and found a pen. The recital was on the following Monday afternoon. She scribbled down the details and put the piece of paper in her pocket.

She wanted a glimpse – just a glimpse – of the future she never had.

Catherine had no dreams of new romance. There would be no fresh conflagration of passion, nothing like that. Instead they would talk. She would reassure herself that, yes, what had happened between them had been true and good – an adventure, long past them now, but true and good all the same. Perhaps there would be a shared, wistful sigh, a quiet reflection of what might have been. Catherine's quiet act of remembrance of those long-lost days would no longer be a solo performance, but – at last – a duet, rich with forgotten harmonies. Then perhaps, just perhaps, she would be able to return home to face her future and her family – finally free from the ghosts of her past.

Ahh, men.

The weekend yawned ahead of her. The hours until Monday lunch time stretched into the distance, stiller than gravestones.

Catherine remained at the kitchen table, cast adrift on an ocean of memories. It was only when the telephone rang – Mrs Perkins from the nursery, worried that nobody had come to pick Florence up – that she realised that the afternoon had escaped her. She muttered her apologies and ran to the car. It was only as she was trapped in the usual Friday afternoon gridlock that she remembered Toby's school play.

By the time she had collected Florence from the nursery and apologised again to a frowning Mrs Perkins, she was over an hour late. The drive to Toby's school seemed to take for ever. Catherine pulled Florence out of the car and ran towards the school hall, grateful that at least Andrew would be able to brief her about what she had missed. She pushed open the door and stared, horrified, at the crowd of cheerful parents who were discussing the play which had just finished. By the door there was a small pile of programmes. Hastily she picked one up and looked at it. There it was in black and white, towards the bottom of the list of credits: *Assistant Stage Manager – Toby Shaw*. One for the scrapbook, she thought. Then she realised sadly: Toby didn't *have* a scrapbook.

Catherine held Florence's hand tightly and moved through the crowd looking for Andrew. The level of chatter rose steadily. Suddenly she saw Toby and ran over to him, beaming. 'Toby!' she cried, bending down and squeezing him tight. As she held him she shut her eyes briefly and silently apologised for what she was about to do. 'Well done! That was a *really* well stage-managed play.'

'Where's Daddy?' asked Toby.

'Well, darling, I don't know.' She stood up and cast her eyes about the room. 'It doesn't look as if he's here.'

'James Macintyre's father came,' said Toby at once.

'Perhaps he got stuck at work,' said Catherine. 'You know how busy he is. But don't worry, I'll be sure to tell him what a wonderful job you did.' She did not want to get into a comparison between Andrew and James Macintyre's gun-toting, women-baiting fascist of a father, partly because she didn't want to discover that James Macintyre's gun-toting, women-baiting fascist of a father was actually the better dad. 'Did you enjoy the performance?'

Toby nodded. 'It feels nice to have done a good job,' he said.

It was all Catherine could do not to give her son another hug for delivering this answer with such a perfectly straight face. 'A job well done –' she began, sure that this was the start of an old saying, but then discovering that if it was, she didn't know how it ended. She ruffled Toby's hair affectionately as she performed one final scan of the crowd, which was beginning to thin out. Andrew was nowhere to be seen. At least, she thought guiltily, that meant that he would never know about her own late arrival. 'Ready to go?' she said.

Toby looked up at her. 'Is Daddy really not here?'

Catherine shook her head. 'I'm sure he'll make it up to you, though.'

'How?' demanded Toby.

'Well, you tell me. What would be the best thing?'

'The *best* thing,' said Toby immediately, 'would be a trip to the Harry Potter Café, obviously, but I know –'

'Then that's what you'll do,' cried Catherine.

'Really?' said Toby.

'Really. How does tomorrow sound?'

'That sounds amazing,' said Toby, blinking.

'Great. Just you and Daddy.'

'At the Harry Potter Café?'

'I promise.' Catherine smiled. 'Come on, let's go.'

'The last day of term,' sighed Toby happily as they walked towards the car.

Catherine stopped dead in the middle of the car-park. The last day of term! She had forgotten.

'What are we going to do next week?' asked Toby.

Andrew crept out of the office at 5.28, two minutes early, and went into the nearest pub. He sat alone at the bar and ordered a pint of lager. As the first mouthful of cold liquid slipped down his throat, he knew that he had never enjoyed a drink more. Real work, he mused, gave you a thirst. As he watched the cool drops of condensation run down the outside of the glass, the squadron of thoughts which had been circling above him all day, waiting for a break in the clouds, finally came in to land.

The two unexplored drawers in Catherine's jewellery box beckoned to him, inviting further betrayal. Andrew was swamped with sadness at his inability to believe in his wife's innocence.

He should have seen this coming. Even as the strands of their lives became more closely woven with each passing year, the resulting tapestry disguised its fragility behind a bland picture of family life. All that was needed was a small tug at the weakest spot for the whole structure to unravel.

There had followed a decline in vigilance, and now the wool had worked itself loose.

Andrew saw his family standing in front of his house, waving him goodbye. He stood on the pavement, clutching an old suitcase. Toby stood sullenly behind his mother's legs, hiding in the folds of her dress. Florence was waving gleefully, shouting affectionate nonsense. Catherine held Florence in her arms and watched him go without saying a word. This woman he no longer knew.

There was nothing left for him here.

He watched himself walk away.

Catherine struggled through the rest of the afternoon, fighting to escape her disappointment.

Her plans to go to Daniel Woodman's recital on Monday had evaporated as quickly as they had arrived. The school holidays made the trip impossible, of course. Toby would see too much, more than was good for either of them.

Catherine retreated to her greenhouse to hide her frustration from the children. She patrolled up and down the columns of plants, systematically examining each one. She pressed her thumb into the soil surrounding the base of every stem, resisting the temptation to water. More orchids were killed by over-watering than for any other reason. Too much love could kill you. Catherine bent down by the pots of *anguloa clowesii* and breathed deeply, inhaling the fragrance which lingered in the cup of golden yellow petals. The sweet aroma filled her with a quiet ache of regret. Her orchids would always remain a pale substitute for her lost career, a reminder of all that she had abandoned. She straightened up and watched Toby riddle his sister with invisible bullets.

Toby was in excellent spirits at the prospect of months without school. Not even Andrew's absence at the play could dampen his good mood. In the garden, brother and sister played in harmonious independence. Toby had immersed himself in an intricately conceived private world of flying submarines and bionic horses with laser guns built into their heads. He set off to save the world, every heroic action simultaneously broadcast to the garden via his own breathless commentary. Florence sat near the flowerbed, patiently ferrying pebbles to and fro with her Tonka truck. As she did so she unwittingly played various roles in her brother's adventure, from an axe-wielding henchman to entire villages of soon-to-be-exterminated peasants. Invisible blows rained down on her shoulders, but she carried on unperturbed.

Catherine watched her children, each content in their own small worlds – together, but wholly apart. They had, she reflected, intuitively grasped how best to live together. If only it were always so easy. She thought of Andrew, and of the silk nightdress which was lying beneath her pillow.

* * *

When Andrew arrived home, Catherine was sitting at the kitchen table, a glass of red wine in front of her. She smiled as he appeared at the door. She looked tired.

'There you are.' She raised her glass towards him. 'Started without you.'

Andrew poured himself some wine. They clinked glasses. He took a sip. 'It's very quiet,' he said.

'The kids are in bed.'

'Oh.'

'It's past their bedtimes.'

'Is it?'

'Andrew,' said Catherine, 'have you been in the pub?'

He coughed. 'Friday night.'

Her eyes met his, unblinking. 'It was Toby's play this afternoon.'

'Oh, *shit*, Cathy. I totally forgot.'

'Well, yes.'

'It was a mad day at work.'

'It always is.'

Andrew shrugged helplessly. 'How was it?'

'The play?' Catherine was silent for a moment. 'If you must know, it was terrible. But Toby was expecting you to be there.'

'Damn,' said Andrew. Apart from anything else, he thought, it would have been an excellent excuse to escape from the post room early.

'How could you *forget*, Andrew?' said Catherine. 'His first school play!'

Andrew stared at his wineglass, thinking of the unexplored drawers of jewellery upstairs. 'I'm sorry.'

'I can't *believe* that you'd do such a thing.'

'Look, I'll make it up to him.'

'Sooner than you think. I promised him that you'd take him to the Harry Potter Café tomorrow.'

191

'Oh no.'

'That's all right, isn't it? We've got nothing special on.'

Nothing special on, thought Andrew sadly.

'If you go for lunch,' said Catherine, 'you'll be home well before your father gets back from the cricket.'

'You're not coming?'

Catherine shook her head. 'This is Toby's treat. He'd object if Florence came along. You didn't miss *her* play.'

'God. Whatever happened to sibling affection?'

'Spoken like a true only child,' observed Catherine drily.

'I might go upstairs for a moment,' said Andrew. 'Change into something more comfortable.'

Catherine nodded. 'I'll start supper.'

Andrew went up to the bedroom and quietly closed the door behind him. He walked over to Catherine's dressing table and pulled out the third drawer of the jewellery box.

It was the bracelet drawer.

He peered in, and was confronted by a complex Venn diagram, glittering circles intersecting in three dimensions. He ran his fingers through the morass of jangling hoops. There was gold, silver, steel, tin, jade, ivory, plastic, wood – just about every material Andrew could think of, in fact, except for white gold. The final drawer contained Catherine's watches, their straps curled up beneath them like sleeping snakes. Andrew closed the drawer and sat down heavily on the bed. So there was no bracelet. He considered this, and wondered why the news didn't provoke even the smallest twinge of relief.

Perhaps Catherine had seen him prying this morning and guessed what he was looking for. She would have had all day to hide the bracelet somewhere else. He took off his shoes and realised that this was no longer about Annabel's bracelet. It was *his* betrayal, not hers, which was weighing so heavily upon him.

He didn't trust his wife any more.

Andrew changed clothes and returned sadly downstairs. Catherine was standing in front of the hob, stirring something in a saucepan. 'Smells good,' he said.

Catherine laughed, a little too loudly. 'Who needs Sinead?'

Andrew swallowed. 'Has she been in touch?'

Catherine shook her head. 'I've been thinking about her, though,' she said. 'You know. Trying to work out what happened, why she left. Wondering whether it was something I did.'

Andrew remembered what Sinead had told him just before she had jumped on him. 'Shouldn't worry,' he said. 'It was probably something to do with splitting up with her boyfriend.'

'Her boyfriend?'

'They broke up. That evening.'

Catherine looked at him strangely. 'How on earth do you know?'

He paused. 'Oh. Well. I saw her, actually. The night before she disappeared. Only briefly, though. It was just before I came upstairs to bed.'

Catherine blinked. 'Why on earth didn't you mention it before?'

Andrew shrugged, suddenly cautious. 'Didn't really think about it, I suppose.' He took a sip of his wine. His mouth was dry. 'Anyway, they had a fight, or something.'

'Oh, poor Sinead,' said Catherine distractedly. 'That must be it.'

'He sounded like a nasty piece of work, though,' said Andrew. 'She turned up late to his gig and he dumped her on the spot, just like that. Cathy? What is it?'

Catherine's hand had flown up to her mouth in horror. 'I asked her to stay a little later that night,' she whispered.

Too late, Andrew remembered that part of Sinead's drunken story.

Catherine stared at the kitchen ceiling and exhaled. 'It *was* my fault, then,' she said. 'If I hadn't asked her to stay late –'

'Come on, Cathy,' said Andrew softly. 'You can't blame yourself. How could you have possibly known?'

Catherine put down her wooden spoon and burst into tears. 'I can't stop *hurting* people,' she sobbed.

Cautiously, Andrew approached, and put an arm around her shoulders. He held her while her sadness spilled into the room.

The meal was eaten in silence.

Catherine seemed to retreat into herself after her tearful outburst. She scarcely looked up from her plate. Andrew watched her from across the table, apprehensive about what she would do next. He wondered whether her unravelling portended some greater ill.

At the end of the meal, Andrew cleared away the dishes. Catherine touched him on the shoulder. 'Back in a minute,' she said, and disappeared upstairs.

Andrew stood in front of the sink and turned the tap on. He let the hot water scald his hands. At some point their marriage had quietly expired, cancelled due to lack of interest.

'What do you think?'

Andrew turned around. Catherine was standing at the kitchen door, her hand resting on her hip. She was wearing a dark blue silk nightdress. She had reapplied her lipstick, the dark gash of colour incongruous against her pale face. She smiled uncertainly at him. The inky flood of despair swamped his heart.

'Cathy,' he said sadly, 'I'm not –'

She took a step towards him, putting a finger to her lips.

'Not now,' she whispered, taking his hand, still wet from the hot water.

Andrew heard the quiet pleading in her voice.

There had been enough hurt, he thought. No more unravelling, not tonight.

He followed her upstairs.

FOURTEEN

The doorbell echoed through the house. Catherine grunted and pulled her pillow over her head. There was a minute's silence. Then the doorbell went again.

'Andrew,' murmured Catherine.

Andrew stared at his alarm clock.

The doorbell rang for a third time, longer and more insistently. 'You're my hero,' whispered Catherine. She nudged him softly with her knee. 'My wonderful, door-answering, hero.'

Andrew sighed and crept out from under the duvet. He pulled on his dressing gown and walked to the front door, still drifting in the soft focus of half-sleep. He peered through the spy-hole. A man was standing on the doorstep. The gold buttons of his navy blue blazer sparkled in the early morning sun. The creases in his cream trousers were razor sharp. Dark glasses glinted beneath a rakishly angled Panama hat. Andrew opened the front door and rubbed his stubbled jaw. 'Hello, Dad.'

Patrick Shaw whipped off his dark glasses. '*Shalom, naim lehakir.*'

Andrew frowned. 'What?'

'I said, Hello, how are you?'

'In what language?'

'Hebrew. Can I come in?'

'You're learning Hebrew?' said Andrew as he shut the door behind his father.

Patrick took off his hat and put down his bag. He followed Andrew downstairs to the kitchen. 'I am. Call it a precaution.'

'Against what?'

'I read somewhere that people are more likely to speak Hebrew in heaven than anything else.'

Andrew blinked. 'You're – this is for when you get to heaven?'

'Well, you'd want to be able to speak the language, wouldn't you? Especially if you're going to be there for all eternity.' Patrick paused. 'Perhaps you think I'm being presumptuous.'

'It's not that.' Andrew shook his head, unsure what he thought.

Patrick cleared his throat. '*Eze mezeg avir nechmad.*'

'Which means?'

'Lovely weather we're having.'

'Do you really think you'll be sitting around discussing the *weather*?'

Patrick shrugged. 'There's also *Cham po, nachon?*, just in case I've miscalculated and end up in hell.'

'What does that mean?'

'Bit hot down here, isn't it?'

Andrew laughed. 'Do you want some coffee?'

'Thank you.'

Andrew yawned as he switched on the kettle. 'You're looking very spiffy,' he said.

'Well, the Saturday of a Lords test match is always an occasion,' replied Patrick. 'Dressing up is part of the fun.'

He smoothed down his MCC tie. 'Makes you feel part of something special.'

'The glories of tradition?' said Andrew. 'The timeless sound of, what is it, leather on willow?'

'For someone who's hated cricket his entire life,' said Patrick, 'you show a flair for its nuances.'

'Now be fair. I haven't hated cricket my entire life. Not yet.'

Patrick sighed. 'How we produced a son like you I'll never know.'

'A triumph of good sense over genetics,' suggested Andrew.

Patrick put a hand on his heart. 'You wound me.' He looked around. 'So where is everyone? Where are my grand-children?'

'Dad,' said Andrew, 'do you know what time it is?'

'I'm probably a bit early,' conceded Patrick. 'I caught the first train from Swindon this morning. Didn't want to be late.'

'When does the game start?'

'Eleven o'clock.'

Andrew looked at the kitchen clock and then at his father.

'Oh, don't worry, I won't hang around here,' said Patrick. 'I'll just drop my things off and then go and find a good breakfast. Wander around a bit and soak up the pre-match atmosphere, that sort of thing.'

'You can stay here as long as you like, you know that.' Andrew spooned coffee into the cafetière.

'So,' said Patrick after a moment, 'what's new?'

What's new?

Last night's lovemaking had been terrible. The more Catherine had whispered and sighed, the more Andrew felt himself retreat, until he had the impression of hovering above the bed, watching the couple below him with empty dispassion. Catherine had betrayed herself by the hollow drama of her responses – the wide-eyed gasps of pleasure, the enraptured writing. It had been a tired exchange of favours – two over-familiar bodies, sweatily trying to ambush their own expectations. An undignified epitaph. When he had finally rolled away from her, dismally spent, his shame barrelled into him. He should have said no; he was *leaving*, for Christ's sake. Andrew was judge, jury, and grim-faced flogger of the guilty-as-charged. By morning he was bloated with self-loathing.

Andrew looked at his father and knew that he would say none of this. Patrick had never shared Rosa's appetite for intimate confidences. She had sought out secrets from anyone who would take her compassion in return, but Patrick was cool and detached – remote, almost. He was a contained man, this retired provincial solicitor. He had hovered like a solitary moon over Rosa's choppy sea, curbing her excesses, marshalling her tides. Andrew had often wondered whether his father's dispassion was just a defence against the chaotic whirlwind of Rosa's existence. For a while after her death his own emotions had finally risen to the surface in all their anguish. Andrew had fielded a succession of lonely phone calls in the dead of the night. The small, lost voice at the other end of the line sought solace in the rambling litany of old memories or raged in baffled fury at the stupidity of her illness, before dissolving in a quiet storm of tears. Words were always defeated, in the end, by the unbearable weight of Patrick's loss.

After some months, the phone calls stopped, and the old, equable Patrick Shaw returned, his pain packed quietly away, out of sight. He had set about conquering his life afresh, calmly determined not to be defeated by his grief. Now here he was, relaxed and resplendent in his outfit, ready for the Members' Pavilion at Lords. Andrew knew his father would be horrified if he began to confess what was going through

199

his head. Patrick had risen above the emotional riots of other people's lives, beyond all that messiness, and that was where he wished to stay.

'What's new?' said Andrew with a small smile. 'Nothing's new.'

Catherine lay in bed, thinking.

The truth behind Sinead's disappearance had triggered a fresh cyclone of guilt.

Sinead had left because she was heartbroken. She was heartbroken because she had broken up with her boyfriend. She had broken up with her boyfriend because Catherine had been too weak to cope on her own, and had asked her to stay late.

It was, in other words, all her fault.

She rolled over and looked at the empty berth next to her. Andrew's scent lingered on in the sheets. The blue nightdress had done its work last night. Andrew had seemed remote all evening, hidden behind a wall of introspective silence, but in the bedroom he had thawed a little. His hands knew their way. Their lovemaking might have had none of the passion that there was with Richard, but familiarity brought its own reward. They had both worked with unselfish industry. Catherine had sighed and murmured, gasped and moaned, wanting it all to mean more than it did. Afterwards Andrew had subsided into the pillows next to her and had quickly fallen asleep. She had remained awake for hours.

Catherine stared at the ceiling and wondered what Daniel Woodman was doing right now. He had never liked mornings. He used to sulk beneath the covers, begging her to fetch him cups of tea, affronted that he should ever be expected to relinquish the comfort of his bed before noon.

She wondered who he was waking up with today.

With a sigh, Catherine climbed out of bed. She stood on

the landing, listening for signs of life from the children's rooms. All was quiet. She went downstairs. In the kitchen Patrick and Andrew were silently drinking coffee. 'My, my,' she said, as Patrick stood up to greet her, 'look at you.' She kissed him on the cheek. 'Very dashing.'

'Hello, Catherine,' said Patrick.

'Good trip up?'

'Very good, thank you.'

'Andrew's been looking after you?'

'Of course he has. Although I prefer your coffee.'

She grinned. 'You always did have impeccable taste.'

Catherine and Patrick looked at each other affectionately. She remembered how much she liked Andrew's father. Patrick drained his mug and looked at his watch. 'Well, I should probably go.'

'Already?' said Catherine.

'I'm sure you've got plenty on.'

'Have you eaten? I can always knock something –'

'Really.' Patrick smiled. 'Sweet of you. I think I'll go and find myself a greasy spoon somewhere urban and insalubrious. Nothing like a breakfast swimming in fat before a day's cricket.'

Catherine shrugged. 'Be sure you don't get ketchup on that lovely tie.'

'Tell me,' said Patrick. 'You do still *have* children, don't you?'

'What do you mean?'

'You haven't sold them into slavery or something?'

'Oh, I see. No, we haven't sold them. I don't think we'd get much for them, to be honest. They're too lazy. Still asleep, you see.'

'A miracle,' observed Patrick.

'For which we give thanks,' added Andrew.

Catherine smiled. 'You'll see them this evening, I promise.'

'Well.' Patrick straightened his tie. 'Wish me luck.'

Catherine nodded. 'Have fun.'

'Hope your team scores lots of goals,' said Andrew.

Patrick performed an elaborate sigh and left the kitchen. Andrew and Catherine listened as the front door opened and closed. Catherine poured herself a cup of coffee and sat down. 'Good morning,' she said.

Andrew looked at her. 'How are you?'

'I'm fine.' She reached across the table and touched Andrew's wrist. 'I enjoyed last night.'

Something shifted behind Andrew's eyes. 'Me too,' he said.

After a moment Catherine removed her fingers.

'Jesus,' sighed Andrew. 'It's not even eight o'clock and I'm already knackered.'

'Look on the bright side,' said Catherine. 'You've got your lunch with Toby to look forward to.'

'Yes, thank you,' said Andrew wearily. 'The prospect of eating expensive junk food in a restaurant full of over-excited children is *exactly* what I need to cheer me up.' He took an ill-natured slurp of coffee.

Toby appeared at the kitchen door in his pyjamas.

Catherine smiled. 'Hello, darling.'

Toby looked from his father to his mother, and then back again. 'Are we going soon?' he asked.

The rest of Andrew's morning was punctuated by Toby's persistent enquiries about the imminence of their departure for the Harry Potter Café. Never did a clock move so slowly as it moved for Toby that morning. He was restless, irritable, and unable to concentrate on anything else. Andrew did his best to remain calm in the face of his son's obsessive nagging.

'Come with us,' he begged Catherine through clenched teeth half-way through the morning.

Catherine shook her head. 'This should be just the two of you,' she said.

'*Please*,' said Andrew.

'Father and son together. Off on an adventure. You wait and see. It'll be fun.'

'Cathy, for God's sake, I'm begging –'

'Remember,' said Catherine, 'this is your way of making up for missing the school play.'

'I remember,' muttered Andrew.

'Anyway, it'll give you a chance for some father and son bonding.'

'Father and son *bonding*? If you really think –'

'Here's Toby!' interrupted Catherine gaily.

'Are we going soon?' asked Toby.

Finally, they left the house. Black clouds were gathering overhead. Andrew hailed a taxi just as the rain began to fall. The cab pulled out into the Saturday traffic and promptly ground to a halt. Through the windows they watched as people ran for cover.

'Do you think we'll see some real wizards?' asked Toby.

'Real wizards?' said Andrew. 'I don't know, Toby. Yes, probably. Why not?'

Toby was clutching his magic wand. 'Can I tell you a secret, Daddy?'

Andrew patted his son's knee. 'Of course you can.'

'My magic isn't real magic,' said Toby.

Andrew frowned. 'What do you mean?'

Toby leaned towards his father and spoke in a low voice. 'They're *tricks*,' he said.

'Oh I see,' said Andrew.

'I'm not a proper wizard,' sighed Toby. 'Not like Harry and Hermione.'

'Hermione?'

'I only *pretend*,' continued Toby. 'I'm probably just a Muggle, like you.'

'A Muggle.' Andrew wasn't sure whether he had heard correctly. 'I'm a Muggle?'

Toby looked at his father sadly and nodded.

By the time the taxi arrived at the restaurant, Andrew was baffled. If he had inferred correctly, Toby's most heartfelt wish was that his family wasn't actually his family; that there had been some administrative cockup, and that he was in fact a wizard (*not* a Muggle) who was patiently biding his time in north London while he waited to be summoned to join the eternal fight between Good and Evil. Andrew wondered whether he should feel put-out by all this. Then he remembered that when he was Toby's age, he wished that Rosa and Patrick would admit that they were just looking after him while his real parents, a beautiful king and queen, were off on unspecified business elsewhere.

Toby's eyes shone as they walked into the restaurant. 'Look, Daddy!' he cried, pointing at a wooden display case mounted on the wall. 'There's Headwig!'

Andrew peered at the case. A stuffed owl gazed impassively back at him. Without warning the owl's head did a brisk three-hundred-and-sixty-degree turn and then resumed its immobile pose. Toby clapped his hands and released an unguarded gurgle of delight. Suddenly he was a different boy. His small features were no longer squeezed into their usual mask of worried concern. Instead his face glowed with pleasure.

My God, thought Andrew, what a beautiful child.

Catherine was trying to persuade Florence to use her crayons to draw a picture rather than as a source of supplemental nourishment when the doorbell rang. She went to open the front door. Richard was standing on the doorstep. She stared at him dumbly for a moment, remembering the letter she had begun but never finished.

'Richard,' she breathed. 'It's you.'

'Yes,' agreed Richard irritably. 'It's me, and I'm soaking. Can I come in?'

'Of course.' Catherine stood back to allow Richard to pass her. 'Well,' she said. 'This is a surprise.'

Richard turned towards her. 'Is Andrew here?'

Catherine smiled and shook her head. 'He's taken Toby out for lunch.'

'Damn,' muttered Richard.

Catherine faltered slightly. 'Was it him you wanted to see?'

'We were hoping to see both of you.'

'We?'

The doorbell went again.

'Annabel's been parking the car,' explained Richard.

'The car,' said Catherine stupidly.

They looked at each other for a moment.

The bell went again. Catherine returned to the front door.

'Hello, Catherine.' Annabel swept into the house without the usual kiss of welcome. She looked at Richard. 'Where's Andrew?'

'He's taken Toby out to lunch,' Richard told her.

'Damn,' said Annabel. She and Richard exchanged looks.

'Well, look,' said Catherine anxiously, 'at least come downstairs.' Annabel and Richard followed her down to the kitchen. Florence had abandoned her crayons and was now sitting in the middle of the floor, scolding one of her dolls. Catherine recognised the piqued cadences of her daughter's diatribe. They were her own. 'Now,' she said with a breeziness she did not feel. 'Coffee? Tea? Something stronger?'

Richard waved the offer away. 'We won't be long.'

'We were really hoping Andrew would be here, too,' said Annabel.

'What's this about?' asked Catherine.

There was a small pause.

'We have some news,' said Annabel.

Catherine's stomach twisted in apprehension. 'Is it –? Are you two all right?'

'Us?' Annabel glanced at Richard. 'We're fine.'

'You're fine. That's good.' Catherine smiled brightly. 'Good for you.'

Annabel coughed. 'The thing is, Cathy, we're leaving.'

'Leaving?'

'We're off. Back to the States.'

Catherine stared at them uncomprehendingly.

'My brother has a place in upstate New York,' said Richard, avoiding her eye. 'He never uses it. We'll stay there while we look around for a house of our own.'

'You're going for *good*?'

'We think it's for the best,' said Annabel. She looked at her shoes.

'It'll be a fresh start,' said Richard. His words collided into Catherine with the destructive energy of a car crash. Richard was going away. For good. For a *fresh start*.

'But this is all so sudden!' cried Catherine.

'Yes, well,' said Annabel. 'There's really nothing keeping us here, is there?'

The words punctured her. Really nothing. 'So, so *wow*. This is incredible.' Catherine squeezed out a smile. 'When do you think you'll go?'

Richard's arm crept around Annabel's waist. 'The tickets are booked. Heathrow to Newark. First class. One way. Next week.'

'Next *week*?'

'No time,' said Annabel quietly, 'like the present.'

206

The speed of the desertion felt like a slap in the face. What were they running from? 'But what about my party?' blurted Catherine.

'What party?' said Richard.

'My birthday party,' said Catherine. 'You *know*.'

'Your birthday's next month, isn't it?' said Annabel.

'Yes, and Andrew's told me about your –'

'We can't possibly come back for a party,' interrupted Richard brusquely. 'There'll be so much to do. We'll just be finding our feet.'

'Richard, listen to me. There's no need to pretend. Andrew's already told me.'

'Told you what?'

'About the surprise party you're planning.'

Richard blinked. 'He told you we were doing that?'

She smiled. 'Not his fault. He's putty in my hands. I can wheedle anything out of him.'

Annabel turned to Richard. 'Why would he do that?' she asked. 'Why would he tell her that?'

Catherine sighed. 'I suppose it's all academic now. You'll be long gone by then.'

Richard frowned. 'Sorry, Cathy. I don't have the faintest idea what you're talking about.'

There was a strained silence. 'If you've got to go,' said Catherine finally, 'then you've got to go.'

Annabel looked at her watch. 'Anyway, we should be getting on.'

Florence wandered up and tugged at Catherine's fingers. 'Mummy,' she said.

Catherine bent down and picked Florence up. She held her close, like a shield. 'Will we see you again before you go?'

'There's so much to do,' said Richard.

'I see. Of course.'

'Be sure to tell Andrew we're sorry we missed him,' said Annabel.

'I will. And once you're settled in, we'll come over and visit.'

'That,' said Annabel faintly, 'would be *great*.'

They walked up the stairs to the front door in silence. At the door Richard and Annabel turned to face Catherine.

'Goodbye, then,' said Richard. He opened the door. It was still raining.

'Do you want an umbrella?' said Catherine helplessly, not wanting to let them go. 'We've got loads.'

'No, thanks, that's all right. We'll make a run for it,' said Richard, turning up the collar of his coat. He put his arm around Annabel and they stepped out into the downpour, shoulders hunched against the rain. Catherine watched as they scuttled down the street together. They did not look back.

Catherine shut the front door and leaned against the wall, holding her daughter tightly.

Florence kissed her glistening cheek.

The wizard approached their table. His thick ponytail emerged from the back of his black pointed hat. Toby watched him intently, anxiously fingering a silk handkerchief.

'What can I get you?' yawned the wizard, extracting a pad of paper from the folds of his cloak.

Andrew picked up the menu. 'Two helpings of fried bats' brains, please.'

'Two bats' brains,' said the wizard. 'OK.'

'And then one sorcerer's sausage sandwich, and one of Hermione's heroic hamburgers.'

'D'you want owl droppings with both of those?'

Andrew wrinkled his nose. 'Yes please.'

'And some magic mushrooms,' added Toby.

208

'Magic mushrooms. OK. And to drink?'

'One purple Potter potion and a black coffee.'

Just as the wizard was turning to go, Toby said, 'Excuse me.'

The wizard stopped and looked at him. Andrew suspected that the wizard might be a little hungover. 'Yes?'

Toby shifted to the edge of his seat. 'Can I show you something?' Andrew watched as his son began to wave his silk handkerchief in the air. A pit of anxiety had been yawning within him since Toby had explained his plan, a few minutes previously.

With careful deliberation, Toby poked the silk handkerchief into his small fist. He nodded to Andrew, who handed Toby his wand. Toby gravely waved the wand over his closed fist. 'And now, hey presto!' cried Toby. He opened his fist. The silk handkerchief had disappeared.

There was a moment's silence.

'Good, isn't it?' prompted Andrew.

The wizard finally understood, and started to nod. 'Very good,' he said. 'Very *very* good, in fact.'

'Good enough to be accepted at Hogwarts?' asked Toby querulously. His voice, pitched high with hope, sliced Andrew open, unpacked and reassembled him in a slightly different configuration. Inside him something shifted, then clicked neatly into place.

'Hogwarts?' said the wizard.

'I know I *look* like a Muggle,' whispered Toby to the wizard, 'but I might not be.' He pointed at Andrew. 'He's not my real dad,' he explained.

'*Toby,*' said Andrew, as his heart flooded with a ferocious love.

'Probably,' qualified Toby reluctantly.

'OK,' said the wizard, glancing uncertainly between the two of them.

'So what do you think?' asked Toby. 'Could I be accepted at Hogwarts?'

'He stands a pretty good chance, wouldn't you say?' said Andrew, calculating exactly what he would do if this idiot demolished his son's dreams with a careless remark.

'Oh yes, I should say so,' replied the wizard, anxiously scratching his ponytail.

'There you go, Toby,' said Andrew. He gave the wizard a sardonic look. 'Thanks very much.'

The wizard escaped.

Toby grinned at his father. 'He said a pretty good chance.'

'He did,' agreed Andrew. Richard Sulzman had been right after all, he thought. Sciamachy, that was his problem. Andrew had always obliquely considered himself pitted in intractable combat against his son. He had come to believe that Toby's sole purpose in life was to thwart Andrew's dreams and schemes. But now he saw that they were allies, playing for the same side. He looked at the precious, vulnerable little boy on the other side of the table. After so many years of steering well away from the rocky promontories of excessive sentiment, Andrew promptly switched course.

'I must keep practising,' mused Toby, and Andrew suddenly understood why he spent so much time in his bedroom rehearsing his magic tricks. Like a prisoner digging a tunnel with a stolen teaspoon, Toby had been patiently and methodically preparing his escape.

'Well, whether you're a Muggle or not, I think you're great,' said Andrew.

'Thanks, Dad.'

'I'm sorry I missed your play yesterday.'

'That's all right.'

There was a pause.

'Are you looking forward to the holidays?' asked Andrew,

who was suddenly desperate to discover what Toby thought about everything.

'I suppose.' Toby thought. 'Although it would be more fun if I had a gun.' This morning at breakfast Toby had used his teeth to fashion a revolver out of a piece of wholemeal toast. He had shot Catherine in the head at point-blank range, and then turned the gun on himself.

Andrew's defences had been decimated by the unexpected tidal wave of affection which had washed over him moments before. He wasn't going to do anything which might sour this moment of grace. Father and son, together again for the first time! 'All right,' he said. 'You can have a gun.'

Toby's eyes widened in surprise. 'Really?'

'Really.'

'*Brilliant*,' breathed Toby.

Andrew smiled. The look on Toby's face was worth every retribution which Catherine would exact upon him for veering so catastrophically off-message.

'How have things been at home?' asked Andrew.

'All right, I suppose,' said Toby quietly.

'Don't you like having Mummy to look after you?'

Toby looked at his father for a moment, and then shook his head, almost imperceptibly.

'No? Why not?'

A pained look passed across Toby's face. 'She's not as good at it as Sinead.'

Sinead. A jolt of residual guilt and disquiet. What the hell had *happened* to her? 'Well, give her time. She's out of practice.'

'Plus she's gone all *weird*.'

Andrew looked at his son. 'Weird?'

'She just seems sad.' Toby stared at the table. 'She doesn't laugh much any more.'

Toby was right, realised Andrew. Catherine didn't laugh

much any more. She hadn't, he reflected, had much to laugh about.

Andrew ruffled his son's hair. 'Tell you what.'

'What?'

'Mummy's going to be fine.'

A hopeful smile. 'Really?'

'I promise. All right?'

Toby nodded gratefully. Andrew was startled by his son's unquestioning faith in him. Daddy said it was OK, so it was OK. Crisis over. Stand down the troops.

What had he done to deserve such trust?

The rain was causing problems.

Catherine and Florence were in the sitting room. Florence was restless. She needed to run around outside and burn off some of her excess energy, but the downpour was torrential and relentless. In the last two hours Catherine had exhausted every tune, every nursery rhyme, and every game she could think of. Florence had suffered her mother's attempts to entertain her with a lofty disdain, but now she was threatening a monumental tantrum. She was systematically dropping every piece of a wooden jigsaw puzzle down the back of the sofa, depositing each piece out of reach with grim purpose and no apparent pleasure. As she worked she emitted occasional squawks of furious disapproval, at what, Catherine was not sure. Her, probably. She sat on the piano stool and peered out of the window at the rain-lashed street.

So Richard was going, and he was taking Annabel with him for good measure. Neither of them had been able to look her in the eye. They were obviously hiding something. She could not imagine why they had pretended not to know about her surprise party. Perhaps they were simply embarrassed. Still, their awkward dissembling hurt almost as much as their decision to leave.

212

Sinead, Richard, Annabel. Soon there would be nobody left – nobody but her, Andrew, and the children.

The last piece of the jigsaw had now disappeared behind the sofa. Florence stood expectantly in front of her mother.

'What do you want to do now, darling?' asked Catherine heavily.

'Thomas video,' said Florence.

Soon Florence's angry hyperactivity had been punctured by the narcotic balm of Thomas the Tank Engine. She sat in rapt attention in front of the kitchen television, sucking her fingers. Catherine watched from the door. In ten minutes, Florence didn't blink.

The doorbell rang again.

Patrick stood on the porch, holding his hat. It was scarcely recognisable from the spruce item he had been wearing that morning. Now its darkened brim drooped, heavy with rain.

'Patrick! What's happened?'

'They've abandoned play for the day,' said Patrick. 'Waterlogged pitch.'

'Oh no,' sighed Catherine. 'How rotten for you. Come on, let me get you something hot and we can see about warming you up.'

Soon they were sipping tea at the kitchen table, watching Florence's unmoving form on the other side of the room. Catherine remembered Andrew's remark about his father and religion a few nights ago. *He's the expert.*

'Can I ask you a question?' she said.

'Of course.'

'Your faith. When did you – how did it come about?'

Patrick thought for a moment. 'I don't know, to be honest. It's always been there, really. There was no dazzling flash of enlightenment, if that's what you're asking me.'

'Oh,' said Catherine, disappointed.

'I'm not sure those sorts of things happen very often, to

tell you the truth. I mean, sometimes you hear about them. You know, a man misses his flight and the plane crashes into the side of a mountain, something like that. He gets a spiritual wake-up call. But I don't think that's really God's style, by and large. He prefers the softly-softly approach.'

'And how does that work?'

'Well, it's probably different for everyone. But say there's a small glimmer of faith within you. Little by little, and with some careful attention, that glimmer will grow stronger and brighter. Of course, to begin with you're sceptical, resistant to it. Who wouldn't be? But if you give that glimmer a chance, then it can develop into something wonderful.' Patrick nodded towards the garden. 'Faith is like your orchids, Cathy. It needs constant vigilance. And you might need a great deal of patience before you're rewarded with a full bloom.' He paused. 'Am I allowed to ask why?'

Catherine shifted in her seat. 'I'm just curious, that's all.'

'Just curious.'

'I don't know.' Catherine ran the tip of her finger around the rim of her mug. 'Stuff happens, sometimes, and you find yourself asking why.'

'Of course you do.'

'And so here I am, I suppose, asking why.'

'What's happened?'

She wasn't ready to tell anyone else about the angel, not yet. Not even Patrick. 'Let's just say I had my own plane that crashed into the side of a mountain.'

Patrick's eyebrows rose. '*Really*.'

'Now, you know me,' said Catherine. 'I've never been one for this sort of stuff.' Patrick inclined his head. 'But recently I've been wondering whether – heavens, I don't know how to put it.'

'Whether someone's trying to tell you something?'

'Sounds ridiculous when you say it out loud.'

'Not necessarily.'

'It sounds ridiculous to *me*.'

'I suppose – well, I don't want to discourage you, but perhaps sometimes it's easy to confuse divine intervention with simple good luck.'

'That's exactly my point,' said Catherine. 'How are you supposed to tell the difference?'

'I have no idea,' admitted Patrick. 'I suppose if whatever has happened has prompted you to turn towards God, then perhaps that's a clue.'

'But that's rather circular, isn't it? You're confusing cause and effect.'

'You're right, I am. But I don't know what else to suggest. What I *do* know is that we can't attribute *every*thing that happens to God. I mean, he may be omnipotent, but that doesn't mean you should take every bit of bad luck personally. Otherwise I'd be worried about what He had against me, what with the cricket and all this rain.'

'Forgive me, Patrick, but this was a bit more than the *weather*.'

'I'm sure it was,' said Patrick mildly. 'I'm just saying that most of what happens is probably *not* the Almighty interfering with things directly. Like I said, that's not the way He tends to go about things.'

'You think I'm imagining things.'

'Cathy, my sweet. How can I, when you haven't even told me what's happened?'

Catherine was silent.

'Do you want my advice?' said Patrick.

'I don't know,' replied Catherine.

'All right, then,' said Patrick. 'Since you've asked so graciously. There's only one way to find out whether what you're feeling, or think you might be feeling, is the real thing or not.'

'And what's that?'

'Simple. Grow your glimmer. Do your horticulture. Nurture, protect. Give it the best possible chance of survival. Then see what happens. After all, if you don't try then you'll never know.'

'Huh. And what's the best way of growing my glimmer?'

'Ah,' said Patrick. 'That's easy.' He smiled at her. 'You go to church.'

FIFTEEN

'That,' declared Toby, 'was the best burger I've ever eaten in my whole *life*.'

'Glad to hear it,' said Andrew. He had hardly tasted his fried bats' brains and sorcerer's sausage sandwich, or the accompanying owl droppings.

'Thanks for bringing me here, Daddy,' said Toby. 'It's completely brilliant.'

Andrew smiled at his son, and another horizon on his emotional landscape came into view. The well of unrefined love which had been lying undetected within him for so long was gushing unstoppably now. As it burst to the surface it caught the light in a dazzling rainbow of truth. The picture was finally clear. Andrew looked on, drinking in the view: he saw, at last, his family – that messy agglomeration of lives lived in the inescapable orbit of others, the entangled strands of hope and history which weave back and forth across generations. At last, he recognised the irresistible pull of his own. Like a satellite launched towards a distant planet, his mother's love had finally reached its target. Now, as Toby moved his straw around the bottom of his glass, noisily hoovering up the last of his drink, Rosa's legacy presented itself. Andrew was suddenly aware of his son's ability to unlock his happiness with a careless smile, and he knew that there was nothing more important in the world. And this astonishing alchemy extended to Florence, too. The interminable guilt of that sabotaged contraceptive had vanished like one of Toby's conjuring tricks, displaced by a rush of adoration. Andrew felt giddy with love.

But in the shadows cast by the brilliance of his new-found devotion lurked a reciprocal terror. He knew that he could never protect his children against the perils which swept through the world. His impotence smashed into his chest as he foresaw a future hemmed in by a litany of menace. A thousand drunk drivers careening along the roads, the suicidal mutation of human cells, the sinister tick of the terrorist's bomb – Andrew was powerless against them all. He would never sleep again. Danger would lurk in the dark of every unbroken morning. A life of unyielding worry scuttled in.

Andrew blinked back tears of happiness.

'Daddy,' said Toby, 'are teenagers true?'

'Yes, Toby, they are. All too true.'

'Will I be one?'

'I'm afraid so.'

Toby sighed. 'I don't want to be a teenager.'

'It's still a long way away.'

'*Six years*,' said Toby.

'Being a teenager is fun, actually,' said Andrew. He remembered his own awkward stumbling towards adulthood. The orthodontic braces. The acne. Being egged on by his mother to talk to girls. Oh yes, enormous fun. Poor Toby, he thought. He was too brittle for the cruel indignities of adolescence. 'Just you wait. You'll have a great time.'

Toby looked far from convinced. 'James Macintyre says that when he's a teenager he's going to get a motorbike and a leather jacket.'

'Then what will he do?'

Toby's shoulders shot up and down in an unconvincing display of indifference. 'He says he's going to have lots of girlfriends,' said Toby hollowly.

'Huh. And what do you think about that?'

'I think he's showing off. He's an idiot.'

Andrew frowned. 'I thought James Macintyre was one of your friends.'

Toby paused, and then shook his head. 'He doesn't like me much, I don't think.'

'But you like him,' said Andrew.

'Not really, no,' said Toby.

'Oh. I thought you liked him.'

'Well, it's not really about whether I *like* him or not,' explained Toby. 'I just want to be his friend.'

'There's a difference?'

Toby looked at his father.

'OK, so there's a difference,' said Andrew, numbed by this playground *realpolitik*. 'But why do you want to be James Macintyre's friend in particular?'

'He's the leader,' said Toby.

'Of what?'

'Our gang.'

'You're in a *gang*?'

'Daddy,' said Toby patiently, '*everyone's* in a gang.'

'*I'm* not in a gang,' said Andrew.

Toby looked at his father sympathetically.

'All right,' sighed Andrew. 'But I still don't see why it's so important that you're friends with him. I mean, there must be *other* gangs, surely?'

'But if *he's* my friend, then everyone else will be my friend, too.'

'Toby –' Andrew stopped, hamstrung by a debilitating rush of sorrowful affection, tongue-tied by the urge to impart

219

some paternal wisdom, to pass on some hard-earned know-ledge. This, it occurred to him, was what fathers had been doing since time began. The thought filled him with a guilty disquiet. Better late than never, he told himself. 'Toby, look. You shouldn't pretend to be friends with someone you don't like just because you think it will make you more popular.'

'Why not?'

'Ah. Well.' Andrew stopped, lost for words. 'You see —'

'Are you all finished here?'

To Andrew's relief, the wizard with the ponytail had re-appeared at their table to take away their plates. Toby ordered some Weasley Waffles for pudding while Andrew tried to marshal his thoughts. In the past he had avoided Toby's awkward questions by discouraging intimacies and keeping his distance. But all that was going to change now. There would be no more dodging of difficult issues, no more ab-negation of his responsibilities. Toby needed his father.

Andrew's chest filled with pride and fear.

An hour later, Toby climbed out of the taxi and waited on the pavement for Andrew to pay the fare. 'Thanks, Daddy,' he said. He took Andrew's hand as they walked up to the front door. Andrew was momentarily unable to speak. He fumbled for his keys.

'Maybe we can do some other stuff together,' he said eventually. 'What do you think about that?'

'That would be nice,' said Toby as they stepped inside.

'How about a game of football? We could go up to Highbury Fields and have a kick around.'

'Actually,' said Toby, 'I don't really like —'

'There's an old ball around here somewhere. It's probably downstairs. Shall I go and look?'

Toby stood frozen in the middle of the hall. 'You want to go and play *now*?'

'Why not?' Andrew mimed kicking a football. 'It'll be fun.'

'But Daddy,' said Toby, 'it's *raining*.'

'Hello, you two,' said Catherine, coming up the stairs from the kitchen. 'How was lunch?'

'Lunch was *great*,' said Andrew. 'And now we're off for a game of football.'

'But Andrew,' said Catherine, 'it's *raining*.'

'A bit of rain never hurt anyone, did it?' Andrew didn't care about the rain. He just wanted to play football with his son, the way fathers do.

'Why don't you wait until the weather improves a bit?' said Catherine. Andrew recognised her tone of voice. It was the one she used for similar negotiations with Toby. 'Then you can play as much football as you like.'

'Actually,' piped up Toby, 'I don't really like –'

'All right, all right,' said Andrew, holding up his hands in defeat. 'We'll skip the football. What shall we do instead?'

'Instead?' said Toby.

Andrew rubbed his hands together. 'Do you fancy another game of Scrabble?'

Toby took a step backwards. 'I thought I might go and do a bit of practice, actually.'

'Don't you want to do something together?' asked Andrew.

Toby's face was pained. 'If you like.'

Andrew's heart melted all over again.

'Don't worry,' he said. 'You go upstairs. We can do all that stuff some other time.' He paused. 'We had fun today, didn't we, Toby?'

Toby turned back towards his father, one hand on the banister. 'It was wicked, Daddy.' He flashed a smile and then continued up the stairs. Andrew stood in the middle of the hall.

'Are you all right?' asked Catherine, who was watching him.

'Hmm? Oh yes, quite all right.' He turned to his wife and smiled. 'Where's Florence?'

'She's in the kitchen with Patrick. He's been here for most of the afternoon. The cricket was abandoned hours ago.'

'Oh no. The rain. Poor Dad.'

'He's being very stoical about it. The forecast is better for tomorrow, he says, so all is not lost.'

'I'll go and see him,' said Andrew.

Patrick was kneeling in the middle of the kitchen floor, watching Florence crawl around the room. She was yapping loudly.

'Andrew, thank goodness,' said Patrick, getting stiffly to his feet. 'My knees are killing me.'

'What are you doing?' asked Andrew.

'Grandpa be a dog, a dog!' cried Florence.

Patrick looked wryly at Andrew. 'There's your answer.'

'Grandpa be a dog!'

'Sorry, Florence, not any more. I'm too old for that game,' said Patrick, brushing down his trousers. 'Perhaps Daddy will play with you instead.'

Florence did not show the slightest rancour. 'Daddy be a dog!' she yelled.

Andrew dropped to his knees and let out a high-pitched bark. Florence was so surprised that she sat back on her haunches and stared at him. Andrew barked again. Florence giggled. Then Andrew released a torrent of joyful yips, glee-fully shaking his head from side to side and pawing at the kitchen floor with his hand, swept along by his own yodel of happiness. Soon his barks were joined by Florence's delighted laughter. After a while she crawled across the kitchen floor towards Andrew. She patted him softly on the head, so gently that he could only just feel her tiny fingers through his hair.

'Good dog,' she whispered.

One thing was for sure. Andrew was not leaving, not now.

Catherine had followed Andrew back down to the kitchen. She watched from the door as he shook his bottom in the air, wagging an invisible tail. She decided not to tell him about Richard and Annabel's imminent departure, not yet.

Richard and Annabel were leaving! Catherine felt lost, abandoned, drifting helplessly towards unspecified disaster with no means of saving herself. And now she had a new problem: this sticky business of *church*.

Since her conversation with Patrick earlier in the afternoon, Catherine had been warily circling the idea. The very notion seemed absurd. There was something vaguely feudal about the whole idea of attending a church service – she imagined the local populace congregating for worship, doffing their caps and humbly offering up their tithes. But to her consternation, Patrick's suggestion had actually made perfect sense. There was nowhere better to discover whether she was experiencing a genuine religious conversion, or merely an excess of pagan superstition. Perhaps she would try and grow her glimmer. This was eternal life they were talking about, after all. It had to be worth at least making a *bit* of an effort.

Still, Catherine wasn't looking forward to broaching the subject with Andrew. She could hear his scornful disbelief. She could see the disdain on his face. She could feel the sarcasm raining down, relentless, pummelling her resolve.

She sighed. Everything seemed to be coming unstuck. She wondered how much the trip to church was just a desperate search for some glue.

The rest of the afternoon slowly unwound. Outside the rain was relentless.

Florence and Andrew chased each other up and down the stairs on their hands and knees. Andrew sat on the floor of Florence's bedroom and watched as she harangued her dolls, a tiny sergeant major. She arranged and rearranged the dolls as she hectored them, her hands a furious blur. Andrew was utterly charmed by her strident bossiness. As he watched her play, a vast weight lifted from between his shoulder blades. Only now did Andrew understand that his daughter had long since spiralled away from the dark secret of her conception. Burdened by guilt, he had never been able to frame Florence in any context other than that of his crime. But she was so much more than that! She fizzed with boundless energy, brimful of mischief and laughter. Florence had effortlessly freed herself from whatever tawdry biological reality had brought her into the world. Andrew looked on, transfixed by the spectacle of this independent flowering. There was so much about her that he still had to discover. As she marshalled her gingham-clad troops, he considered the journey which lay ahead of him. He could not wait to begin.

So he was going to stay, after all. As he watched Florence play, he realised that no matter how far apart he and Catherine had drifted, it was time to forgive and forget.

This, though, brought him up short. He realised that there was nothing to forgive Catherine *for*. In the end there had been no sign of Annabel's bracelet in her jewellery box. It had been Andrew who had been unable to trust his own wife, Andrew who had flirted with Clara, Andrew who had bounced the au pair up and down in his lap. The only person who needed to be forgiven was him. The shadowy aggregate of Andrew's failures and betrayals skewered him with silent accusation, and at once he resolved to redeem himself. There was to be no more self-pity, no more mournful introspection. Instead he would do everything he could to reconnect their fractured lives. And anyway, he thought, if he could suddenly discover new happiness with his children, who was to say he couldn't perform a similar trick with his wife? A galaxy of possibilities soon began to twinkle in his imagination. They could take a trip to Venice, just the two of them, and drink Bellinis on the terrace of the Cipriani, the southern shore of the city glowing pink in the twilight. Or they could visit Manhattan. The Four Seasons, perhaps. Andrew imagined himself arm in arm with Catherine, strolling down Fifth Avenue, glamorous, cosmopolitan lovers once more. All of a sudden the world burst with fragrant possibility.

Andrew played with Florence for the rest of the afternoon. He submitted willingly to all of her demands. He fed, he undressed, he bathed, he dressed again. Florence accepted her father's sudden attention with regal detachment, as if it were no more than her due. From time to time Catherine looked in on them, an unreadable look on her face. At Florence's insistence, Andrew read the same bedtime story five times. With each reading her eyelids grew heavier. Finally he bent down to kiss her good-night. She turned sleepily away from him and without a word subsided into stillness.

He closed the bedroom door, euphoric.

Catherine had made lasagne for dinner. It was burnt, but only slightly. She dished up enormous platefuls of it and passed the food around the table.

'This looks delicious,' said Patrick, peering at his plate.

Catherine took a sip of wine. 'It's an old family recipe.'

'The best sort,' said Patrick, nodding. He put a forkful into his mouth and began to chew thoughtfully.

'So, Toby, we've hardly seen you all afternoon,' said Catherine brightly. 'How was the Harry Potter Café?'

'Completely brilliant,' said Toby, glancing gratefully at Andrew. Catherine felt a small twinge of resentment. *It was*

225

my idea, she wanted to remind him. 'I showed the wizard my trick,' continued Toby.

'And he liked it, didn't he?' said Andrew.

Toby nodded. 'He said I had a good chance of getting into Hogwarts. If, you know, I'm not a Muggle.'

'A Muggle?' said Catherine.

Long story, mouthed Andrew.

Catherine saw Andrew's eyes drift towards Toby. There was a warm fondness in his gaze which Catherine had not seen before. She watched him, curious. First he had spent all afternoon playing with Florence, which was unheard of, and now this.

'Well, I have some news,' she said. 'Or I suppose you might say it's more a sort of request.'

'This sounds interesting,' said Andrew.

She took a deep breath. 'I want us to go to church tomorrow morning.'

Silence.

'Really?' said Andrew.

'*Church*?' said Toby.

Patrick coughed. 'Actually, Catherine –'

'All I'm asking is that we give it a go, that's all. I know it's not something we've done before, but you should try everything once, don't you think?'

'Is this to do with that conversation we had last week?' asked Andrew. 'All that stuff about grander schemes?'

'Yes,' said Catherine, steeling herself. 'It is.'

Andrew grinned. 'You see? I *told* you it was to do with religion.'

She looked at her husband, too surprised to speak.

'Which church?' asked Toby.

'Actually, Catherine,' said Patrick, 'when I suggested church, I meant you should go on your own, not with the whole family.'

226

'What?' said Catherine. 'Why?'

'Well, you're there to talk to God, after all. It won't be easy if you have to wipe Florence's nose every ten seconds.'

'Nonsense,' said Catherine. 'We're all in this together.'

'All in *what* together?' asked Andrew, putting down his fork and looking between Catherine and Patrick. 'What have the two of you been cooking up?'

'Nothing,' said Catherine. Andrew raised a sardonic eyebrow. 'I just thought we should go to church, that's all.'

'Well, yes, I gathered that much,' said Andrew. 'My question is, why?'

'Oh.' Catherine paused. 'I feel that sometimes we drift along, without bothering to question why we're here. A lot of big questions go unanswered.'

'Which church?' asked Toby.

'Oh, I see,' said Andrew. 'And you think that going to church is going to give us instant spiritual salvation.'

Catherine shrugged. 'I don't know. Perhaps not. But it must be worth a try, surely?'

They sat around the table in silence.

'All right, then,' said Andrew.

'What?' asked Catherine.

Andrew leaned back in his chair. 'Let's do it. Let's go to church.'

'Are you sure?' said Patrick.

'Why not? I'm game. I'll try anything once.'

'Heavens, Andrew, I don't know what to say.' Catherine smiled anxiously at him. 'Thank you.'

'Will someone *please* tell me which church we're going to?' whined Toby.

Catherine turned towards him. She had been too worried about Andrew's reaction to consider the rest of her plan in any detail. She thought furiously, trying to remember where the nearest church was. 'The one with the blue door,' she said. 'You know. A couple of streets away.'

Toby swallowed. 'St Andrew's?'

'That's right,' said Catherine. 'St Andrew's.'

'Well, I approve of the name, at least,' said Andrew. 'As long as you realise that I know nothing about any of this stuff. I'm no good on ecclesiastical etiquette, you know. I'll probably embarrass you terribly. Try and snog the organist, that sort of thing.'

'You'll show us the ropes, won't you Patrick?' asked Catherine.

Patrick put his hands up. 'Oh, I'd love to, obviously. But the game starts at eleven. I don't want to miss a ball, especially after today's disaster.'

Catherine stared at him. 'You're not – but won't it rain again?'

Patrick smiled affably at her. 'Let's hope not.'

There was a long sob from the other end of the table. Toby was holding his head in his hands.

'Toby? What is it?'

He looked up. His face was smudged with tears. 'I don't want to go.'

'Why ever not?' asked Catherine, shocked.

'You wouldn't understand,' mumbled Toby, his words half-swallowed by another choking sob.

'Toby, if you don't actually give us a reason, how are we supposed –'

'I've just remembered,' said Toby, rubbing his eyes with the back of his fists, 'I'm busy tomorrow morning.'

'Oh really,' said Catherine flatly.

He nodded. 'I have to do a thing.' He paused. 'A thing for school.'

'School broke up yesterday,' Catherine reminded him. 'It's the holidays now.'

228

Toby was silent for a moment as he considered this, his small face pinched with tension.

'Come on, Toby, one church service won't kill you,' said Catherine.

'But you don't *understand*,' cried Toby. He slipped off his chair and ran out of the kitchen. His footsteps thumped angrily up the stairs. Seconds later his bedroom door slammed shut with a reproachful thump. Andrew, Catherine and Patrick looked at each other.

'Do you think you should make him go, if he really doesn't want to?' asked Andrew.

'But he hasn't said *why*,' complained Catherine.

'Perhaps he's inherited his grandmother's aversion to religion,' said Patrick with a sigh.

'Dad, he's seven years old,' said Andrew. 'When he runs out of the room in tears, it's not because of theological reservations.'

Catherine stared at Toby's abandoned plate, still full of food. 'Perhaps he just didn't want to eat my lasagne,' she mused.

To her disappointment, neither Andrew nor Patrick disputed the possibility.

SIXTEEN

'Toby!'

Silence.

'Come on, Toby. We're going to be late!'

There was a shrill blast of petulance from the top of the stairs: 'I'm not going!'

Andrew watched Catherine as she shifted Florence from one hip to the other. She was wearing a floral dress and flat beige pumps. She had scraped her hair off her face; it was being kept in place by a faded old hair band. She wasn't wearing any make-up. She looked as if she were going to court, not church. 'Of course you are,' she called. 'Come on. It'll be fun.'

'No way is this going to be *fun*,' shouted Toby.

Andrew fingered the knot of his tie. 'Shall I try and lure him down?'

'Don't lure him,' muttered Catherine. '*Threaten* him. We're already late.'

Andrew started up the stairs, relieved to escape. Catherine had become increasingly agitated as the morning had gone on. She had changed her own outfit three times, and Florence's twice. Now, with their departure imminent, the faint shade of impending hysteria had crept into her voice, and she looked ready to punch someone. Andrew did not want it to be him.

It was all rather perplexing. Catherine did not appear to be looking forward to this morning's expedition to church any more than the rest of the family. Perhaps, reflected Andrew, he should have put up more of a fight last night, but he had been caught with his guard down, still dreaming of long weekends in New York. Besides, his instinct for confrontation had been blunted by his wondrous afternoon with the children. He hadn't felt inclined to spoil his good mood by wading into an unwinnable argument.

Still, Catherine's suggestion about church *had* dented his spirits a little. This bewildering new interest in religion was just another manifestation of her disconnection with her old self, and fuelled Andrew's lingering disquiet. Who *was* this woman he was planning to fall in love with all over again? But he had hidden his reservations and had cheerfully agreed. If there were to be no Bellinis without a slug of communion wine first, then he could live with that.

Now, though, he was wondering whether this was really such a good idea.

Andrew knocked on Toby's bedroom door.

Silence.

'Toby, it's *me*,' said Andrew through the door.

'Go *away*,' said Toby after a moment.

Andrew felt a little bit of himself break off, lost for ever in the tiny cracks of casual heartbreak.

'Look, Toby, you've never *been* to church before,' said Andrew, trying to sound reasonable. 'So how can you possibly know whether or not it's going to be fun?'

'I just *do*.'

'What sort of an answer is that?'

'You wouldn't understand.'

Andrew opened the door. Toby was lying on his bed, playing with a hand-held computer game. He didn't look up as his father came into the room. 'Maybe I would,' said Andrew. Toby snorted and the computer game simultaneously emitted a short raspberry, a double-barrelled blast of contempt. Andrew sat down on the end of the bed. 'Good game?'

'I'm on level four.' Toby's thumbs were a blur as they pounded the plastic buttons.

'Is that good?'

'It's all right. James Macintyre got to level seven. He got the extra pineapple which sits behind the castle, though, and that gives you two more booster things, and an extra life. It was completely fluky. So it hardly counts.' Toby's eyes narrowed in concentration as he spoke.

'Listen, Toby,' said Andrew. 'If you told me *why* you don't want to go to church, then maybe I could help.'

'It's complicated,' said Toby.

'Is it to do with God?'

'God,' muttered Toby. 'I'm fed up with *God*.'

'What's wrong with God?' asked Andrew, genuinely curious.

'We have Divinity, with Mr Cole? Stories from the Bible and stuff like that? It's so *boring*.'

'Your grandmother felt the same way,' said Andrew. He leaned forward. 'Have you learned about the disciples yet?'

Toby nodded, still not taking his eyes off the small screen in front of him.

'Well, Grandma always said that there was actually another disciple, who nobody ever talked about. The thirteenth. And this guy was a bit of a villain, you know, always up to no good. He used to play tricks on the other disciples. Fed their donkeys beans to make them fart, that sort of thing. So they

232

kept quiet about him. Didn't want the bad publicity. That's why he doesn't appear in the Bible.' Andrew paused. 'He was called Frank. Frank the Disciple.'

A small grin.

'Grandma used to go on and on about him,' said Andrew. 'It used to drive Grandpa *mad*.'

There was a volley of electronic blips. 'Oh *rats*,' sighed Toby. For the first time, he looked up at Andrew. 'What was she like, Daddy?' he asked.

'Grandma?' Andrew paused. 'She was amazing, Toby. A force of nature. She swept through people's lives like – like a breath of fresh air, I suppose. Everyone she met, she touched. Nobody ever forgot her.'

'I'd like to be like that.'

'I think we'd all like to be like that,' agreed Andrew sadly.

'I wish I could have met her.'

'So do I, Toby, so do I. She would have loved you. More than you could imagine.'

'And she didn't like God, either.'

'You could say that.'

'She sounds nice.'

Andrew could feel the hot squeeze of unshed tears behind his eyes. He looked away. 'You still haven't told me why you don't want to go to church,' he said after a moment.

'No,' agreed Toby.

'It's nothing to do with God, is it?'

'No,' said Toby. 'It's not.'

A pause.

'Well, all right,' said Andrew. 'But even if you won't tell me, you've still got to come. We're all waiting for you down-stairs.'

'But I *really* don't want to go.'

'I know you don't. But we all have to do stuff we don't want to do from time to time. That's life, I'm afraid.'

233

'You don't want to go either, do you?' said Toby after a moment.

With a thrill Andrew realised he was about to tell his son the truth. 'Not especially, no,' he said. 'But it's important to Mummy, so I'm going to go anyway.' He ruffled Toby's hair.

'*Hachayim, ze lo picnic*,' said Toby.

Andrew looked at him. 'Grandpa?'

Toby nodded.

'What does it mean?'

'It means, I don't know, Life's Tough.'

'Well, you know what? Grandpa's right. Life *is* tough. And the good guys get through the tough stuff.' He held out his hand. 'Come on. It'll be you and me. We'll get through the tough stuff together. Keep each other company on the way. *Hachayim* – what was it again?'

'*Hachayim, ze lo picnic*.'

Andrew snapped his fingers. 'Picnic. Right.'

Toby clambered off the bed.

'At last,' sighed Catherine.

Toby came down the stairs first, followed by Andrew, who was beaming at her over Toby's head, doing a thumbs-up sign. Florence squirmed in Catherine's arms.

'Duncan,' said Florence.

'Come on Toby,' said Catherine. 'For heaven's sake. We're *so* late. Get your jacket on. Chop chop.'

'Success,' whispered Andrew as he reached the bottom of the stairs.

'What was the problem?'

Andrew shrugged. 'I don't know.'

She stared at him. 'What do you mean?'

'I asked, he wouldn't tell me, we chatted about some stuff, and he came downstairs. End of story.'

234

'My God, Andrew. How could you manage *not* to find out what the problem was?'

'Duncan,' shouted Florence.

'He didn't want to tell me,' said Andrew. 'What was I supposed to do? Torture it out of him?'

'Oh, don't be so melodramatic,' sighed Catherine. 'Good grief. You could have sat up there all morning and you *still* wouldn't be any the wiser.'

'Your point being?'

'My point being that you have *no* idea how to talk to your children.' At once Catherine knew that she had gone too far. She bit back the words, too late, too late.

'He's here, isn't he?' said Andrew stiffly. 'That's the important thing.'

'You don't think the *important* thing might be to find out why he's so upset at the prospect of going to church?'

'You just told me to get him downstairs as quickly as possible,' said Andrew.

'I know I did. I just would have thought –'

'*Duncan*,' shrieked Florence, prodding Catherine viciously under her armpit.

'Oh, Florence, all *right*. Where's Duncan?' Florence pointed towards the stairs just as Toby appeared. 'Toby, pop down to the kitchen and fetch Florence's dinosaur.'

'Why?' said Toby.

'Because I'm *asking* you to,' said Catherine, who could feel her composure slipping away with every passing second that they remained in the house.

'No, I mean why does she need her dinosaur in church?'

Catherine shut her eyes. 'Just go and fetch it. Now. Please.'

'But I only –'

'Toby, go and get the dinosaur *now*.' Andrew's voice was full of authority and infuriatingly relaxed. Catherine's temples began to throb. 'Florence needs something to play with during the service. Otherwise she'll get bored.'

'Can't *I* have something to play with too, then? My Gameboy's got a mute switch so nobody would ever –'

'No, you can't. You're far too old for that sort of thing. Now, quickly please. Go and find the dinosaur.'

Toby stomped off with a mutinous sigh.

'Thank you,' muttered Catherine through gritted teeth.

'Oh, that was all right, was it? For someone who doesn't know how to talk to his children?'

'Look, Andrew, I'm sorry, all right? I'm *sorry*. I'm just a bit on edge.' In fact Catherine couldn't remember the last time she had felt so nervous. This had the potential to be a real life-changing moment, one to tell her grandchildren about. Although if she were being honest, the prospect of spending the rest of her life as a *Christian* did fill her with disquiet. She knew what people would say behind her back. They would make the same patronising jokes that she had always made.

Catherine felt she had every right to feel apprehensive.

Toby reappeared, holding a large yellow dinosaur. It had a long spotted tail, two huge front teeth, and an imbecilic grin. Florence grabbed it from her brother.

'Duncan,' she sighed.

'Right,' said Catherine, glancing at her watch. 'Come on.' She opened the front door. The sun was shining warmly again after yesterday's deluge. Catherine's shoes pinched her feet as she hurried along the pavement. She did her best to ignore the pain; instead she filed it away with the other accumulated resentments of the day. She would revisit them later, after this was all over, when she could wallow at leisure in a private stew of self-righteous fury.

Of the morning's many trying moments, the most galling had been Patrick's cheerful departure for Lords. He had strolled off down the pavement half an hour earlier, and Catherine was still reeling from his desertion. When she woke this morning to the treacherous, shining sun, she had dared to hope that Patrick might still change his mind. He'd never be so callous as to abandon his family on their inaugural visit to church, just to watch a game of *cricket*. But that was exactly what he had done. She felt tricked, betrayed. Patrick had talked her into this and had then left her to get on with it on her own.

Catherine strode ahead, propelled forwards by her indignation. All three generations of Shaw men had been exasperating today. In addition to Patrick's disappointing behaviour and Toby's reluctance to come downstairs, Andrew's relaxed good humour had been a source of aggravation all morning. Ever since he had unexpectedly agreed to come to church last night, Catherine had been frothing with suspicion, wondering what she had missed. Andrew was a creature of habit, reassuringly predictable, and Catherine was utterly wrong-footed by his good-natured willingness to go along with her plan. As a result, a creeping paranoia had begun to tug at the edges of her equilibrium. Something was going on, but she had no idea what.

As Catherine marched on, ignoring the pain in her feet, Florence sang softly to herself and hit her mother affectionately over the head with her yellow dinosaur. Catherine turned down a side street, and at once the dark bulk of the church rose up in front of her, casting the pavement into shadow. She stopped. All of a sudden *church* was no longer just a notional concept, a peculiar way of spending your Sunday mornings – suddenly it was imbued with a physical reality, a heavy truth. For a second she considered turning on her heels and making a run for it. Then Andrew and Toby arrived behind her.

'Having second thoughts?' asked Andrew.

'Of course not,' said Catherine. 'We were just waiting for you two slowcoaches.'

'That's all right then,' said Andrew, giving Florence a quick tickle. Catherine walked up the stone steps in front of the church. An elderly lady in a grey dress and a crumpled brown cardigan was standing by the front door, a sheaf of papers in her hand.

'Good morning,' said Catherine. Andrew and Toby fell into line behind her.

The old woman looked at them suspiciously, infidels storming the temple.

Catherine gestured inside. 'May we –?'

The woman shrugged a shrug of monumental indifference. She licked her thumb and forefinger and slowly counted off three sheets of paper. 'Order of Service,' she croaked. She extended a craggy finger. 'Hymnals at the end of each pew.'

Catherine took the sheets. With a brief glance behind her to check that Andrew and Toby were still following, she stepped inside. She stood for a moment on the threshold, waiting for her eyes to adjust. The peaty aroma of long-settled dust and cold stone filled her nostrils. The floor was a collage of old tombstones, inscriptions worn away by the feet of generations of worshippers. A blue carpet ran the length of the nave, separating two armies of dark pews. At the far end of the church sat the altar, a disastrous modern confection of polished pine. The altarpiece was embroidered with chunkily impressionistic crucifixes of varying sizes and colours. To one side, a huge spray of lilies sat resplendent in a large pot.

All of a sudden Catherine was a young girl again, ambushed by the familiarity of these unchanging sights and smells. The church of her childhood, a tiny chapel sheltering beneath a quiet canopy of oak trees deep in an Oxfordshire

238

valley, could not have been more different from this vast ship of urban Victorian gothic, but both buildings shared the unmistakable aura of hushed piety. Reassured by her memories, Catherine set off hopefully down the aisle.

The church was about a third full. A silent sea of greys, browns and blacks spread out before them, a stony-faced aggregation of pensioners. There was nobody under the age of sixty. Each person was staring with watery eyes at the back of the person in front, waiting for the service to begin. Nobody moved, nobody talked. Nobody turned to look as Catherine led her family to the nearest empty pew.

Andrew sat down and looked around him. 'The church disco must be a riot,' he whispered.

Frowning silence, Catherine opened the faded red covers of the prayer book which sat at the end of the pew. She lowered her nose to the open spine and breathed deeply. Her nostrils were filled with the pungent aroma of old paper, ochre-stiff pages fighting off the slow, relentless trudge of mildew. She turned the pages, scanning the chopped lines of prayer. *Hi*, said all the thees and thines. *Welcome back*. Catherine closed the book and lowered her head to pray. Come on, then, she thought. Here I am. I'm ready if you are. Show me what you've got.

She waited for a beatific sensation of profound holiness to descend upon her. Catherine stared at her knees, willing God on. The earlier sensation of warm familiarity had vanished. Now she just felt lonely and anxious. She was waiting for divine visitation with the twitchy impatience of an adolescent waiting for a boy to call. Catherine was shocked to discover that she wanted this to work, very much. Andrew had been right: religious faith *was* a wonderful thing, if you could pull it off. She shut her eyes and tried to pray. *About the angel you sent to rescue my daughter –*

The organ erupted in a syrup of noise. Catherine raised

her head and turned to watch as the vicar made his way down the aisle. He was a small man, trapped in a cassock several sizes too large; its hem dragged along the floor behind him. His hands were clasped tightly around a black leather-bound book. The journey towards the altar seemed like a titanic effort. He struggled on, bent forwards in an embattled stoop. He was followed by a boy of about Toby's age, also in a cassock, who carried an ornate gold cross which was larger than he was. The cross wobbled precariously as the boy advanced. At the altar the vicar turned towards the congregation and cleared his throat. To Catherine's surprise, he did not look much older than she was, but he seemed pegged back, burdened by his lot. His eyes were fogged over by defeat.

'The peace of the Lord be always with you,' he said – a triumph, it seemed to Catherine, of hope over experience.

The vicar rattled through the parish notices – this week's Bible reading class and next Thursday's rescheduled coffee morning in aid of Famine Relief. Andrew listened to it all with a certain anthropological interest. His mother would have been disgusted, but this was no time for principles, his own or anyone else's. He had a marriage to rescue.

'And now,' said the vicar, 'let us join together in worship by singing hymn 352, "He Who Would Valiant Be".' He paused, and then added, with feeling, ' " 'Gainst All Disaster".'

As the organ ponderously began to pipe out the tune, the pensioners crabbily unfolded themselves from their pews in a chorus of muted coughs. The women warbled, their frail voices piously off-key. The men dispensed with melody altogether and delivered the words in a low, rumbling monotone, a sanctified, slow-mo rap. Toby stood with his face half-hidden by his hymn book, solemnly singing in his wobbly treble. Catherine was staring at her hymn book, her mouth clamped firmly shut. Florence stood on the pew between Catherine and her brother, looking around with interest.

When the hymn ended, the vicar said, 'Let us pray.' Andrew sank to his knees and rested his forehead on the wooden shelf in front of him. 'Christ, the light of the world, has come to dispel the darkness of our hearts,' began the vicar.

Andrew looked at his watch.

Another voice joined the vicar's. '*Oh wow,*' it breathed, '*tickle me there.*'

The vicar paused for a moment, and then continued cautiously. 'Lord God Almighty, who taketh away the sins of the world –'

'*Oh, yes,*' murmured the second voice, enraptured. The words floated over the bowed heads of the congregation.

Andrew was aware of a mild commotion at the other end of the pew.

'– and who gave his only son, our saviour Jesus Christ, to die upon the cross –'

'*Duncan just loves being tickled!*'

Andrew looked along the pew just in time to see Catherine snatch the dinosaur out of Florence's arms. She ripped off the top of its head and plunged her hand inside. After a moment she pulled out two large batteries and the dinosaur fell silent. Florence started to screech hysterically.

'– grant us your peace,' said the vicar defeatedly.

Duncan the Dinosaur lay in Catherine's arms. The strip of yellow fur which Catherine had removed from between his ears now sat unevenly on top of his head, like a mohican on a King's Road punk. Florence, traumatised by Catherine's improvised lobotomy of her favourite toy, was sucking her fingers, leaning into her mother's ribs, her eyes half-closed. 'Duncan,' she murmured faintly.

Free from interruptions, the vicar had now acquired a good head of steam, and was rattling through his prayers at a fair whack. Catherine, though, was too disappointed to pay much attention. There was going to be no luminous revelation here. Patrick had been right, she thought. She should have come on her own. There were too many things vying for her attention. God should not have to compete with talking dinosaurs. She stared at the top of Duncan's head, dismayed by the resolute emptiness within her. This had been a waste of everyone's time.

By the time they reached the sermon, Florence's mourning for Duncan was over. She had slithered off the pew and was examining the embroidered prayer mat which hung on the small hook in front of her mother. (Catherine had not used the mat: she prayed with her buttocks perched on the edge of the pew, her knees pushed forward in mid-air genuflection. She did not want to spoil her dress.) The vicar stood in front of the altar, shuffling a pack of index cards. Finally he looked up. 'My text this morning is taken from the Gospel of St Mark, chapter 10, verse 14.' He cleared his throat. '"Suffer the little children to come unto me, and forbid them not: for such is the kingdom of God."' He paused. '"Suffer the little children",' he repeated, in a voice which suggested that when it came to little children, the vicar had done more than his fair share of suffering. 'Now, what was Jesus telling us with these words?' Catherine saw Andrew swallow a yawn. 'He was saying that he wanted to share the word of God with *everyone*. Not just the elders, or the wise men, or the people of influence, but the children, too. And so, in the spirit of Mark, chapter 10, verse 14, I'm going to take Jesus at his word. The love of God is not just for grown-ups. To illustrate the point, I'm going to conduct a little experiment.' The vicar rubbed his hands together in what Catherine supposed was meant to be a display of eagerness. 'I'd like a volunteer to come up here and join me in front of the altar. Are there any *young* members of the congregation who'd like to help?'

The vicar's eyes scanned the pews. Toby sank slowly towards the floor until he was slumped like a slothful invertebrate, almost horizontal along the pew.

'Surely there must be at least one little boy or girl who wants to help,' said the vicar, narrowing his eyes. 'Aha! I think I can see a young lad back there.'

He was looking directly at Toby.

'No,' gasped Toby in horror. 'Mummy, don't let him –'

'Come up to the front, why don't you?' said the vicar. Ancient necks had begun to twist creakily towards them.

Toby looked up imploringly at Catherine. The look of desperate supplication in his eyes almost broke her in two. Hating herself, she smiled and nodded cheerfully. 'Go on,' she whispered. 'It'll be fun.'

With a sigh, Toby clambered to his feet. 'Excellent,' said the vicar, with evident relief. 'Ladies and gentlemen, we have a volunteer.' Toby walked towards the front of the church like a condemned man on his way to the scaffold. The vicar was waiting for him, his hands clasped in front of him in a wholly unconvincing gesture of delight. When Toby arrived at the altar, he was turned around to face the congregation. His eyes finally settled on his mother, full of reproach.

'Jesus said, "Suffer the little children",' declared the vicar again, his hands resting on Toby's shoulders.

'I'm not *that* little,' said Toby, his voice small.

'How old are you?' asked the vicar.

'Seven and a half,' replied Toby.

'Little enough,' said the vicar briskly. Toby's shoulders slumped in defeat. 'Now then, what's your name?'

Toby thought for a moment. 'Marcus.'

Catherine and Andrew exchanged looks.

'All right. Marcus. Good. Now, I don't think I've seen you here before. Is this the first time you've come to this church?'

Toby nodded.

'Well, Marcus, I've got a surprise for you,' said the vicar. 'In fact, you *have* been to this church before.'

'No I haven't,' said Toby politely.

The vicar smiled. 'Yes, Marcus, you have.'

Toby shook his head. 'No, really, I haven't.'

'Let me explain why,' said the vicar, switching tactics. 'When we talk about going to church, we're not talking about the building where the service takes place. We're not talking about these walls, these beautiful stained-glass windows, or even our lovely altar. You see, Marcus, the church is not the *building*, but the people inside it.'

Andrew leaned towards Catherine. 'What has this got to do with suffering little children?' he whispered.

Catherine shrugged.

'When we speak of God's church,' continued the vicar, 'we mean his family throughout the world, wherever and whenever and however they may congregate together to praise his name. The first modern church, you might say, was established by the disciples. They may not have had a beautiful building in which to worship, but that didn't matter. These twelve men, joined together by their shared devotion to Christ, met to praise their –'

'Thirteen,' said Toby.

'What?' said the vicar.

'There were thirteen disciples,' said Toby.

'Ah, no,' laughed the vicar, 'I'm *pretty sure* there were only twelve, Marcus. I checked in the Bible last night.'

'Well, that's why you've made the mistake,' said Toby. 'The Bible doesn't talk about the thirteenth disciple.'

'It doesn't?' said the vicar.

'They kept quiet about him,' explained Toby. 'He wasn't very nice.'

The vicar thought about this for a moment. 'Perhaps we should get back to what I was saying about the first modern –'

'He used to feed beans to the other disciples' donkeys,' said Toby.

Catherine looked down the pew. Andrew's head was in his hands.

'He did?' frowned the vicar. 'Why?'

Toby suddenly looked guarded. 'I don't know,' he mumbled.

There was a pause.

'Right, well, how fascinating. You learn something new every day.' The vicar laughed humourlessly. 'Does he have a name, this disciple?'

Toby nodded. 'Frank.'

'St Francis?' suggested the vicar. 'Of Assisi?'

Toby shook his head impatiently. '*Frank*. Frank the Disciple.'

Catherine leaned across Florence. 'Andrew,' she hissed, 'what have you *done*?'

Andrew did not look at her, but simply shook his head in horror.

'Well, Marcus, perhaps this neatly illustrates the point I was trying to make about God's church being more than bricks and mortar,' said the vicar. 'We all bring new light to the Scriptures. You've learned about this, this – *Frank*, in your previous church, I suppose, and now here you are, spreading the Word, telling us all –'

'Oh, no,' said Toby. 'I've never been to church before.'

'What?' said the vicar.

'My parents don't believe in God,' explained Toby.

Catherine's skin began to crawl. The people in the pew

245

in front had begun to peer round at her. She stared straight ahead, mortified.

'You've *never* been to church?' said the vicar, shocked. 'Not *ever*?'

Toby shook his head.

The vicar was beaten. He stared at Toby, finally lost for words.

At the end of the service, Andrew and Catherine sat silently as the rest of the congregation filed out into the sunshine. Florence was using her mother as a climbing frame; Toby had wandered off somewhere. Andrew kept his head bowed to avoid the looks of righteous disapproval from the passing parishioners, suddenly ashamed of his family's flagrant godlessness.

The vicar had finally got his sermon back on its rather tenuous track. Toby had returned to his seat, looking shaken – although not quite as shaken as the vicar. The service had limped painfully on without further interruptions.

Now the ordeal was finally over. There was just one last hurdle to negotiate: the vicar was standing at the front door of the church, saying goodbye to the dwindling crowd. Andrew had already looked around for alternative exits. There were none.

Catherine leaned across and touched him on the elbow. 'Come on,' she sighed. 'We can't very well stay here for ever.'

They stood up. 'Where's Toby?' asked Andrew.

'He'll be around somewhere. If he's got any sense he'll have escaped already.'

Andrew picked up Florence and they walked towards the exit. He briefly considered making a run for it, but as they approached the door the vicar spread his hands out towards them. Andrew wasn't sure what the gesture was supposed to mean, but it seemed friendly enough.

Catherine stepped up and grasped the vicar's hand.

'Hello. Catherine and Andrew Shaw. We're *so* sorry about – all that,' she said.

The vicar produced a thin half-smile.

'I can't think what my son was talking about,' gushed Catherine, 'all that business with the thirteenth disciple.' She performed a high little laugh. 'High spirits, I suppose. Honestly, the things these children get in their heads! Such imaginations!'

'I *was* a little taken aback,' admitted the vicar. 'It's not every day one of the most fundamental –'

'And that *nonsense* about never going to church!' Catherine put a fluttering hand to her chest.

'So you *do* attend regularly elsewhere?'

Catherine looked around her. 'And of course now he's vanished.'

Just then Toby appeared in the open doorway. The boy who had followed the vicar down the aisle at the start of the service stood next to him, no longer dressed in his ceremonial garb.

'There you are, darling,' breathed Catherine. 'What have you been up to?'

Toby turned to the boy beside him. 'I've been talking to James.'

'I'm so sorry,' said the vicar. 'I've been frightfully rude. I haven't introduced myself. I'm Julian Macintyre.' He put a hand on the other boy's shoulder. 'And this is my son, James.'

There was a stunned silence.

Catherine stared at Toby, who grinned guilelessly back. This, she realised, was why he had been so reluctant to come to church this morning. He hadn't wanted to run into James Macintyre, or, presumably, James Macintyre's father, who was standing in front of her now, in his oversized robes, his hands clasped together in benevolent holiness.

'Well, this is a bit of a surprise,' she said carefully.

'Do you boys know each other?' asked the vicar.

'We go to school together,' said James Macintyre, scuffing his shoe against the flagstones.

Toby looked at his parents. 'Can I spend tomorrow at James's house?' he said.

'Well,' began Andrew, frowning, 'I don't know –'

Catherine turned to the vicar and smiled. 'I think you need to ask Mr Macintyre, sweetheart, not us.'

The vicar looked suspiciously at Toby. 'We'd love to have Marcus for the day,' he said. 'That would be tremendous fun.'

'Actually,' said Andrew, 'his name is Toby.'

'Oh.' The vicar looked confused. 'But he said –'

'This *boy*!' squawked Catherine, mussing Toby's hair more roughly than was strictly necessary. 'I don't know what you were thinking, Toby, really I don't. Honestly. Giving Mr Macintyre a false name, indeed!'

'Please,' said the vicar reluctantly. 'Julian.'

'Well, *Julian*,' said Catherine, beaming at him, 'thank you. Toby would love to come and play. That would be wonderful.'

There was an awkward pause. It dawned on Catherine that Julian Macintyre's reactionary opinions on guns, women, piano lessons and other topics were almost certainly lies fabricated by his son. She wondered whether the vicar had any idea what sort of libellous fictions were being circulated about him in the playground. Had any of his parishioners been young enough to have children of school-going age, James's stories would probably have percolated back to him by now, but he seemed oblivious. Once again, she marvelled at the deviant genius of seven-year-olds. Julian Macintyre was obviously not a bad man; Catherine felt guilty for so readily believing every word she had heard about him. Still, she would leave it to someone else to tell him about his son's attempts to besmirch his good name.

'We really should be going,' she said.

Julian Macintyre shook Catherine's hand, then Andrew's, and finally Toby's. 'Goodbye Toby,' he said gravely. 'Thanks for all your help today during the sermon. Most illuminating.'

Before Toby could answer, Catherine grabbed him by the wrist and propelled him out of the door, waving over her shoulder at the vicar and his son. 'Bye! Bye! Thanks again! See you tomorrow!' She marched Toby off down the street. Andrew followed, carrying Florence.

'There, Toby,' said Catherine, when they were a safe distance away from the church. 'That wasn't so bad was it?'

'Actually,' said Toby, 'it was quite good in the end. You know, with James.'

'I'm surprised you want to go and play with him,' said Andrew quietly, 'given that the two of you don't actually *like* each other.'

'Well,' said Toby with evident satisfaction, 'we're going to be friends from now on. I went up to him afterwards and said that unless we could be friends then I'd tell everyone what a dork his father was, and that *he* has to wear a dress every Sunday.'

'It's a *cassock*,' said Catherine.

'Anyway,' said Toby cheerfully, 'after that he said he supposed it would be all right. So now we're friends.'

They walked in silence for a few moments.

'So you've blackmailed him into inviting you over tomorrow,' said Andrew.

Tomorrow, thought Catherine. Tomorrow is *Monday*.

'What's blackmailed?' asked Toby.

'Never mind,' said Andrew sharply. 'No son of mine uses those sorts of tactics to win friends.'

'Andrew,' said Catherine.

'There is absolutely no *way* you'll be going to the Macintyres' house tomorrow,' said Andrew. 'You should be ashamed of yourself.'

Toby looked dismayed. 'But –'

'I think,' said Catherine, 'that Daddy and I need to have a little chat about all this when we get home. In private.'

'What on earth is there to discuss?' asked Andrew.

She looked at him. 'Plenty.'

Plenty: if Toby were to spend Monday with James Macintyre, then Catherine could take Florence to Bloomsbury for Daniel Woodman's recital.

Florence would never remember. She'd never tell.

Catherine had gone to church, and God had dropped a little miracle right into her lap.

SEVENTEEN

It was past midnight. The bedroom air hung still in the darkness. Catherine lay next to her sleeping husband, lost in plaintive Schumann melodies, and the pale autumn sun creeping across four skylights. The images and sensations washed over her with a quiet, elegiac dignity, for Catherine was returning for one last visit.

Bloomsbury beckoned.

Catherine wondered what the new day would bring.

Did she sleep? She could not remember.

Andrew spent much of Monday morning trying to return his office to the state it had been in when he had last used it. In his single day's tenure Damian had made a number of small but aggravating changes. The desk had been repositioned. The contents of his drawers had been gone through and rearranged to no apparent purpose. Worst of all, the room reeked of stale cigarette smoke. Andrew pottered with distracted industry, rehabilitating paperclips. As he reimposed his own brand of order, he thought about Toby's behaviour the previous day.

Love, he was beginning to understand, imposed higher

251

expectations on everyone involved, both the adorer and the adored. Two days ago Andrew would not have especially minded how Toby won friends, but now he cared, deeply as it turned out. He was ashamed of Toby's blackmail trick, but to his bewilderment Catherine seemed unconcerned. In fact she had insisted that he should go and spend the day with James Macintyre. Andrew had wondered whether she was pursuing some sinister plan to gain access to the higher echelons of the local bishopric. He was baffled. A familiar twinge of disquiet: *We all keep secrets, even from our loved ones.*

And so they had fought, for the first time in months. It was a fractious, loose-limbed brawl, spiked by impatience and frustration. A river of misunderstanding ran fast and treacherous between them, their words pulled down by the onrushing current. With every parry and barbed put-down Andrew watched Catherine retreat into her private cocoon of hurt.

In the end, he had capitulated. He was supposed to be winning Catherine back, not pushing her further away. Toby would go to James Macintyre's. The rest of the day had been spent in an uneasy armistice.

There was, he thought, a long way to go to regain the intimacy which they had so carelessly lost.

The telephone rang. Andrew wearily picked it up.

'Hello?'

'Andy?'

'Oh God.'

'Look, buddy, I just thought I'd give you a holler.' Richard launched straight into his bluff good-ole-boy routine. 'I haven't heard from you since our drink and I wanted to check that everything was OK.'

'No, Richard, you wanted to check whether I'd found Annabel's bracelet.'

There was a silence.

'And have you?' asked Richard.

'Of course not.'

'But you have looked.'

Andrew shut his eyes. He didn't want to admit his doubts about Catherine to anyone, least of all to Richard. But Andrew also wanted him to know that he had been *wrong* – gloriously, emphatically mistaken.

'Yes,' he said eventually. 'I looked.'

'And?'

'Nothing.' Quiet triumph.

There was a pause.

'Where did you look, exactly?' asked Richard.

'What do you mean, where did I look? In her jewellery box, of course.'

'Yes, and where else?'

'Where *else*? Where else would she put a bracelet, for God's sake?'

'Well, think about it for a minute. If – and I'm just saying if – if Cathy *has* stolen the bracelet, then she's not going to put it in her jewellery box, is she? She's going to *hide* the damn thing.'

'Oh, for heaven's sake,' sighed Andrew.

'I'm not asking you to turn your whole house upside down,' said Richard. 'But try a little harder, would you please? Look under the bed, that sort of thing.'

'I'm sorry but no. I won't do your tawdry spying for you.'

'But you already did,' said Richard.

'No,' said Andrew hotly, already regretting opening his mouth, 'what I did had nothing to do with your –'

'And I wouldn't push, but it would be nice to know before we go.'

Andrew frowned. 'Before you go where?'

There was a moment's silence. 'Catherine hasn't *told* you?'

'Told me what?'

'We came round to tell you on Saturday. You were out. We're leaving. We're off to the States next week.'

'Oh. She didn't mention it, no.'

'That's strange,' said Richard. 'I wonder why not.'

'How long will you be away for?'

'We're going for good, Andy. I'm going back to the homeland.'

Andrew blinked. 'Bullshit.'

'Really. No bullshit. We're selling up and moving on.'

'You're – bloody hell, what's brought this on?'

'We were stagnating. I needed a change of scene. We both did. The East Coast has been calling. So we're off.'

'Well, congratulations,' said Andrew. 'God. Next week! What's the rush?'

'You know how it is. Once you make your mind up, you just want to get on with it. No point hanging around.'

'I suppose not.' Then the news hit home. Richard Sulzman was leaving! 'But this is terrible news,' said Andrew, beaming.

'Well, these decisions are never easy,' said Richard. 'We'll miss you both, you know that. But these things happen.'

'I'm devastated, obviously,' said Andrew.

There was a pause as both men silently considered this lie.

Richard cleared his throat. 'So as far as you're concerned, this business with the bracelet is over?'

'As far as I'm concerned, Richard, this business with the bracelet never *began*.' The Sulzmans were leaving! There would be no more patronising lectures or pretentious dinner-party conversation. Catherine would no longer be distracted by Richard's superior vocabulary, or his preening erudition, or his fame. The game was up, and Andrew had won. He put the phone down and walked over to the window. At no

254

point over the weekend had Catherine mentioned the Sulzmans' imminent departure. He wondered why she had kept the news to herself.

Then, at the back of his head, a new question began to disseminate tiny waves of freshly-minted chaos.

Catherine *wouldn't* hide a stolen bracelet in her jewellery box, would she?

The morning crept forward. Catherine tried not to look at the clock. Largely she failed. Time was dragging by in ever-decreasing increments.

Catherine had driven a beaming Toby to James Macintyre's house an hour earlier. On the doorstep Toby had greeted James with effusive triumph; James had hovered behind his mother's legs, eyeing Toby with overt distrust. Catherine had smiled blandly at the vicar's wife and then fled.

Still. Had it not been for the Macintyres' invitation to Toby yesterday morning, Catherine would have dismissed the expedition to St Andrew's as a disaster, and would have concluded that she was not in fact undergoing a religious awakening. But now Sunday's experiment remained frus-tratingly inconclusive, because her prayers, quite literally, had been answered: she was able to go to today's recital in Bloomsbury, after all.

First, though, Catherine had to catch her daughter.

She inched forward, clutching a small white sandal.

Florence backed away, hissing like a cornered animal. Catherine lunged for her right foot. With a scream Florence toppled over on to the floor. She kicked her legs in fury, ramping up the volume of her yells as she did so. Catherine lost her grip on Florence's sock.

'Florence, *please.*'

Rather than surrendering to the ferocity of Florence's

255

struggle, her daughter's resistance made Catherine more determined not to be defeated. She carefully manoeuvred herself in front of Florence, who was lying on her back, her feet now flying back and forth in a blur of pink cotton. She grabbed a leg and wedged it in between her knees. Florence howled in protest as Catherine forced her foot into the sandal. As Catherine did the buckle up, Florence slumped into defeated torpor. The other sandal was sitting on the kitchen table, out of reach. Catherine relinquished her grip on Florence's leg. Florence did not move. She was phlegmatic now, defeated, waiting for the worst to be over.

'Right,' breathed Catherine. 'Wait there.' She got to her feet.

Even with her lopsided, one-shoed gait, Florence was too quick for her mother. Before Catherine reached the table, she had disappeared out of the kitchen and up the stairs. Catherine finally cornered her three floors up, and quickly wrestled her to the ground. Florence's shouts of anger felt like hot acid in Catherine's veins. Every yell twisted viciously through her, coiling her into a tight, jagged fireball of fury. *Stop it*,' she hissed as she tried to catch Florence's unshod foot.

Some minutes later, the second sandal was finally in place. Catherine was kneeling over her daughter, regaining her breath, when without warning Florence sent her right foot flying upwards in a violent arc of revenge. The tip of her foot connected squarely with the underside of Catherine's chin. There was a hollow *clack* as Catherine's lower jaw smashed into her head and her teeth bit crisply into her tongue. Her mouth erupted in a blast of pain. The only thing that she could see through her shock was an impudent grin on Florence's face. She could taste the sharp tang of her blood and her eyes filled with tears. '*Florence!*' she shouted, suddenly angrier than she could remember being in her life.

256

'You *bad*, ungrateful little –' Catherine's arm rose above her head, ready to beat her own pain away against her daughter's body. 'Don't you ever, *ever* –'

Catherine stopped, choked into sudden silence by the sound of her own rage, and her arm dropped back down to her side, icily, guiltily still. *I was going to hit her*, she thought. I was going to hurt her, because she hurt me.

'Oh Florence,' faltered Catherine, horrified. 'I didn't mean –'

But it was too late. Catherine's mask of maternal composure had slipped, and Florence had glimpsed the unguarded fury on her mother's face. She began to recoil from Catherine, terror in her eyes, scrabbling away down the corridor. As she slithered across the floor a scream grew from deep within her, which boiled and bubbled and finally emerged from her lungs at a harrowing pitch, cutting Catherine like a knife.

'*No*, Florence, no,' cried Catherine, following her down the corridor on her hands and knees, desperate in supplication. 'Florence, *darling*.'

Florence came to a halt outside Toby's closed door. Still screaming, she turned and watched Catherine approach. Her tiny face was crumpled with fear, unrecognisable. Her cheeks were bright red and striated with hot, terrified tears. Twin columns of glistening snot crept towards her upper lip. Her mouth was open as wide as it would go, yelling for help, begging to be rescued.

Catherine slowed her approach. She tried to speak softly but was drowned by Florence's cries. 'It's all right. It's all right. I wasn't going to hurt you. Really I wasn't.'

Tears escaped her eyes. The lie scorched her.

'Andrew,' said Joel. '*Hi*.'

'Hello Joel,' said Andrew, looking up from his paperwork. 'Good weekend?'

'Have you got a minute?' asked Joel.

'*I* had a *great* weekend,' Andrew told him.

Joel blinked. 'You couldn't –? Just in my office. Cheers. Won't take a sec.' He disappeared.

Andrew yawned and stood up. He crossed the corridor and pushed open the door of Joel's office. 'So, Joel, what can I do you for?'

'Ah, Andrew, there you are. Good to see you again.'

'*Freddie?*'

Trident Television's Overseas Corporate Development Officer was perched on the edge of Joel's desk, twiddling his luxuriant moustache.

'Surprise!' said Freddie Larssen.

'What are you doing here?' said Andrew.

'I am here to see *you*,' said Freddie.

'Me?'

Freddie pointed at Andrew. '*You.*'

'Good gracious. What an honour. Joel, did you know about this?'

Joel was busy delving through a drawer behind his desk and did not answer. There was a brisk knock on the door.

'Come in,' said Freddie. Tilly Tyler walked in.

Andrew turned to Joel. 'What's this all about, Joel?'

Joel mumbled something inaudible into the wall.

'We have some things to discuss,' explained Freddie.

Tilly Tyler moved across the room without looking at Andrew and stood next to Joel.

'OK,' said Andrew, starting to feel anxious.

'Andrew, the thing is this. This is the thing.' Freddie's eyes drooped sorrowfully. 'We've received a complaint.'

'A complaint?' said Andrew. 'What sort of complaint?'

'A serious one,' Freddie told him. 'Against you.'

'Me?' said Andrew. 'From whom?'

Freddie glanced down at a piece of paper. 'Clara Burgess.'

Andrew stared at Freddie for several moments in mute shock. Finally he found his voice. 'Freddie, you have to believe me, absolutely *nothing* happened, whatever she's –'

Freddie held up a hand. 'Andrew, please. Don't make this worse for yourself.'

'I swear, *nothing* ever –'

'We have her testimony in writing,' said Freddie.

There was a pause.

'What has she said?' asked Andrew dispiritedly.

'That you abused your position to secure sexual favours.'

'Freddie, look. This poor girl is deranged. Honestly. She's not right in the head. I never touched her. There's obviously been a terrible –'

'These allegations are very serious, Andrew. But what also concerns me is that you appear to have been purporting to act *ultra vires*.'

'Ultra what?'

'From a corporate governance perspective, you promised things that you were not in a position to promise.'

'From a *corporate governance perspective*?'

'At least you're not trying to deny *that*,' observed Freddie.

'I'm not sure what it is I'm supposed to be denying,' said Andrew.

'I'm talking,' said Freddie, stroking his moustache, 'about your plans to move into *film* making.'

'Oh,' said Andrew flatly. 'That.' He looked reproachfully at Joel.

'Do you have anything to say for yourself?'

Andrew shrugged. 'I didn't mean any of it. It was a silly misunderstanding, that's all.'

Freddie frowned. 'But you promised this girl a position as executive producer on a *film*.'

'Well, yes, that's true, in a way, but I never thought for a moment –'

'And *Cock*. What sort of film is called *Cock*?' Freddie paused. 'I will tell you. A *pornographic* film.'

'Freddie,' sighed Andrew, 'you've got it all wrong. This is utterly –'

'Then there's your e-mail.'

Andrew frowned. 'What e-mail?'

Joel coughed and spoke for the first time. 'After she left your office last week, Clara Burgess forwarded me an e-mail you had sent her. About Trident.'

Andrew's stomach sank. So that e-mail had come back to haunt him, after all. Clara had had her revenge.

'Oh,' he said. 'That one.'

'Was that a stupid misunderstanding, too?' asked Freddie. Andrew could hear the sinister creep of acid in his voice.

'It's just a question of context,' said Andrew weakly.

'Do you really think of our audience as a bunch of, let me see, "gormless morons"?' asked Freddie.

'No, of course not,' scoffed Andrew. He touched the side of his nose. 'It's the English sense of humour, Freddie, that's all. Doesn't quite translate.'

'I didn't think being called a "prissy monomaniac" was very funny,' said Joel. 'And *I'm* English.'

'And you called *me* a "talentless old goat",' interjected Tilly.

There was a pause.

'I believe that History will say that I was charitable,' declared Andrew.

'The thing is,' said Freddie, 'this sort of behaviour really isn't acceptable. We have a corporate identity to maintain, and it can't be compromised by this sort of thing, especially from one of the directors.'

For some reason Andrew was suddenly struck by the realisation that Freddie Larssen was speaking in what was probably his third or fourth language. This knowledge was suddenly a terrible torment. 'It was just an e-mail,' he said sullenly. 'It didn't mean anything.'

'Perhaps not to you,' said Joel bitterly.

Andrew turned to him. 'Joel, I'm *sorry*. It was a mistake.'

Joel's sideburns twitched. 'You don't think I'm a prissy monomaniac?'

Andrew thought. 'I don't think you're a monomaniac,' he replied.

'Oh, thanks a bunch.'

Freddie put up his hands. 'Look, Andrew, try to see it from Stockholm's point of view. This is *not* how we foster a working environment of harmony and understanding.'

'Oh,' said Andrew, 'but your Staff Displacement Scheme is, I suppose?'

'Well,' said Freddie. 'Actually, I was coming to that.' He turned to Joel and nodded.

Joel picked up a sheet of paper, cleared his throat, and began to read. ' "Why can't he try out his hare-brained schemes on someone else for a change? We're not a colony of corporate guinea pigs, Joel. We have a business to run." '

'Oh, for God's sake,' muttered Andrew.

'And on Friday he was seen leaving the building at 5.28,' continued Joel. 'Which is two minutes before the designated clock-off time for post-room personnel.'

Freddie shook his head. 'A poor example to set your colleagues, wouldn't you say?'

'You're surely not –'

'And during the afternoon,' interrupted Joel, 'he refused to fetch a tall, skinny latte for the acting creative director. Or a wholemeal cinnamon muffin.'

Andrew looked at Joel's face and realised that somewhere along the line, he had been guilty of a grave miscalculation.

* * *

The top of the bus barrelled into the hanging foliage. Florence giggled as the leaves hit the front window and then disappeared, whipped upwards and out of sight. The heavy branches scraped along the roof of the bus and then fell silent. Florence stared out of the window, thrilled by this new perspective from the upper deck. She had escaped the turgid immediacy of her usual, pavement-bound world. The road into the middle of the city unfolded a little more around each new corner. From up here Florence could look ahead, and see what the future held.

Catherine sat beside Florence on the faded orange seat, gently holding on to her daughter's arm. She had no idea what the future held for her. She was more preoccupied with the recent past. Florence had eventually calmed down enough to be coaxed downstairs, where Catherine had showered her with a guilty cargo of treats, anxiously cooing apologies. Lunch was a procession of lollipops, sweets and ice-cream. Florence's usual good humour had eventually returned and she had happily eaten everything Catherine had put in front of her, oblivious to her mother's fretful shame.

What sort of a monster was she, Catherine wondered as she gazed down at the passing streets. She remembered the muscled tension in her arm as it had risen above her head. It had been taut with violent intent, primed to inflict real pain. This would have been no idle smack. This was worse, so much worse, than all of those months when she had simply abandoned the children to Sinead's doleful care. *Abuse.* The word ricocheted around Catherine's head in demented tandem with the memory of her raised hand, waiting to strike.

What chilled her most was how terrifyingly *natural* it had felt. She couldn't persuade herself that the episode had been some nightmare aberration. The corrupting, debilitating rush of unconfined power, the instinct to lash out, had made a terrible sense to her. A slap, a pinch, a punch: release. It would have been so simple, *so easy*. Nobody would have known.

Catherine was crushed with remorse. All of a sudden, she was terrified of what she might be capable of.

Freddie put the tips of his fingers together as if he were about to pray. 'What I'm seeing in all this, Andrew, is a regrettable refusal to accommodate and respect the feelings of fellow employees.'

'But I'm the *creative director*,' complained Andrew. 'Shouldn't fellow employees have to accommodate and respect *my* feelings? Isn't that the right way round?'

'It's a two-way street, my friend,' replied Freddie, blandly sanguine.

'A two-way street,' echoed Joel.

'Anyway, look,' said Freddie. 'You'll probably want to consult your lawyer.'

Andrew swallowed. 'My lawyer.'

Freddie nodded. 'Clause 19 of your service agreement is the relevant provision. Summary Dismissal for Gross Misconduct. Our legal department tells us that we've got enough gross misconduct here to dismiss you several times over. But we don't want to do that, obviously.'

'You don't?' said Andrew.

Freddie shook his head. 'Of course not.'

'Oh, thank Christ,' breathed Andrew. 'You had me going there for a moment. I really thought you were –'

'We want you to *resign*,' interrupted Freddie.

There was a long silence.

'But this is a disaster,' said Andrew.

'The board has decided that Damian will replace you as creative director,' continued Freddie. 'I'm sure you'll want to wish him well in his new job. He has a big pair of shoes to fill.'

'Damian,' repeated Andrew dully.

Freddie stood up. 'Your assistant will arrange all your personal items to be sent on to you.'

'There's no notice period?' said Andrew. 'No carriage clock?'

'Your resignation is accepted,' replied Freddie smoothly. 'With regret, of course. And with immediate effect.'

'But you can't *do* this,' protested Andrew. 'This is *my* company.'

The Swede shook his head. 'Not any more, Andrew. Not any more.'

Daniel had gone everywhere by bus. He despised the Underground. To him, travelling beneath the surface of the city was an arrant absurdity. The inside of one dark tunnel looks just like another, he used to say. People shuttled from home to work, work to home, and never saw the spaces in between. So they had always travelled over London rather than under it. Before she knew Daniel, Catherine had rarely given the city much thought. But on top of the bus, London soon ran into her veins. Little by little the streets revealed themselves. Connections were made, clues pieced together, slabs of geography painstakingly joined up. Before long narrow ribbons of knowledge criss-crossed the metropolis, illuminating her mental map of the city like strings of fairy lights. The complex topography of her experience slowly coalesced into a unique whole, a town all of her own.

And now all this carefully accumulated information was leading her back, back.

Andrew perched on an empty bench in Soho Square, beneath the shade of overhanging trees. A few early lunchers sat on the grass in the full glare of the sun, skirts hoicked up high to expose their blue-white legs. He watched as they ate their sandwiches and blew thin columns of smoke into the air. A small bird landed at his feet and pecked enquiringly at the ground, looking for dropped crumbs.

So, there it was. Andrew had been sacked. Caught squarely in Clara's spiteful cross hairs, he had never stood a chance. He sighed. The rumours would already be crashing around town, becoming more outrageous with each new deflection they took, every new fictitious spin. What hurt Andrew the most was knowing that Joel had been the principal architect of his downfall. He was scraped raw by the memory of Joel's expression as he denounced him. It was not a look of triumph or malice. Joel's face had simply been loaded with regret, and it was this which was crucifying Andrew slowly from within. For he knew that the genesis of this disaster was not Joel's betrayal of Andrew, but rather the reverse.

Andrew's only defence against Joel's generous offer to participate in his new television venture all those years ago had been to treat him with unpardonable contempt ever since. He had heaped a never-ending barrage of ridicule and humiliation on Joel in order to maintain the fiction that he was not going to be indebted to his friend for the rest of his life. In fact Andrew meant very little of what he had said, but Joel's failure to react to his taunts just spurred Andrew on to acts of increasing meanness. Joel's implacably sunny countenance was like an abandoned football sitting in front of empty goal posts; Andrew couldn't walk past without taking a shot. Nothing he ever said or did seemed to have any effect, but that sort of unthinking rudeness was habit-forming, and so he had carried on anyway, safe in the knowledge that Joel would never take offence.

Now it seemed that he had been wrong all along. Beneath Joel's unruffled exterior beat a vulnerable, sensitive heart.

He had been assiduously cataloguing Andrew's casual abuse for years. Each fresh volley of spite had slowly nudged up the index of hurt, until Joel could take no more. And this was his revenge. Or was it an act of self-defence? Andrew did not know which was worse.

The bus was nearly full. Catherine usually enjoyed the relief which crowds could bring. She liked to lose herself in their anonymous dementia. She liked the sensation of being gently erased, just another faceless body in the thronging mass. Liberated by this cloak of invisibility, she was able to think more clearly, uncluttered by self-consciousness. But with Florence in tow, she could not slip away. She had to remain vigilant. Now crowds represented nothing more than the threat of uncontainable danger.

Across the aisle of the bus sat a young woman, engrossed in a paperback. Catherine peered surreptitiously at the book. It was Richard Sulzman's most recent novel. At once she was pierced by an acute sense of loss. Of course, Richard had continued to write successful books after their partnership had been broken by her maternity leave. The corporate publishing machine had carried on without her, monstrous and efficient, oiling Richard's creative wheels, helping him along to his next fat royalty cheque. Someone had stepped in to fill her shoes, and that was that. And now Richard was escaping back across the Atlantic, gone for ever. There was no way back for her now.

She watched as the woman's forefinger and thumb extended towards the top right-hand corner of the page. There they hovered, in calm suspense. And then an intricate little dance: finger and thumb sweeping languidly from right to left, the book repositioned by a fraction of an inch, the woman's head adjusted to address the fresh collection of sentences. She did not blink. It was seamless, graceful, unthinking. As she watched the woman read, freed by another's words, Catherine was struck by the simple beauty of the moment. A new page.

Ten minutes later, Catherine crouched on the pavement, the smoke of the departing bus still blackening the air. She snapped Florence into the push-chair and handed her a box of raisins. Catherine looked at her watch. The recital was due to begin in fifteen minutes. She set off.

They soon arrived in front of the church. Behind them the traffic rumbled past. A notice board was attached to the iron railings which separated the church steps from the pavement. On it was pinned a single piece of paper, advertising the concert that was about to begin. Catherine stared at the poster. The anxious fluttering in her stomach compacted into a tight knot of nausea.

A flight of steps led up to the door of the church. Catherine began to drag the push-chair upwards. People at a nearby bus stop watched her slow progress, not moving to help. Florence giggled each time the wheels of the push-chair crept backwards over another step. When she reached the top Catherine wheeled the push-chair to one side of the church's open door and took a moment to compose herself.

Suddenly she was paralysed by doubt, unsure what she was trying to achieve. She did not know the Daniel Woodman who was waiting inside. It had all been too long ago. Catherine wanted to pick Florence up and run back down the steps, to jump on the first bus and escape. But she did not move. Something was fixing her in her place. The caesura of seventeen years, an infinity of ignorance, beckoned her inside.

As she rocked the push-chair back and forth, battling the agony of indecision, a trio of elderly ladies slowly climbed up the stone steps. One of them smiled at Catherine as she stepped into the church.

'You should come in, dear,' she said. 'It'll be nice.'

Sprung from her trap, Catherine stepped forwards.

The church was huge and dark. The building swallowed the light which fell through the narrow, lead-latticed windows, pulling it into distant, impenetrable corners. The spine of the building was a row of vast columns which soared into the shadows of the vaulted ceiling. There were no pews, but rows of identical wooden chairs, stretching towards the altar. A space had been cleared on one side of the church. A concert grand waited, its lid open, its sound board up. Chairs were arranged around it in a respectful semicircle. About twenty people were already sitting, waiting for the recital to begin. Catherine advanced slowly. She could feel her heart thumping in her chest.

Finally she saw him, standing near the piano, watching the small group of people.

Catherine stared through the half-light.

Daniel Woodman was wearing a dark suit and an open-necked white shirt. He wore a pair of steel-rimmed glasses. His dashing Byronic locks had been lost to a thinning crop of greying curls, squirreling tightly to his scalp. His face was heavy and drawn, now a weary battleground of creases and pocked imperfections, pinched shut by the years.

Catherine leaned weakly against the handles of the push-chair. What rushed back to her was not the expected symphony of chocolate-box memories, but, instead, the long-forgotten truth. It was his eyes – cold and lifeless as they flickered across the small audience – which unlocked the secret she had buried so deeply within her.

She had disintegrated under that same blank stare.

Without warning Catherine was ambushed by the brutality

of Daniel's refusal to explain why he had broken her heart. All the anguish and despair of their last days together crashed down around her once more, as virulent and poisonous as it had been the first time. She let out a small gasp of pain. She had not been expecting this. Her defences were amassed elsewhere, ready to resist other, warmer memories. The truth stormed in unopposed, rampaging and destructive.

'Mummy, I want more raisins,' said Florence.

Catherine pulled herself unsteadily back to the present. 'Have you finished those already?' she whispered.

Florence turned the little box upside-down to demonstrate.

'I'm sorry, darling, I haven't got any more,' Catherine told her. 'You shouldn't have eaten them so quickly.'

Florence shook her head. 'I want more raisins,' she insisted, more loudly.

People nearby were half-turning in their seats. 'Florence, I *can't* give you any more. I don't have any. You'll just have to sit tight.' She opened her handbag, looking for the emergency toy she always carried with her. 'Look, let's see if I can find –'

'*No!*' Florence's voice rose. 'I don't want the bag! No bag! I want *raisins*!'

Catherine bent down towards her. 'Florence, darling,' she pleaded. 'Please don't. We've got to be quiet now. We're going to listen to some music.'

At this Florence extended her legs out in front of her, rigid with fury. Her tiny feet twitched in impending apoplexy. Her mouth opened and closed, but no sound came out. Catherine looked on, helpless. There was a gentle tap on her shoulder.

'Excuse me.'

Catherine straightened up and turned around. She was standing face to face with Daniel Woodman. He stared at her.

269

EIGHTEEN

Andrew stepped through the front door of his home and was greeted by silence. He stood in the hall, listening. The house was empty. His shoulders felt heavy with sorrowful relief. He walked up to the bedroom and sat down on the bed. He pulled off his shoes, and put his head in his hands.

No more job: what did that *mean*, exactly?

No more salary, for one thing. They were still rich, of course, or at least he supposed they were. The proceeds from the sale of the company to the bastard Swedes were somewhere, scattered through an opaque collection of offshore bank accounts, high-yield stock portfolios, Liechtenstein investment funds, Dutch Antilles blind trusts, and other befuddling things. Andrew was proud of his ignorance of his own financial affairs. It was a mark of success, he believed, not to know exactly how much one was worth. He once read about a rock star who'd been robbed by his own accountant. The accountant had stolen six million pounds, and the guy hadn't even noticed. Six million quid! That was something to aspire to. Andrew reluctantly decided to call his own accountant. He couldn't afford ignorance, not right now.

He lay back on the bed and stared at the ceiling. It wasn't just the money, though. It was the *ignominy* of it all. He hadn't even been able to orchestrate his departure in the manner of his choosing, which would at least have been memorable and dramatic. Instead Freddie had told him to collect his jacket and leave immediately, and that was what he had done, shamefaced, without protest. Joel had followed him back to his office, silently watching as he collected his things. He was escorted to the front door of the building like a common criminal, craven and humiliated.

Andrew wondered how to break the news to Catherine. He considered a number of different approaches. He painted himself in turn as innocent victim, misunderstood genius, and uncompromising idealist. None seemed convincing. Then he thought: perhaps he could make it out to be *his* idea. He could recast the whole episode, and present it not as a disaster, but an opportunity. This was not an end, but a new beginning. He had not lost a job, but gained his freedom. If he piled it on good and thick, fattened Catherine up with the usual clichés, she might just buy it. Then Andrew saw the flaw in his idea. It would never work without a credible new venture to dangle in front of her, some evidence of a *plan*. And that was his problem. He had no idea, not one, what he was going to do next.

They looked at each other in silence. Catherine's insides yawned with trepidation. Given the onslaught of unwelcome remembrance which had just scythed through her, she was no longer sure whether this was what she wanted after all.

Florence continued to splutter furiously in her push-chair. The noise eventually shook Catherine out of her trance. 'Yes?' she said, rather curtly.

Daniel Woodman took half a step backwards. 'I'm sorry.'

Catherine suppressed a snort of hysteria. The first thing

he'd said to her in seventeen years was an apology! 'What are you sorry for?' she asked.

'For bothering you. It's only –'

'You shouldn't apologise,' said Catherine. Her voice sounded a million miles away. 'It's your recital, after all.'

'Oh. Yes, well. I suppose it is.'

The familiar voice, enriched and deepened by the intervening years, threatened to destabilise her. She cleared her throat and looked away. 'Are you starting soon?' she asked.

'Well, we were about to, actually. That's why I'm here.' Daniel Woodman paused. 'I need to talk to you,' he said, his voice barely more than a whisper. 'I saw you as soon as you walked in. And I knew I'd never be able to begin without talking to you first. Impossible to concentrate.'

'Yes,' said Catherine. A shy half-smile. So!

'It's about your child.'

She had misheard him. 'My child?'

He put his hands in his pockets and gave an apologetic shrug. The gesture was so familiar that it took her breath away. 'Please don't think me intolerant. This is a free concert, and we're obviously happy for anyone to come in and enjoy the music. But I don't want the performance to be ruined by a crying baby.'

Catherine stared at him. All she could think to say was, 'Florence isn't a *baby*.'

'Whatever.' Daniel Woodman waved a bored hand. 'The important thing is –'

'She's *two*,' insisted Catherine.

He looked at her oddly, and then down at Florence. 'I'm afraid I'm going to have to ask you to leave.'

'But that's ridiculous.'

Those cold eyes turned on her. They flickered over her face with a contemptuous disdain. There was not, Catherine

272

saw, the faintest glimmer of recognition. 'Ridiculous or not,' he said, 'I'd still like you to leave.'

A wrecking ball smashed into her chest, obliterating half a lifetime of memory and regret. She stood before him, cold and numb, and finally able to see. 'Very well,' she murmured. She turned the push-chair around and walked stiffly back towards the door of the church.

Catherine sat in the back of the taxi and hugged Florence to her.

Her act of selective remembrance had finally betrayed her. Her concocted story was exquisite, the fuel which had sustained her through endless lonely nights, but it simply was not true. The deliberate erasure of everything which was not perfect had shackled Catherine to a myth which – she saw it now – had crippled her with the weight of impossible expectations. She stroked her daughter's hair, and looked back again into the past, unblinkered now.

There had been fights. There had been boredom, frustration, and irritation. Of course. Sometimes they had argued themselves to defeated standstill across a vast chasm of misunderstanding.

Daniel had always been fascinated by himself, consumed with his own importance. It was this dazzling display of self-possession which had so captivated her. Blinded by adoration, Catherine was a loyal acolyte, a devoted sidekick. Most importantly, she was someone in whom Daniel's own glory could be reflected to maximum effect. He was too self-absorbed to consider other people except in terms of their function in the drama of his own existence. In the end, she was just the accompanist. Today she had simply changed roles. Small wonder he had failed to recognise her.

That young couple of long ago had not been blessed by unassailable harmony or heroic, poetic sympathy. Years of painful memorial were smashed beyond hope. Here was the truth which Catherine had been running from for so long:

They had been just like everyone else.

Andrew heard the key in the front door. He climbed off the bed and walked slowly down the stairs. Catherine and Florence were standing in the hallway.

'Daddy!' cried Florence.

'Andrew?' said Catherine. 'What on earth are you doing here?'

He couldn't tell her, not yet. 'Quiet day at the office,' he said. 'Cancelled meeting. I thought I'd come home and surprise you.'

Catherine hung up her coat, looking perplexed. 'I see.'

'That's all right, isn't it?'

'Of course,' said Catherine, not quite looking at him. 'I just wasn't expecting you. It's a bit of a surprise.'

'A nice one, I hope.'

'Very nice. Thank you.' She smiled briefly.

'Where have you two been? Somewhere nice?'

'Just for a little trip into town,' replied Catherine. 'Nothing special. We needed to get out of the house.' She turned to Florence. 'We went on the bus, didn't we, Florence?'

'A big red bus!' agreed Florence.

Andrew thought of his plans for Venice and New York, all those child-free romantic getaways. Catherine was looking rather beautiful. Her cheeks looked flushed; her eyes were shining. She seemed healthy, full of rude life. He took her hand in his and kissed her cheek. 'Well,' he said. 'That's good.'

Catherine looked at him and started to cry.

'Cathy?' He squeezed her hands more tightly. 'What's wrong?'

'It's nothing,' said Catherine. 'Sorry. I'm tired, that's all. I'm not used to this constant –'

The sound of smashing glass splintered the conversation into jagged silence.

Without another word Catherine ran down the stairs to the kitchen. Andrew picked up Florence and followed her. They peered through the French windows into the garden. Catherine grabbed Andrew's arm. 'There's somebody in the greenhouse,' she whispered. A moment later, the greenhouse door opened, and a woman stepped on to the lawn. In her hand she was holding a pair of garden shears.

'I don't believe it,' breathed Catherine.

Andrew was paralysed as he watched the woman approach the house.

'Come on,' said Catherine. 'This won't do. This won't bloody do at all.' Before Andrew could stop her she flung open the doors.

The intruder stopped at once. 'Oh,' she said, 'I didn't think you were –'

Florence ran into the garden. 'Sinead!' she cried.

'Sinead,' said Catherine, stepping through the doors, 'where have you *been*?'

'I just went back to Dublin for a couple of days,' said Sinead. Florence was clinging on to her leg. Andrew stepped into the garden, trying to quell the riot of conflicting emotions inside him. Sinead was safe! There had been no blood spilled on those deserted railway tracks, after all. His conscience, at least in that regard, was clear. But Sinead was also *back*, and looking decidedly volatile.

'Dublin,' said Catherine.

'I needed to get away,' explained Sinead. 'Then my boyfriend came to get me.'

'Your boyfriend?' said Catherine. 'But I thought –'

'Yeah, well. That's all sorted out now. I'm staying at his.' Sinead ruffled Florence's hair.

'How did you get in?' asked Andrew.

She looked at him for the first time. 'I've still got my keys, haven't I?'

'And what exactly,' said Catherine, 'were you doing in my greenhouse?'

Sinead held up the shears. 'Bit of gardening.'

Catherine's face went pale. 'You haven't –'

'I've cut them all off,' said Sinead calmly. 'Every single one of them.'

Catherine's hand went up to her mouth. 'But *why*?' she gasped.

A new dimension of dread opened up inside Andrew's gut. 'Why?' said Sinead. 'I'll tell you *why*.' She waved the shears in Catherine's face. 'This is for all the times you've been unable to say please or thank you. It's for that look in your eye when you handed over my wages each week, as if I was a piece of shit you'd just found on your shoe.'

'Andrew?' screeched Catherine. 'Surely you aren't going to let her talk to me like that?'

'Well,' began Andrew cautiously, who was waiting to see what Sinead would say next, 'perhaps we –'

'And it's for the never-ending, nosy questions about me.'

'I wasn't being nosy. I just –'

'And the endless crap about soap operas.'

'Soap operas?' said Andrew.

Sinead turned to him. 'It was the only thing she thought I was interested in,' she explained. 'Patronising cow.'

'I was just trying to be *friendly*,' whined Catherine.

'Friendly? You treated me like a *dog*.'

As Andrew watched the anger flash across Sinead's face, the thought occurred to him that perhaps the episode at the kitchen table had also been an act of revenge. Sinead had simply been using him to get at Catherine, a final settling of scores before she left.

Suddenly he felt rather stupid.

276

'Anyway, maybe without your stupid flowers you'll spend some time with your children for a change,' said Sinead.

Tears had begun to roll down Catherine's cheeks. 'I *am* spending time with –'

'There's somebody else in the greenhouse,' said Andrew. 'I can see them crouching down between the tables.'

Sinead turned towards the greenhouse. 'You might as well come out,' she called.

The greenhouse door opened again and a man stepped out. Catherine uttered a small cry and collapsed on to the grass.

'Hello again,' said Gabriel.

Catherine struggled up on to her elbows. 'It's you,' she said.

He grinned sheepishly. 'Like a bad penny, aren't I?'

Sinead looked at Gabriel, and then at Catherine. 'How do you two know each other?'

He turned towards her. 'I came round. The day after our fight. I wanted to see you were all right.'

'Gabriel saved Florence's life,' said Catherine. 'There was a van –'

'Ah, you didn't spin her all that Gabriel bollocks, did you?' sighed Sinead. She turned to Catherine. 'His name's really Pete. He just likes to *call* himself Gabriel, the big ponce. Thinks he looks like Gabriel Byrne, if you can believe it.' Sinead snorted.

'Well,' said Pete, 'it's more because of Peter Gabriel, you know, the guy who used to be in Genesis. Pete. Gabriel. Peter Gabriel. See?'

Sinead snorted again.

Catherine slumped backwards on to the grass and stared at the clear blue sky above her. Supine on the lawn, she remained motionless, stunned by her own stupidity.

There had been no angel, no divine intervention. It was just Sinead's feckless boyfriend, back to beg forgiveness. Catherine remembered the envelope she had found stuck in the letterbox just before the accident. SHINAID, it had said. In a way, she reflected, she had been right all along: his presence there *wasn't* simply good fortune. He had been waiting for Sinead to return. Catherine closed her eyes as the world realigned itself along more familiar axes.

What now? she wondered, as she watched an airplane crawl across the sky.

'Where are you living, Sinead?' asked Andrew, somewhere above her.

'Wouldn't you like to know?' said Sinead.

'I just think, given what's happened, that if we knew where we could find you –'

'Worried about the flowers?'

'The flowers, yes, and the glass in the greenhouse that you've obviously broken,' replied Andrew. 'You've come into our house, without our permission, and committed these acts of, of –'

'Forget it, Andrew,' said Catherine.

Andrew looked down at her. 'What?'

Catherine didn't move. 'Get them out of my house.'

There was a pause. 'Right,' said Andrew. 'You heard her. Get out, the pair of you. And consider yourself lucky. If it were up to me –'

'Just get *rid* of them, Andrew, for God's sake.'

'All right, all right. Jesus. Come on, you two.' Andrew, Sinead and Pete went silently into the house. Catherine remained, staring at the sky. *My orchids*, she thought. All that work, destroyed with a few vindictive swipes of the garden shears. Another escape route closed off. Catherine knew already that the greenhouse would no longer be a sanctuary for her. The bitter truth of Sinead's accusations would rebound endlessly between the panes of glass, an eternal echo.

Catherine climbed to her feet. Florence was playing at the foot of the climbing frame, the intruders already forgotten. 'Come on, Florence,' sighed Catherine. 'It's time for lunch.'

Catherine scooped a few spoonfuls of cold baked beans on to a plastic plate. She added some old mashed potatoes that were lurking at the back of the fridge, and two fish fingers. She put the plate in the microwave. Florence waited patiently in her highchair, playing with a spoon. Catherine moved about the kitchen, struggling to combat an overwhelming sense of unreality.

The microwave pinged. Catherine dipped her fingertip in the baked beans to check their temperature. She put the plate down in front of Florence as Andrew came back into the kitchen.

'They've gone,' reported Andrew.

'Do me a favour,' said Catherine. 'Can you give Florence her lunch? There's strawberry yoghurt in the fridge for pudding.' She looked at her watch. 'Then it'll be time for her nap.'

They both looked at their daughter, who had already begun to shove baked beans into her mouth with her spoon.

'What are you going to do?' asked Andrew.

'I just need a moment on my own. To think about what's happened.'

'You never mentioned that Sinead's boyfriend had been here.'

'Didn't I?'

'You looked rather shocked to see him.'

'Can we please just forget it?'

'I'm just saying.'

'I'm upset, can't you see?'

279

He nodded. 'Is it to do with your orchids?'

'Oh, Andrew. It's to do with *everything*.'

She stood amidst the jungle of chintz, gazing at the piano. It sat in the corner of the room, crowned by a phalanx of silver photograph frames.

Everything was gone – Richard, Annabel, Sinead, her orchids. One by one, her defences against the baffled emptiness of her days had been smashed. Even her faith hadn't survived. (Pete the angel. Such idiocy. She sighed.)

There was nothing left to hide behind.

Catherine sat down on the piano stool. Perhaps, she thought, none of it matters any more.

Daniel Woodman, that mythical creature!

All swept away now.

A space had been cleared inside her.

Catherine lifted the lid of the piano and gazed at the keys. Somewhere in the back of her brain, a matrix of synapses, hard-wired into her memory banks, fired into life.

The black and white keys danced before her, beckoning her on.

She turned and sat squarely in front of the piano. Her feet instinctively caressed the brass pedals below. She adjusted the stool. Straightened her back. Stretched her fingers.

Andrew looked up in surprise as the melody spilled down the stairs. His spoon stopped midway between yoghurt pot and Florence's mouth. The kitchen was filled with the familiar patterns of notes which he hadn't heard in years. Catherine was playing her personal coda to each recital, that quiet epilogue to those long-distant evenings. Andrew wanted to run upstairs and watch. He wanted to see Catherine's hands over the keys, precise, poised, controlled.

'Daddy!'

Florence's impatient cry jolted Andrew out of his reverie. Smiling a silent apology, he spooned the strawberry yoghurt on to her tongue.

'Do you hear that, Florence?' he said softly. 'Mummy's playing the piano again.'

Florence looked unimpressed. She pointed to the yoghurt pot. 'More!' she demanded.

Andrew fed Florence the rest of her lunch, listening as Catherine played the same piece, again and again and again. The silence between performances grew shorter each time, until she was playing an unbroken cycle of melody. Andrew listened as he remembered the music which had once illuminated their marriage. Catherine was playing again! His heart filled with new hope. He looked at his daughter, who grinned back. 'Right, young lady. Time for your nap.' He lifted Florence out of her high-chair and carried her up the stairs to the hall. They stood outside the closed door to the sitting room, listening. Andrew put a finger to his lips, and then quietly pushed open the door.

On the far side of the room, Catherine sat at the piano. Her hands moved with an easy grace over the keys. Her head remained completely still as she played. She did not turn around. Andrew took a cautious step into the room, then another. He moved silently across the carpet until he could see her face. Catherine's chest rose and fell with the slow pulse of the melody. Her eyes remained shut as she played.

On her face there was a wide, peaceful smile.

Andrew watched for a moment, and then retreated. He closed the sitting-room door. Florence looked at him. 'Daddy,' she whispered, her eyes impossibly wide and impossibly green. How extraordinary, thought Andrew. This girl is the most beautiful thing in the world, literally the most beautiful thing I've ever seen in my life. 'Come on,' he said, kissing her forehead. 'Time for bed.'

Florence allowed herself to be lowered into her bed. Andrew drew the curtains and crept out of the bedroom. He stood outside the door, listening to the muted sounds of contented snuffling as Florence settled down for sleep.

Andrew walked into their bedroom and listened to the music as it floated up the staircase. All these years of silence, and now this. Catherine could still surprise him. And he was grateful for it.

He remembered then that he hadn't told Catherine about his job. He stopped, bewildered at how he could have forgotten to tell her the news. Sinead's dramatic appearance from the greenhouse had diverted his attention. Andrew sat down on the bed, grateful that at least that secret had been preserved.

Secret. The word ricocheted inside his skull.

Richard's remark of earlier that morning crept up on him, a silent assassin.

Catherine wouldn't hide a stolen bracelet in her jewellery box, would she?

While he could still hear Catherine play, he would be safe from detection.

Andrew dropped to his knees and looked underneath the bed. There was nothing there. He allowed himself a small grunt of relieved triumph. He got back to his feet, more confident now. His eyes scanned the room as he tried to remember where he used to hide things when he was young. The wardrobe. Andrew grabbed a chair.

On top of the wardrobe sat a shoe box.

Andrew reached for the box and carried it to the bed. He sat down and removed the lid.

Downstairs, the piano continued its mournful song.

He stared into the box.

A single sheet of folded paper rested on top of some jewellery.

Andrew looked up at the bedroom ceiling and exhaled slowly, expelling hope. He didn't want to examine the jewellery, not yet. Instead he took the sheet of paper out of the box and unfolded it.

It was an unfinished letter.

CODA

'Promise.'

'I promise.'

'Cross your heart and hope to die?'

'*Andrew.*'

'Come on, it's important.'

'Cross my heart and hope to die,' muttered Catherine.

'It'll be good, Mummy,' said Toby.

'Oh, I know, Toby,' said Catherine. 'It's not that. I'm just –'

'Your first nativity play,' said Andrew. 'It must be quite a challenge, marshalling all the sheep and cows and camels and what not.'

'Well, they're not real ones,' Toby told him.

A horrified hand flew up to Andrew's mouth. 'They're *not*?'

'There wouldn't be enough space backstage,' explained Toby. 'You'd need lots of room if you had real animals.'

'Lots of room,' nodded Andrew. 'Right.'

'And this is on Friday,' said Catherine.

'At four.'

'At four. Got it.' Catherine scribbled something in her diary. 'Consider it booked.' She looked up. 'Where did I put my briefcase?'

'It's in the hall,' said Andrew. 'Although I could hardly pick it up.'

'I know,' said Catherine with a grimace. 'I've got manuscripts coming out of my ears. All my authors have delivered on time. It's most peculiar.'

'A lot must have changed while you were away,' said Andrew.

'Maybe, but this is ridiculous. I mean, whoever heard of authors meeting deadlines? The world's gone mad. It never would have happened in the old days. Richard was always at least six months late. It was a point of honour for him. He tried to screw up our schedules whenever he could.'

'Good old Richard.'

Andrew Shaw often thought about his drink with Richard Sulzman on that summer afternoon in Soho, when Richard had warned him of the perils of fighting imaginary opponents. This from the one adversary who had been so much more dangerous than Andrew could have imagined.

'You'll be back at the usual time tonight?' he asked.

Catherine shook her head. She finished her coffee and stood up. 'I've got that rehearsal in the Barbican. You remember. The mad cellist. She's very talented, but an absolute lunatic. Conspiracy theorist. She reckons that just because we're doing the Shostakovich sonata, she's going to be put on a Communist blacklist in Whitehall.'

'You do pick them,' said Andrew.

'*Au contraire*,' said Catherine, grinning. '*They* pick *me*.'

'So when will you be home?'

'About ten, I should think.'

'There go my plans for dinner,' sighed Andrew.

Catherine's head tilted sideways. 'Can't I warm it up when I get in?'

'Course you can.'

She leaned over and kissed his cheek. 'I should run. We've got a production meeting at nine. Bye, Toby.'

'Bye, Mummy,' said Toby, fingering the knot of his tie.

Catherine kissed the top of Florence's head. 'Sweet pea,' she murmured.

'See you this evening,' called Andrew as Catherine headed out of the kitchen. A brief wave and she was gone.

Andrew sat back in his chair and looked at his children. They looked back expectantly. He rolled his eyes conspiratorially. 'Phew,' he said.

'*Phew*,' agreed Toby.

'Phew!' shouted Florence.

'Listen, kids,' said Andrew. 'I thought we might forget about school today. I thought we could maybe go and ride some ponies and then buy a whole sweet shop.'

Toby and Florence looked at him, smiles bursting off their faces.

It had been nearly five months since Andrew had quietly folded up his wife's unfinished love letter to Richard Sulzman and replaced it in the shoe box, and then put the shoe box back on top of the wardrobe, exactly where he had found it. In the days which followed he had constantly fought the temptation to fetch a chair, retrieve the box, and discover more than he ever wanted to know. Andrew sought refuge behind what remained of his ignorance. When, some weeks later, the shoe box finally disappeared from the top of the wardrobe, and with it all evidence of Catherine's crimes, Andrew was relieved. There were already enough stories which trailed off into darkness.

His wife was an adulteress and a thief. Andrew had

wrestled with the news in solitary misery. No amount of fretful analysis altered the facts. Catherine had had an affair with Richard. She had stolen Annabel's bracelet, and a lot more besides. There it was: impossible, yet somehow also true.

Andrew did not – he could not – begin to understand. Instead he sought solace in the innocence of his children. Their fresh-faced joy helped him through his wounded bewilderment, and their love tied him in place more firmly than the lash of steel ropes. But Catherine's crimes still crowded out serenity, filling the long nights with a riot of unanswered questions.

In the end it had been the piano which had shone a light on to his despair. Every morning Catherine played for an hour while Andrew got the children ready for school. At the end of each practice, just before she sat down to breakfast, the familiar melody would float through the house, just as it had done on the day Andrew had finally learned the truth. In those falling clusters of notes, delicate and full of grace, he heard the promise of a new future. If Catherine was playing again, he told himself, determined that it should be true, then anything was possible. And so quietly he had learned to forgive, to work back towards her.

Sometimes, though, he still wondered. What was it that Catherine had longed to touch?

Outside the temperature hovered a few degrees above freezing. The cold December rain sliced viciously through the grey sky. Andrew ran to the car, carrying Florence. Toby hurried along behind him and hopped into the front seat. This change in seating arrangements for the school run had polarised the Shaw family directly down gender lines, but Andrew's decision had stood. On the evening of Sinead's sabotage of the orchids, he had sat Catherine

287

down and told her that he had lost his job. Then he had offered to become a full-time househusband, and suggested that Catherine might want to return to work. They didn't need the money, he said, but the house would get crowded with both of them at home. Catherine had been comically unable to conceal her relief and delight. Two weeks later, she was the new senior commissioning editor for a thriving independent publishing house, and Andrew was immersed in domestic chores and daycare. Catherine had been so grateful that she had never objected to any of his subsequent policy reversals.

'Right,' said Andrew as he slid in behind the steering wheel. 'Everyone ready?' He reached to switch on the stereo. Toby put out his hand to stop him. 'Daddy, can we not listen to that old stuff today?'

'Don't you like it?'

'Not really,' admitted Toby. 'It's kind of boring.'

'Oh. Yes, I suppose I can see that. All right, then.' Andrew pulled out into the street. 'Let's enjoy each other's company instead. How's that?'

They drove for a few minutes in total silence.

Finally Toby looked across at his father. 'Daddy,' he said.

'Yes, Toby?'

'I was wondering – well, will we have to go to church on Christmas Day?'

Andrew laughed. 'No, don't worry, Toby. No more church, I promise.'

Toby looked relieved. 'OK,' he said. A fresh cloud of worry passed over his face. 'What about Grandpa? He'll want to go, won't he?'

'If Grandpa wants to go, then he can go on his own.'

'Won't he be lonely?'

'Don't worry, Toby,' said Andrew fondly. 'I think he's used to it by now.'

Toby thought about this. 'I'm glad we're not going. To church, I mean.'

'Me too,' agreed Andrew.

To Andrew's relief, Catherine's brief obsession with religion had vanished even more quickly than it had arrived. Since their disastrous visit to St Andrew's, she hadn't mentioned her theological disquiet again. Toby had played with James Macintyre throughout the summer holidays, and Julian Macintyre had been discreet enough never to ask whether the Shaws were ever intending to come back to another service.

Toby was now James Macintyre's loyal lieutenant. They ritually executed each other in the playground every lunch time with their matching replica automatic rifles. Toby's gun sat across his lap as they drove towards school.

Andrew pulled up about fifty yards away from the school gates. From here there were still two busy roads to negotiate. As a reward for this thoughtful behaviour, Toby always allowed his father to lean over and kiss him on the cheek. Toby climbed out of the car. With a happy wave, he walked up to the zebra crossing and crossed the road. From where he was parked Andrew could monitor Toby's progress all the way into the school. He watched until Toby's blazer disappeared through the gates in the bobbing river of boys.

His son had gone. Andrew sat in thoughtful silence for a moment, still astonished by the sweet pain in his chest each morning as he gave his children up to the care of others. He drove the short distance to Florence's nursery.

Florence was babbling with excitement as she dragged him by the hand through the wide glass doors of the building. In the corridor there was cheerful chaos. Small children hurtled to and fro with no apparent purpose, shrieking gleefully. Parents begged them to stay still long enough to shed their winter coats, hats and gloves. The noise was phenomenal.

Father and daughter made their way through the knee-high swarm towards Florence's coat peg. Florence waited patiently as Andrew pulled off her outdoor clothes. Then they set off again to Florence's classroom.

Her teacher was waiting by the door. 'Good morning, Mr Shaw,' she smiled.

'Daphne. Are you well?'

'Very well, thank you. How is young madam today?'

'I think young madam is just fine.'

'I'm just *fine*,' concurred Florence seriously, nodding her head. She gazed up at Mrs Perkins, as adoring as ever, but she did not let go of Andrew's hand.

Finally Andrew extracted himself from Florence's tiny grip and returned to the car. He glanced at his watch as he pulled out into the Highgate traffic. There was still plenty of time to get home before *Tilly!* began.

Since he had left Trident, Andrew had become addicted to his own creation, but now he had developed a newly refined, consumer's sensibility to the product. Andrew adored its trashy awfulness. He watched transfixed as Tilly Tyler shamelessly wound up her unfortunate guests, egging them on to fresh audience-pleasing acts of violence and vitriol. He allowed all of his emotional buttons to be pushed: every day he was rocked by groundswells of empathy, sympathy, anger and outrage. As the credits rolled after every show he felt sated, delightfully bloated on the misfortunes of others.

Andrew switched on the stereo, and Billie Holiday filled the car. The rain began to fall more heavily. The windscreen wipers flashed back and forth, constantly clearing his vision of the road ahead. Andrew whistled along with the tune and tapped his fingers against the steering wheel. When *Tilly!* was over, he would perform the usual battery of domestic chores, efficient and focused, never stopping until he was finished. For when he was finished, he could open his secretly purchased laptop, and begin a fresh chapter of his new novel.

And the words were flowing with an ease which he could never have hoped for. Every phrase which sprang up on to the screen from his fingertips strengthened his resolve a little more, and pushed him onwards to the next. His mind frothed in a deliciously secret cocktail of plot and character. There was none of the ponderous agony of his earlier effort, all those years before. Ideas and characters spilled on to the page, chaotic and rudely alive. And Andrew saw that the words were good. Perhaps they did not dazzle with the brilliant genius of Richard Sulzman, but Andrew no longer cared.

Yes, there was a lot to do before it was time to collect the children again.

The children! Even now, after all these months, he found himself blinking in amazement. Finally he had discovered his mother's gift, the love of family which threads unbroken across the years. Now his children had ignited his own hard, gemlike flame, and it burned brightly, illuminating his life.

And Catherine – well, it didn't matter any more that she *had* slept with Richard Sulzman. It didn't matter that it was Richard who ended the affair, or that Catherine had begged him to take her back. It didn't matter that she only returned to the piano, seeking solace, because the Sulzmans were escaping to America.

None of it mattered. Their long weekend in Venice at the start of November had marked a cautious return towards the mutual affection which Andrew feared had been lost for ever. Some of the old warmth had begun to creep back into Catherine's eyes, a distant echo from their first years of marriage. Her job had given her a fresh focus. She was re-invigorated and cheerful. The music was pouring out of the piano once again, both at home and across the city's rehearsal rooms and recital halls.

Slowly, they were inching back towards better times.

So he had won. And he had discovered that when you won, it was easy to forgive – especially when there was still so much else to lose.

Andrew Shaw drove home.

Lady Day sang on.

With all your faults
I love you still
It had to be you –
Wonderful you!

Love You Madly

Alex George

Matthew Moore is madly in love.

He's one of the lucky ones: after thirteen years, he still idolises Anna, his wife. What's more, his first novel is about to be published. Life could not be better. So why can't he just enjoy it?

'Here's the thing: Anna has changed. It's nothing big. She hasn't grown horns. But there's a little green dot flashing angrily on my screen, telling me there's something out there . . .'

Neither his beloved Duke Ellington records nor his saxophone can distract Matthew from the relentless nudge of his obsession. And so he begins to spy on his wife, until a chance discovery sends his worries spiralling out of control. As he pursues Anna from the streets of Camden to the boulevards of Paris, Matthew is caught in a vortex of jealousy which culminates in an unforgettable climax beneath the family Christmas tree.

Hilarious and devastating, *Love you madly* is about having everything you ever wanted – and having everything to lose.

ISBN 0 00 711795 7

Before Your Very Eyes
Alex George

New Man: remember him? Didn't think so.

Simon Teller is the last of a dying breed. He's such a New Man he's sparkling. Struggling magician, gourmet cook and jazz freak, he's been doing Conversation and Quiche for as long as he can remember, but he's so sensitive that all he's managed to conjure up is a number of awkward crushes and infatuations. And now the women are staying away in droves.

Enter stage left Joe, the Houdini of the one-night-stand and the man who, in the cause of true friendship, is determined to show Simon how to pull women as easily as he pulls rabbits out of hats. Under Joe's expert tutelage, and armed with an array of cynical – and secondhand – seduction techniques, Simon embarks on a radically different approach to dating. The results are disastrous. A number of close encounters of a very peculiar kind with desperate divorcées, nymphomaniac Canadians, and alcoholic doctors leave Simon wondering if the beautiful American magician Alex might be different . . .

A comedy about love, friendship and magic, and about how, sometimes the trick is to see what's before your very eyes.

ISBN 0 00 651333 6

ENJOYED THIS BOOK? WHY NOT TRY OTHER
GREAT HARPERCOLLINS TITLES – AT 10%

Buy great books direct from HarperCollins
at **10%** off recommended retail price.
FREE postage and packing in the UK.

☐ **Working It Out** Alex George 0-00-651332-8   £6.99

☐ **Before Your Very Eyes** Alex George 0-00-651333-6   £5.99

☐ **Love You Madly** Alex George 0-00-711795-7   £6.99

☐ **Man and Boy** Tony Parsons 0-00-651213-5   £6.99

☐ **One for my Baby** Tony Parsons 0-00-651481-2   £6.99

☐ **Man and Wife** Tony Parsons 0-00-651482-0   £6.99

Total cost _____

10% discount _____

Final total _____

To purchase by Visa/Mastercard/Switch simply call
08707 871724 or fax on **08707 871725**

To pay by cheque, send a copy of this form with a cheque made payable to
'HarperCollins Publishers' to: Mail Order Dept. (Ref: BOB4),
HarperCollins Publishers, Westerhill Road, Bishopbriggs, G64 2QT,
making sure to include your full name, postal address and phone number.

From time to time HarperCollins may wish to use your personal data
to send you details of other HarperCollins publications and offers.
If you wish to receive information on other HarperCollins publications
and offers please tick this box ☐

Do not send cash or currency. Prices correct at time of press.
Prices and availability are subject to change without notice.
Delivery overseas and to Ireland incurs a £2 per book postage and packing charge.

www.ingramcontent.com/pod-product-compliance
Ingram Content Group UK Ltd.
Pitfield, Milton Keynes, MK11 3LW, UK
UKHW022247180325
456436UK00001B/41

9 780007 117963